ICE
OUT

ICE
OUT

A Novel

Susan Speranza

SHE WRITES PRESS

Published 2022
Printed in the United States of America
Print ISBN: 978-1-64742-324-7
E-ISBN: 978-1-64742-325-4
Library of Congress Control Number: 2021921259

For information, address:
She Writes Press
1569 Solano Ave #546
Berkeley, CA 94707

She Writes Press is a division of SparkPoint Studio, LLC.

*For Gene, who assured me that morning
would come again*

and for Anne, who remembered the first line. . .

"Are you sure
That we are awake? It seems to me
That yet we sleep, we dream."

A Midsummer's Night Dream, William Shakespeare

Contents

FRANCESCA

3:50 in the afternoon, December 10, 2017

I wish there was a god, so I could hate him.

This was the thought that flew from Francesca in her desperation as the darkness of the icy waters enveloped her. It passed through her like a stiff wind shooting out into the world, an arrow toward a tree. A plea. A shout. A cry. Why? She shivered amid the murky waters. Why did this happen? To her? To Addie? One moment, one unanticipated moment, and everything changed. Swept away. Gone.

Forever.

Francesca loved Ben deeply. Fully. She believed absolutely in his devotion. She trusted him more than she had ever trusted anyone. He was the one constant in her life. The one comfort other than Addie. He was steadfast and dependable, generous and caring, a sensible man who always anchored them and their lives to safe land. But it took only one senseless moment and now everything was lost. He betrayed them. Turned his back on them. Abandoned them when they needed him most. Why? She never would have done this to him.

Despair and bitterness encircled her like a tightly wound rope. Was this to be her destiny? Trapped in an icy prison from which she was powerless to break free?

No, she thought as she forced herself up toward the light, toward the air. She refused to accept this. Perhaps this was nothing more than a terrible dream from which she needed to awaken. She shuddered.

A dream.

Or was it? What if this was real? What if they were unable to escape this dismal prison where fate had randomly tossed them?

She closed her eyes and fought her way to the surface.

Eight Years Earlier

It is an ordinary Monday in early December when the children gather around her as they often do. "Miss Bellini! Miss Bellini," they call and shout, surrounding her like a pack of tail-wagging puppies. Little hands reach out to touch her, tugging at her clothing, grasping at her elbow, anything to get the attention of their beloved music teacher. Francesca looks around the room at her young students and smiles, content and elated to be working at this school on Eastern Long Island where she has recently been hired, her first teaching job out of college.

"Shhhh!" she says, pretending to chide. "One at a time. I can't answer all of you at once!" Francesca pats one, then the other, trying to settle them. They look up at her with adoration, believing she is the most beautiful of all the adults in the building. Indeed, fate has blessed her with a loveliness that has only deepened with age. Tall and slender, graceful and refined, her long black hair cascades behind her and around her whenever she moves. She doesn't really move, though, but rather glides through her world, confident and full of life—as only one can who has never known disappointment or misfortune.

"Miss Bellini," a small dark-haired boy taps her, trying to get her attention. "Look what I got for my birthday yesterday!" He holds his arm high as the afternoon light, filtering in through the large windows, glints off his new watch.

Francesca touches his wrist, admiring the black, red, and silver timepiece.

"What a lovely present," she tells him. "Now you can keep time for us and make sure we don't run over."

He nods. "Yes. I'll be the bell! He beams as he imitates the familiar sound.

"That's louder than the real bell!" She laughs and gestures. "Softer, softer." He cocks his head and gazes up at her.

As if by a spell, the children are lured in by her lilting voice and rhythmic speech, for she talks *to* them, not *at* them. Enticed and unafraid, they look up into her large dark eyes that shimmer like a lake at midnight. Eyes that are full and deep.

Perhaps it is the passion she feels toward her beloved music. It stretches out like open arms toward them, enveloping them in its fervor, wrapping around them with warmth and tenderness. It is no wonder then that these urchins go willingly, captivated by the melodies and the comfort she provides.

They are therefore remarkably attentive. The other teachers and the principal are astounded. The same little savages who insist on dancing around the room, shouting at and hitting one another, throwing pencils, papers, and an occasional ball or hacky sack instead of working at the tasks at hand, such as math or reading, willingly settle themselves in a half-circle in front of her. Their eyes follow her every move, their heads tilt toward her every word. On the playground during recess, even the rough and tumble boys stop their play and run to her, standing as close as they can get to her, basking in the radiance of her smile, the glow of her being.

For this is the effect she has on people, young and old. A beauty and warmth, a passion and grace that attracts and captivates, but never overwhelms or frightens.

Eagerly then, they take up their instruments and from them she extracts beautiful music, unnatural in such young and undisciplined children. Perhaps because they know if they try hard and perform well, she will reward them with the one thing they long for most: that she play her flute for them. Only for them. Thus, at the end of each class, she promises if they behave, she will do just that.

Francesca loves performing as much as they love listening to her. Music has always been her first language. Even before she could speak, she would sing (so Mama Maria often tells her). Her halting first words were not for her mother or for her father (much to Dominic's feigned displeasure), but for something more abstract, for music itself. At a mere eight months of age, she uttered "song" and soon after, while listening to an aria playing in the background at her parent's Italian restaurant, she pointed toward the ceiling from where the music magically emanated and voiced: *pretty song*. Music itself is so intertwined with her being that the desire for it boils up from her soul, like a fallen sparrow scrambling up toward the water's surface for air.

It is this same passion for and desire to speak in the language of music that compelled her to join a New York City–based chamber group while still in college. Performing—filling the world with unspeakable beauty—is her true love; it comes as naturally to her as breathing.

So, it is on this morning, after quieting the group of eight-year-olds who sit cross-legged around her on the floor, wide-eyed and silent, the beautiful notes filling the room, burrowing their way into each child's heart, that three gentlemen stand unobserved in the open doorway.

As the last note hangs in the air, a long, quivering sigh that fades and slips toward silence, the children leap up then and, gathering close around her, chatter simultaneously. The room, once harmonious, now becomes a disorganized land of babel. Francesca smiles and tries to answer each student in turn. Suddenly, the din ceases as rhythmic applause rises and expands into the space, replacing the children's excited voices with thunderous approval.

This is the first time that Miss Bellini or the children are aware of the men in the doorway. Francesca, still holding her flute, turns toward them.

One gentleman is familiar to everyone in the school. Josh, a little older than Francesca, often takes time out from his custodial duties to drop by her classroom whenever she is playing; sometimes he even brings his three-year-old daughter to listen to her. But on this day, he has another reason for being there. He is escorting the other men through the building, pointing out the structure and function of this wing of the school.

The two strangers look alike except for a noticeable difference in age. They appear at once casual and formal, wearing similar khaki pants and green tweed jackets, but also beige dress shirts and ties. Both have similar expressive smiles as they glance around the room at the children. Francesca notes the younger gentleman looking at her shyly. His eyes sweep over her, then dart away. There is something about this tall, quiet, fair-haired man she immediately likes. And she is certain at this moment he will like her too, for she has never been rejected by someone whom she has desired. She understands her power and uses it intuitively for the one thing she wants—an abiding love. That same steadfast affection she observed between her parents through the years.

"Hey, Francesca," Josh greets her, oblivious to her interest in the younger of the two strangers. "Don't mean to disturb you, but these are the architects who'll be working on renovating this part of the building."

Ignoring Josh, she continues to focus her attention on the dignified young gentleman next to him. She basks in his reserved and reflective gaze. He isn't like so many of the others whose eyes hover over her seductively, vehicles of a conqueror's game, instruments sharpened from need and desire enough to cut her into irregular pieces while disassembling her. Rather, his look leaves her whole and unbroken. She smiles as she glances up into blue eyes that seem as clear as the sea, and as bottomless.

"I've heard the board approved it, but I wasn't aware it would start this soon," she directs this off-handed comment about the renovation, which she couldn't care less about, to the object of her interest, as a way of engaging him. The older man, gray peppering his faded blond hair, touches his wire-framed glasses, repositioning them. He bites his lip, suppressing a quivering smile, and looks away from them.

"We're in the initial phase," the young man tells her, adopting a professional tone. Then tilting his head, he gives her a sidelong glance. "That was a beautiful rendition of *Thaïs*'s "Méditation" you played there."

She laughs. A throaty and infectious laugh. "You know that piece? Most people our age aren't very familiar with classical music."

Certainly none of the men she has ever dated.

He chuckles, his eyes glinting even before his lips turn upward. "My parents' influence." And he nods toward the older man.

The other architect steps forward and shakes Francesca's hand. "I'm Dan Bodin, Bodin Associates. This is my son and partner, Ben." He takes a business card from his pocket and gives it to her. She looks down at it and smiles. Ben extends his hand to her, and she slips hers into his. He doesn't shake it, though. He merely holds it. His hand is large and warm, but his grip, gentle and steady. It is the clasp of kindness, the touch of protection.

It seemed like an eternity before Francesca reached the surface. When she emerged into the light, she choked and gagged and gasped for air. She tried to shout but could barely breathe. She slapped her hand to her chest again and again, as if that would help her clear her lungs. All she could manage was a panicked whisper. "Addie! Where are you?" She stifled a sob. "Please!" she begged the heavens, the earth, the very ether around her.

The frigid waters lapped at her like a thirsty dog. She looked across the icy expanse and frantically scrutinized the area, hoping to discern the pink of her daughter's jacket and bibs. But all she saw were the contrasting shadows of the late afternoon sky that seethed with churning clouds.

She blinked, as if noticing her surroundings for a first time. She saw the picturesque landscape of her life—the forest where she had spent many days hiking through, the lake that had refreshed her on warm summer afternoons, her beloved meadow beyond, where she often roamed with Addie and Cruz when her world was stressful and harried. There, pausing amid the wildflowers, she would find peace again; it would rain over her, a blessing from on high, enveloping her like a protective sheath. This was home. All of this. Their home. *Her* home. Where the drama of her life played out in an orderly and perfect sequence, where her passion and happiness echoed through the mountains like a triumphant song.

Francesca shook her head, heaving the memories from her like foul beads of sweat. She no longer wanted to see any of it. She no longer wanted to remember. All she longed for now was safe, dry land. And for Addie.

From the beginning of their time together, Ben tells her he wants to share with her the one place he loves most. The place that has been so much a part of his childhood and youth that he can't look back on any of it without seeing the sheer majesty of the land or remembering the peace and happiness it brought.

Thus, six weeks after their first meeting, Ben suggests they spend a long weekend at the family's vacation home in Central Vermont. A large log cabin set deep in the woods at the end of a private dirt road, it looks out on a few hundred acres of forest, fields, a large lake, and several streams, a nature lover's haven, conceived by his father who dreamed of living in the country since he was a boy and who brought it to fruition twenty years before by sheer determination. For Ben, it is paradise, an enchanted Eden from which he draws his inspiration and his strength. Francesca readily agrees to go.

She had been to Vermont only once, when she was ten. Her parents gathered the money from their struggling restaurant to send her to music camp for a week. It was such a memorable experience, full of breathtaking sunrises, stunning sunsets, dramatic storms, and mesmerizing tranquility. She always meant to go back. Now, as they pull into the long driveway at dusk, she has indeed returned.

Francesca steps from the car and looks in awe at the beauty that surrounds them. The full moon, just risen, glistens down upon the freshly fallen snow, turning night into day. The trees stand tall against the early evening sky. They are brushed white and sway as the wind kicks up a bit.

"Come on," Ben says, "I'll show you around the property."

"Now? But it's dark!"

"The moon's full and clear. It'll give us enough light to guide us. It won't take long. By the time we get back to the house, we'll be ready for dinner and a fire."

"How are we going to walk in all this deep snow?"

Ben laughs and kicks the snow with his foot, sending a powdery cloud toward her. "It's not that deep, only eight inches or so. This isn't Long Island. We're in Vermont now. We don't walk when it snows, we ride. Come on."

Francesca follows him into the garage where five snowmobiles sit side by side, different colors, different sizes. He selects two helmets from a group of five that occupy a nearby shelf. He hands one to her. "Here, put this on."

She looks at it, frowning, and turns it over and over in her hands. It seems alien and complicated.

He smiles as he brushes her long hair from her face and gathers it behind her. "Like this," he says and, taking the helmet, eases it onto her head. Then he goes to the longest, largest snowmobile—a two-up—mounts it, turns it on, and guides it out into the snow.

He puts on a matching helmet. "Get on."

She freezes.

"In back of me. Put your feet on the floorboards and your arms on the armrests. They're heated so you should be comfortable. Press your knees into me. I'll go slow. I promise."

"I don't know about this," Francesca shouts above the roar. "It doesn't look very safe!"

He revs the engine. She jumps back, startled.

He cocks his head. "Well?"

She doesn't move.

"C'mon. Where's your adventurous spirit?"

"I left it home on Long Island!"

He extends a hand to her. She hesitates.

He waits, then calls, "You've told me you're never one to turn down a challenge."

She looks at him and smirks, then takes his outstretched hand. She tries twice before she is able to mount, finally climbing on behind him.

"We'll pick up the trail over there," he tells her, pointing toward the forest line. "When I was a kid, my father and I logged most of the trees ourselves and created our own private trail. It goes all around our property, through the woods and down by the lake. It's a beautiful ride, you'll see."

So begins their moonlit journey. Francesca grips the armrests and at times clutches onto Ben himself; with each slip and sway of the machine, she is certain it will catapult her into the air. But her fear subsides as she learns to sway with the sled, relax into it—surrender to it—and become one with its movements. As they glide through the trees, the moon guiding their way, she senses she has found something beautiful, something rare.

Soon, the path opens into a clearing, and she sees the lake stretch out before them, vast and tranquil. Ben stops and points. There in the distance, standing at the edge of the frozen water, are three deer who look warily up at the intruders. They don't move, however, and Ben, cutting the engine, takes his camera, which he always has with him, climbs from the snowmobile, and cautiously moves toward them. Maintaining a comfortable distance, he captures the scene in shot after shot.

Francesca smiles. She has never seen wildlife this close. In suburbia where she has always lived, she sometimes catches sight of small nuisance creatures like squirrels and rabbits, who live their lives unseen, hiding out in backyards between shrubs and fences that often separate one property from another. But never such majestic creatures as these, standing so stately in such an expanse. Here, as the moonlight glistens on the frozen lake, with Ben beside her and only the deer as witness to her existence, an overwhelming joy floods her, and she believes, no, she *knows,* she has found paradise.

The deer turn away from the intruders and amble on around the lake, disappearing into the woods on the opposite side. Ben and Francesca get back on the snowmobile and press on with their evening journey through the forest. He stops now and then, pointing out places that were meaningful to him as a child. "Here's where my father and I built my first tree house," Ben tells her when they pause amid a group of tall pines. "The remnants of it are up there. See?" And later, near a clearing, deep in the forest, he says, "We used to have a food plot right over there to attract the wildlife. I have a great photo of a bear that used to come every night at ten on the dot."

She shudders. "A, a bear? Deer are one thing, but a big black bear is something else!"

Ben laughs. "Yes, there are bears here. And coyotes. And fishers. And even bobcats."

She holds up her hand. "Please, I don't want to hear anymore."

He chuckles as they continue their evening trek through the woods, circling around to the other side of the house. Once inside the garage, he brings the sled to a halt, turns off the engine, and takes off his helmet. He helps Francesca climb from the sled. She shakes her hair loose as she hands him her helmet.

"Well?"

"It was scary at first," she admits. "But I've never seen such beauty! It doesn't seem real."

"I know," he says as he takes her hand, leading her into the house. "I try to capture it in my photographs, but it's impossible to replicate. It's perfection. That's why I love it here."

That night, then, bathed in the warmth of the wine, sated by the elaborate dinner her mother packed for them from the restaurant, surrounded by the images of the moonlight on the snow, the deer by the lake, in the shadow of the fire as it crackles and sputters, she lies down with Ben, inviting him into her very being. He takes her in his arms and kisses her, wrapping himself around her and her heart, so she can no longer tell where she ends and where he begins. From that moment of abandon, two souls merge. She understands then that he is her fate, her destiny.

And their separate stories now become one.

Francesca struggled to raise her black-gloved hand out of the icy waters. With what strength she could muster, she pushed it high above her and gazed up at it, an appendage, numb and foreign, a dark rocket shot into the overcast skies, a silent plea for help. She turned her hand one way, then another. It seemed nothing more than a useless limb jutting up from the thin ice like a splintered, solitary branch that the wind had carelessly tossed from the forest. Would Ben see it? Would he even care?

She fell backward, for the raising of her hand forced her beneath the water again; instinctively, her arms dropped to her sides as she struggled to keep herself afloat. Though her strength was fading, she forced herself upright and latched onto the ice that surrounded her, hoping it would steady her. She coughed and gagged once more.

Francesca shouted Addie's name as her eyes swept over the lake. She longed to see what was not there, hoping to glean an inkling of pink, of color, of life. Instead, everything seemed bleak and ashen. Had she in her fear lost the ability to see color, or had the landscape really turned gray?

Her hands slipped from the ice; again, she sank beneath the surface. She no longer fought it, she no longer struggled. She gave into it. Surrendered to it. Closing her eyes to the grayness and the world. "Oh, Addie . . ."

It is spring of their first year together. They sit on a large rock deep in the woods of Vermont where nature's perfection resounds in every leaf and blade of grass, in every drop of water that expands and flows toward placid lakes, in every stone that yields to august mountains.

"Architecture's how I make my living," Ben tells her as his long arm drapes over her, surrounding her, drawing her into him. "I love the feel, the look, the smell of different structures. But photography's my passion." He takes his phone and scrolls through the myriad of photographs he has taken over the years.

"Here's the church at Peacham. I took this last fall. I think it was the beginning of October."

"Wow, what a gorgeous scene," Francesca says as she examines the striking shot: the vivid autumn grass spreads out in the foreground, spilling toward the white church and the adjacent red barn, like a welcoming sea of jade; the barn's half-rusted metal roof and the church's white steeple stand in contrast to the oranges, reds, and yellows of the trees on the mountains beyond.

"Wow," she says again. "When I look at this, I hear Beethoven. His sixth. Or Zipoli's "Elevazione." A beautiful setting always requires beautiful music." She pauses. "It doesn't seem real."

"It isn't."

"What do you mean?"

"It's only a photograph."

Francesca rolls her eyes. "Of course. I know that. It's not the *actual* church, barn, meadow, or mountain. I get it." She frowns then. "I only meant that the beauty doesn't seem real. It's too perfect to be real. Perfection's something we can only imagine, never experience."

He laughs. "Well, I'm pretty perfect. Aren't you experiencing my perfection now?"

"Oh, shush." Smiling, she nudges him, then pauses. When she speaks again, her voice is solemn, her expression pensive. "Take my music, for example. I'm constantly trying to recreate all the perfect sounds I hear in my head, but I just can't do it. It always falls short. I can imagine it, but I can never replicate it. It's something that's just beyond my grasp, something that always eludes me."

He shrugs. "I've never really thought about it in that way. I guess I accept that perfection doesn't exist. That's just the way things are."

"I can't accept it. I don't *want* to accept it. If we can imagine perfection, why can't we create it? I'll never give up trying."

He smiles at her. "Trying to be perfect?"

"Yes. And trying to make things perfect. Why not?"

"It just seems doomed to failure, that's all." He runs his hand down her back. "If it eludes you, how do you forgive yourself when you fail? And how do you forgive others when they fail? What do you do then?"

"I never forgive. Myself or anyone else. When I fail, I just keep on trying. And I expect others to keep on trying, too." Francesca pauses, then lowers her head and gives Ben a sidelong glance. "I guess I'm not a very forgiving person," she says quietly. "I'm like my mother. I can be very stubborn. Just to warn you."

"I see that," he replies thoughtfully. "Stubborn can be good. Sometimes." He puts his arm around her and squeezes her. "But sometimes not. At some point you'll have to learn to accept things as they are and forgive life and the world and people for not being perfect."

Francesca throws her head back and laughs. "Never!"

He smiles and brushes her cheek with his hand. "You're bad!"

"No, just determined."

"Well, when you finally attain perfection will you please let me know?" Ben laughs and puts his arm around her again.

"Oh, I will. Definitely."

He scrolls to another photograph. "Maybe you need to see these scenes in real life if you think they're impressive as photos."

"I'd love to. When can we go?"

"I'll take you there. Soon. For these scenes, though, we need to go in the fall."

"Great. Can't wait. Then I'll be able to tell if what I see is perfect and if that perfection is real or not."

He holds out his phone for her to see.

She tilts her head and looks from the phone to him and back again. "Sometimes I wonder if anything's real. If all of this isn't just one big dream. Maybe that's why we can't find perfection. Or recreate it. Because none of this is real."

"You mean all of this?" He looks around and motions with an outstretched arm. "These woods? Or this tree?" He leans back and pats the trunk, then runs his hand through the dirt, gathering up a clump. He takes her hand in his, turns it palm up, and sifts the loose dirt into it. "Feels real to me."

She smiles. "I mean everything. Even you."

He brushes the dirt from her upturned hand, then bends down and kisses it. "Isn't this real?"

She laughs. "It seems like it is. Like it should be. But then, again, maybe it's all just a dream."

"A good one, I hope!" He smiles, still holding her hand, then leans close to her and kisses her. "I'll tell you what," he whispers, his lips hovering near hers. "I'll take you to all these wonderful places I've discovered. That's a promise. Then you can judge for yourself. If it's all just a dream or not." Slowly, he sits back, picking up his phone. "At Peacham, we'll climb the hill—that's where I took this photo from— and you can tell me what you see, if you really see the colors or the shadows or the church or the barn or the mountains behind it. Maybe I'm just delusional."

"Maybe you are." Francesca laughs and examines the picture. "It's a deal. I'll see it for myself, and I'll make my decision about the state of existence. *And* your state of mind, too. Whether or not you're delusional."

"I might be. Will you still want to be with me if I am?"

"I don't know. The jury's out on that one."

He winks at her. "Stick with me and I'll show you things you've never even dreamed of."

Again, she throws her head back and laughs. "I might."

"Glad to hear that!" And he shows her other photographs of East Corinth and Waits River.

"I see you like churches," she says, giving him another sidelong glance.

"Only because they're interesting architecturally." He meets and holds her gaze. He scrolls again. "I like farms, too. See? Here's the one at Sleepy Hollow. And this is the Jenne Farm, the most photographed farm in all of New England. In all of North America, for that matter. And it's in Reading. Not far from here. I'll take you to see that, too. But it's a morning shot. I had to get there real early in order to catch sunrise, so when we go, be prepared to get up in the middle of the night." He shows her more photos. "I also like water.

Lakes, rivers, brooks, ponds. Here's Kettle Pond. I took this from Owl's Head Mountain. What a climb that was. We'll go hiking there this summer."

"I'll plan on it then." She stands up, throws her head back as she stretches out her arms as wide as possible, ready to embrace the surrounding forest. "I want to see it all, I want to experience it all for myself. Be my guide and lead me onward, like Virgil led Dante, to these otherworldly sites."

Ben rises, taking her by the waist. He swings her around, answering, "But it'll be to paradise I'll lead you, certainly not into hell." And he plants a quick kiss on her lips as she laughs.

"It better be!" she nudges him.

While his color photographs are most impressive, it is his black and whites that are breathtaking. A creek seen through the trees in the morning mist. A buck barely visible through the thicket as a shaft of light falls through the canopy, illuminating it.

He sees things with the camera's lens that escape most people—the intricacies of the intertwining branches of a barren tree in winter; the melting of icicles that hang from the roof of an old barn near the family's home. His photographs are a chronicle of devotion teeming with life: the fleeting moment before a bee alights on a flower, two fawns eating apples from the trees in a meadow, peaceful country roads, lakes and ponds, mountains and old churches, sunrises and sunsets. Francesca understands that the spirit which awakens the photographer in him is the same that calls forth the musician in her. So she feels a bond with him.

And he feels one with her, for after they meet, his photographs change in content. He no longer limits his vision to nature. She now makes up an integral part of the picture.

On a sultry late afternoon in July during their first summer together, he keeps his promise to show her the hidden, wild beauty of Vermont as he leads her down a concealed path to Buttermilk Falls.

"Not many people know this way," he says as he helps her step over a fallen and splintered, half-rotten tree trunk. "It's not really a path, just the way I like to go to get down here."

"No kidding!" She clutches onto one tree, then another, preventing herself from tumbling down the steep incline. "There's a reason no one goes this way. It's certain death."

"Yes, but it'll be so worth it," he calls over his shoulder.

As they descend, the roar of the water grows louder, and the oppressive air turns chilly.

When the terrain levels out, they walk along the ledge that is formed from the bedrock. They have come down behind the falls.

"If this was the weekend, there'd be people here. Only locals though. They're the only ones who know about this spot. And me, of course. Everyone comes here when it's really hot, to swim and get cool." He points to the sizeable area bounded by immense boulders on three sides where the water pools as it runs off the falls. "Let's go down there. The water's cold, even at this time of year." He leads her along the ridge as a frosty spray drifts over them like a fine, chilling rain. "And there's where we can get the best look at the falls." They walk until they come to the spot opposite the waterfall.

"This is impressive," she says, looking at the rushing water.

"That's the photograph I want." Ben points and jumps from the ledge onto a large rock that juts out of the swirling pool. He extends his hand to her. "Come on. This will make a great picture of you with the falls in the background."

She joins him on the rock, then sits down as he leaves her, climbing to a higher position. "Smile!"

"Yes, sir," she laughs and salutes him. He ignores her teasing, concentrating on taking countless photographs of her perched like a mermaid in the middle of a sea while behind her, the raging white water cascades between the dark gray boulders like a thick bridal veil.

No more scenes of empty woodlands or barren lakes in morning mist. Now he places her as the centerpiece of the photograph, sitting like she is on the mound, smiling up at him with the white foamy waterfall as a backdrop. Or alone in the lane in Belmont, the surrounding trees ablaze with yellows and oranges. Or arms outstretched, head thrown back, her laughter radiating from the still picture caught at the very moment she emerges from an old covered bridge.

She is there at the very heart—the subject—of his present life.

Francesca, limp and exhausted, drifted well beneath the surface. Though her eyes were closed, images rose like unwanted specters, creating a kaleidoscope of the past which crowded her, taunted her. She bolted upright, as determined to flee these remembrances as she was to find air and light. With ebbing strength, she forced herself to the surface again; once there, she inhaled the bitter air in long, desperate gasps. But her rapid breathing made her light-headed, and the frigid air made her cough and choke.

She looked around the lake once more. A sense of dread and doom crept over her with each passing moment. Where was Addie? Why couldn't she see her?

She spun herself around. Her desperation mounted. The ice trapped her on all sides. Perhaps if she could get the height she needed as Ben had done, she could land on the frozen surface and drag herself to shore. She would mimic her beloved Cruz and, lying belly down, crawl to safety. Once there she would surely see Addie and help her. But first, she had to get out. First, she had to leap. High.

She drew in another deep breath, but it made her so dizzy she almost fainted. Recovering, she plunged beneath the water, then using what strength she had left, pushed herself upward, trying to gain the momentum to leap high enough to clear the ice. But her efforts were futile; she fell back with a force, clipping her head on the jagged surface as she sank.

Her instinct was to fight it. Instead, she allowed herself to drift downward as her arms floated out from her. Through the dimness, she gazed at her hands and the thick black gloves she had donned earlier that day. They were new and fit so snuggly that she had to remove her ring to get them on. It was only with great reluctance she did so, for from the moment Ben asked her to marry him, presenting her with the brilliant gem, it never came off. Until today. The very day the bond ruptured. Was there some sort of magic attached to this ring? she wondered, growing giddy at such an incredulous thought. Maybe if she could reach it, place it back on her finger where it belonged, she could turn back time and return to her life as it was.

It is their second Christmas together. Francesca's family does something they have never done before: They close the restaurant for the holiday and join the Bodins at their Vermont house. What precipitates this unusual behavior is the sense that something momentous is about to happen, and they want to be a part of it.

The families have previously met. Ben's father and his mother, Laura, along with Ben's younger sister, Danielle, have been Maria and Dominic's guests at the restaurant many times in the past year.

Francesca's parents have come to love Ben, often referring to him as the son they never had. They have warmly embraced him and his family, opening their home and their lives to them. In the same fashion, Ben's parents have grown to love Francesca. It is this mutual affection and concern for these young people that bring the two families together. They hope that in due time, they will be united by a stronger commitment. And by blood.

They, therefore, gather for the holiday with anticipation. It is Christmas eve and in the tradition of Vermont, snow turns the meadows white and dusts the bare trees silver. Dan, Ben, and Danielle, who is home on vacation from her last year at Stanford had, a few days earlier, gone in search of the tallest, fullest evergreen they could find in their forest. They hoped such a tree would lend a festive atmosphere to the room it was destined to grace. When they finally found one that suited them, a beautiful white spruce, they cut it down and with much effort dragged it from the woods using the snowmobiles to transport it back home. There they installed it in the center of the living room, where, in the heart of the house, it now rises, majestic and imposing, stretching high into the vaulted ceiling. It can be seen from every room, upstairs and down, and from every nook and corner, shining brilliantly with lights and keepsake ornaments the family has collected over the years; trinkets that mark special events and passages of their years together. It stands like a beacon in the middle of their lives.

On this night, a sumptuous Italian feast that Francesca's parents willingly spent the afternoon preparing is served—antipasto, fried calamari, clams oreganata, their signature dish of mussels, scallops, shrimp over linguini, and struffoli to end the meal. Afterward, the two families retreat to the living room where they gather around the tree, the fire raging nearby. There they talk, laugh and exchange gifts.

Francesca, sated and warmed by the hearth and the flowing of red wine, settles into the plush leather sofa, nestling into Ben who, seated close to her, drapes his long arm around her.

This is the first vacation her parents have had in years. Her mother looks suddenly younger, laughing and chatting as she sits with Laura on the opposite couch. Maria, always beautiful, whose thick, dark, unruly hair is lately streaked with silver which has crept in unnoticed during the past year, relaxes the constant furrow in her brow. The two women banter and quip, leaning into one another and clutching onto one another's arms as they laugh and giggle like schoolgirls. They are so different; Maria is dark and petite, gregarious and impassioned; her large black eyes fade and brighten with intensity depending on the emotion of the moment. She is an avid storyteller and has a way with words; when she speaks, others listen intently. Laura, on the other hand, is taller and thinner, her fading blonde hair worn short and straight. She is aristocratic and graceful, soft-spoken and retiring. She has grown even more retiring and reticent in recent years following the death of her oldest daughter, Ben's twin sister, Lucy, whom the family rarely mentions. There is a darkness about Laura, a heaviness of her spirit even when she smiles, as if she is trapped within the walls of a silent prison from which she is never free.

Their backgrounds are just as dissimilar: Maria never attended college. Instead she went to work full time right after graduating from her Brooklyn high school. She married Dominic, her high school sweetheart, soon thereafter. With what money they received from their wedding and saved up by hard work, they moved to Long Island and opened the restaurant right after their first child was born; the restaurant became Francesca's second childhood home. Laura, conversely, grew up in luxury on the North Shore of Long Island, a neurosurgeon's daughter, who graduated from Sarah Lawrence.

It was early in her college years that she met Dan Bodin, the tall, handsome, fair-haired Architecture major at Columbia, the quiet, gentlemanly honor student whom all the girls had their eyes on.

Dominic sits back in the chair nearest the fire and sips his wine, his eyes drooping, a smile wavering on his lips.

Dan, opposite him, swirls his after-dinner drink at intervals and touches the side of his glasses, readjusting their position. He leans forward and talks to Dominic about their common interest—sports. "You have to be real careful about showing your love for the Yankees around here. We're in Red Sox territory up here. And believe me, everyone takes baseball and the Sox very, very seriously."

Dominic chuckles. "I guess I shouldn't wear my Yankees hat or tee shirt when I come to Vermont!"

"No, not if you value your life." Dan grins and takes another sip from his glass.

Dominic throws back his head and lets out a resounding laugh.

"I mean it," Dan snickers. "It's true. Really. These people are crazy when it comes to their teams. And that includes the Patriots, too."

"Sure sounds like it." And Dominic, shaking his head, laughs again. "I'll remember not to root for another team when I'm up here."

Francesca has never seen her father this relaxed.

Dominic, whose ample frame bears well the extra twenty-five or so pounds he has gained through the years, is a good-natured, industrious man. He carries the business with him every hour of every day and often quips that the stress of running such an enterprise has caused his hair to thin to such a degree that it is easier for him to shave off what little remains. He loves good food, good wine, good company, and all manner of people. So much so that he always makes it a point to speak with every person who enters his restaurant. Over the years, he has accumulated many strong friendships among his clientele. People love Dominic as much as he loves them. There is no one in their community who doesn't speak well of him. His laughter can be felt miles away, and every Sunday when he and Maria enter church before Mass, everyone pushes toward them to shake his hand and ask how he is doing. He responds with a broad smile, an affectionate pat on the back and a loud, "Come on down and eat with us this week!" Francesca has inherited her mother's beauty, and it seems, at times, her intense temperament, but she is sure it is from her father that she gets her passion for living, her appreciation for la dolce vita.

Her sisters Teresa and Angela, still college students, sit off on the opposite side of the room with Danielle where they talk and laugh about such mutually interesting subjects as college classes, dorm living, boyfriends and frat parties.

It is then, as Francesca sighs, contentedly surveying the room, that Ben rises from the couch and going to the tree, selects from the pile beneath it a small present wrapped in gold paper. He turns toward Francesca and says, "This is a little something from me to you." And smiling, he holds out the gift to her. A hush falls over the room as all eyes turn to her. Francesca puts down her glass and stands to face him. Taking the present, she pulls off the wrapping with one tug, but her hands quiver, and she nearly drops the small, red box. She hinted several times in recent weeks that she thought the amethyst pendant she saw in a local jewelry store was lovely. Expecting that he took the hint, she looks down at the present, but when she opens the box, she gasps. What she sees instead is a large diamond ring. She holds the box out from her as if she is afraid of it, of its spell, its magic and draws her other hand to her mouth. Ben takes the box from her, and grasping the ring, sinks to one knee in front of her. He holds her hand gently, lovingly.

"Francesca," he says quietly, "marry me. Live with me. Grow old with me. I can't think of any other woman I want to spend the rest of my life with more than you."

Overcome, she can only stand close to him, her head bowed, tears streaming down her cheeks as she places her hand over her heart. Suddenly, her future stretches out before her, long and joyous. In one sweeping vision, she sees their lives together—the home they will build, the children they will have. She observes them years later, near the end of their lives having grown old together, peaceful and contented, their children, grandchildren, and even great-grandchildren gathered around them. It seems as if this present melts and merges into the future which she can almost touch.

Through her sobs, she nods. Ben places the ring on her finger, then stands, taking her head in both his hands, kissing the top of it. "I hope these are happy tears. You did say yes, right?"

She laughs though still weeping and nods again. The room, previously silent, hums with excitement as they crowd around the young couple. Dan and Dominic pat one another and Ben on the back, shaking the others' hands vigorously. Maria and Laura hug one another as they wipe their eyes and sniffling, embrace Francesca. Each, in their turn, takes her hand in theirs to admire the ring.

Dominic, kissing her forehead, firmly envelopes her in the same bear hug he perfected upon greeting her when she was a child. In his strong arms, she feels safe and loved, as she always has. He tells his soon-to-be son-in-law, "I expect you to treat my baby well."

Ben beams. Dan puts his arm around his son's shoulders and remarks, "Don't worry, I've taught him to be a gentleman in every sense of the word."

"Wow, it's gorgeous!" Teresa hugs her older sister. "So, does this mean I'm going to be your Maid of Honor?

Francesca laughs. "Of course, you are. Unless you don't want to be, then I'll have to ask Angela." And she tugs at her sister's long pony-tail that drapes over one shoulder like a dark scarf. Teresa grins and slaps Francesca's hand away, just as she did when they were children.

Angela leans toward Francesca and hugs her with great warmth. "I guess I'll have to settle for being a bridesmaid!"

"Yes, a bridesmaid," Francesca laughs, still holding her. "Even though you're the baby of the family, you're too old to be a flower girl." Angela giggles and nudges her, as Francesca, in return, ruffles her sister's dark curls.

Danielle then hugs Francesca, patting her as she holds her. "Once a bridesmaid, always a bridesmaid!"

"Shush, Danielle, I'll tell you what I tell my sisters—that you're too young to even think about getting married. Finish college, then we'll talk!"

Danielle chuckles and brushes her long, blonde hair from her face. "Ha, first I need a boyfriend!"

Dan bends forward and kisses Francesca on the cheek. "Danielle will never get married if she keeps breaking up with everyone she dates."

Laura smiles through tears and embraces Francesca. "Welcome to our family." She hugs Francesca a little longer and a little more firmly than the others as if she doesn't want to let her go.

"Oh my god," Maria exclaims as she blinks away tears and rotates her daughter's hand first one way, then another so the diamond catches the festive lighting of the room. "It's beautiful! It's perfec-tion!" She leans forward, takes her daughter's face in her hand and gazes lovingly at her, then hugs and holds her. "Ugh, it's all gone by too fast, too fast."

Francesca smiles. "Mama . . ." And she wipes a tear from the older woman's cheek. "Be happy. I am!"

And indeed, she is. She thought earlier, as she sat serenely in the heart of all the people who meant the most to her in the world, that she would never know any more joy than this. But she was wrong. At this very moment, with her parents and sisters and her new family gathered around her, as Ben takes her in his arms, clutching her close, stroking her hair, kissing her, she knows she has found what most people do not—an abiding love and true happiness. And she wants it to last. Forever.

Francesca drifted farther down toward the bottom, as exhaustion blanketed her like a shroud. She closed her eyes. If only she could sleep and dream, she knew she could regain her strength. She wanted to rise to the surface; she longed for light and air and warmth. But the weight of the water, and a creeping despair, impeded her.

Suddenly, Francesca heard a child's cry. A familiar sound she would know anywhere.

She moved her head from one side to the other, slowly at first, struggling to throw off the fatigue and heaviness that immobilized her. She fought to break through the water's resistance. As her strength resurged, she shook her head faster and faster and mouthed, "No!" And "no" again.

Vowing then that she would not allow herself or her daughter to be swallowed up like this, she gathered up her courage and clawed her way to the surface.

Francesca enters the restaurant after school on one of the worst days of her young life yet. Her best friend, Brittany, had offered her a puppy from their dog's unexpected litter. There was just one left, and she said Francesca could have him. Francesca discussed the prospect of taking the puppy with Dominic and Maria and presented a cogent argument (for a nine-year-old) as to why they should allow her to have him. Together with her sisters, she promised they would participate in the care, training, and raising of said puppy. Dominic, through the years, had instilled in them the importance of honoring promises, so Francesca knew that this was a commitment she could not get out of. But she wanted that puppy, especially when he jumped into her lap, tail wagging, and bestowed innumerable puppy kisses upon her. So, she promised her parents, and Brittany had promised her this one.

She places her backpack behind the counter as she always does, then takes a seat in the far corner of the unoccupied rear dining room and broods.

Her father enters this room from outside and pats her on her head as he walks past her toward the kitchen. "Hi, Sprite, how'd your day go?" He expects her to follow him around the restaurant as he goes about his chores, the way she always does, laughing and chattering about the things that happened at school. On this day, however, she utters a quiet, "Fine," without lifting her head from her hands or her eyes from the table. Almost to the kitchen door, Dominic stops, turns, and looks at his melancholy daughter. He walks back to her. "Francesca, what's up?"

Too upset to speak, she shakes her head as a tear slips from her eye and pools on the tablecloth.

"Francesca, tell me. What happened to make you so unhappy?"

The dam that holds the anguish breaks and she sobs. "Brittany promised I could have that puppy. But he's gone. They gave him to someone else."

Dominic puts down the stack of cloth napkins he holds, then pulls up a chair next to his disheartened daughter.

"Maybe Brit's parents didn't know she promised you that puppy?"

"They knew!" Francesca wipes her eyes and sniffs. "She gave him to another friend. A *boy* she likes."

Dominic sits back and frowns. "Well, if that's the case, that was very wrong of her to do, since she promised you could have the puppy."

"People are always breaking their promises," she blurts out in despair.

"No, not always. Some of us keep our word."

Francesca wipes her eyes again.

"Brittany was wrong to do this. She should never have promised you that puppy then turned around and let someone else have him. Once you give your word, you should always keep it." Dominic pauses and looks at his daughter whose head is still lowered. "If we went around always breaking our promises, no one would ever trust us."

"I don't trust *her* anymore. I've never broken a promise to her."

"Which is the right thing to do. Your mother and I have taught you girls well. To give your word and to keep it is the most important thing you can ever do. And to break it is the greatest form of betrayal."

"I hate her."

"But please, honey, don't hate her. You may never be able to trust her again, but you need to forgive her."

"Why?"

Dominic runs his hand over his forehead. "Because the anger and hate will only hurt you."

"I don't care. I'll never, ever forgive her."

Dominic sighs. "People shouldn't do things like this, but they *are* human. They aren't perfect. They make mistakes and hurt others along the way. But you have to forgive them."

Francesca looks up at him and glowers, her lips clenched. "No. Never." She wipes away another tear. "She's not my friend anymore."

He reaches over and puts a comforting arm on his daughter. "I know how much you wanted that puppy. I'm sorry your best friend betrayed you. We were all looking forward to having him too. I'll call her mother and tell her how upset you are. But I also think you should tell Brittany yourself. When you calm down, tell her how you feel."

Francesca shakes her head. "I'm never going to speak to her again."

"Please, honey, don't do this. Are you really going to let this end your friendship? She's been your best friend practically since you were born."

"Not anymore." She stares coldly ahead.

When Francesca reached the surface, she flailed, then anchored herself to the ice and spit out a mouthful of freezing water with the same vehemence that she hurled her anger toward shore. When this was done, and she was home safe with Addie, she would wipe Ben from her life for this betrayal. He had promised so many things. To love her always. In sickness and in health. In times of need. All the days of their lives. What did promises mean, if they were broken so readily? A person's word meant everything. That's what Dominic always told her. He was right. And when people broke the promises they made, for them, there could be no forgiveness.

She never would have done this to him.

They decide on an autumn wedding and where best to have that autumnal celebration but in the heart of the most beautiful fall scenery—Vermont.

However, Francesca's parents are less than thrilled with this option. Maria and Dominic envisioned their girls being married at their local church on Long Island with the reception, grand and lavish, held at their restaurant. There they would invite the entire town to come celebrate along with them. When Francesca tells them she and Ben are planning otherwise, Maria, especially, is upset.

"Why do you want to have the most important day of your life in a place so far from all your friends and family?" Maria asks her daughter one evening when Francesca stops by the restaurant for a late dinner.

"Mama . . ." Francesca lays down her fork, the food barely touched, and frowns across the table at her mother, as they sit together in a quiet corner of the rear dining room. "You've seen the invite list. We won't leave anyone off. Everyone will come, I guarantee it. Vermont isn't so far away, only four hours. Well, maybe three and a half if there's no traffic. . . ."

"There's always traffic, and because it's so much trouble, nobody will come. It's too far away." Maria looks at Francesca and pouts. "And I can't believe you won't have a church wedding. You've been raised Catholic, and you won't be married by a priest? Shame on you."

"Please, let's not go there now." Francesca sighs and, picking up the fork, pushes the food around on her plate.

"Now is as good a time as any." Maria leans back, crosses her arms on her chest and presses her lips together. She stares unflinchingly at her daughter.

Francesca meets and holds her mother's pained and defiant gaze, which she has seen many times throughout the years. "Look, I know how important the church and religion are to both of you," she says, lowering her eyes against Maria's unwavering glare. "I respect that.

I really do." She draws figure eights on her plate with her knife. "All I'm asking is for you to respect that to me it's just not as important."

Maria grimaces. "It's all those science and philosophy courses you took in college. They make religion seem, seem—" and she hesitates "—*stupid*."

Francesca rolls her eyes. "Actually, they provided me with an alternate way of thinking about things. That maybe this one world is all there is. That maybe this one life is all we have, and we'd better make the best use of it while we can." She stabs a piece of meat with her fork. "Is that so bad?"

Maria, softening, leans across the table, placing her hand on Francesca's arm. "You're still young, yet. Maybe this is just a phase. Maybe when you're married and have children, you'll think otherwise, you'll come around."

"You mean, when I'm older I'll see the light?"

"I hope so!" Maria purses her lips. "Look, there are other reasons to have a church wedding."

"Which are?"

"Well, if you don't have one, you might look back at your wedding a couple of years from now and say how perfect it all could've been if only you had it in a beautiful church. Then you'll be full of regrets."

Francesca lays down her knife and fork and sighs. "Oh, Mama . . ."

"I know you, Francesca. You've done things like that since you were this high."

"Done what?"

"Looked back on things and regretted that they weren't as perfect as you tried to make them, as you wanted them to be."

"My wedding *will* be perfect, whether it's in a church or not!"

"But if you regret it, you'll never forgive me for not speaking up, for not pushing you. You're not very forgiving when things don't go your way."

"Well, I *am* your daughter, aren't I?" Francesca slides her mostly full plate away and dabs her mouth with the napkin.

Maria smiles, nodding. "Yes, you certainly are. The two of us, stubborn, unforgiving, perfectionists. Two peas in a pod."

Francesca laughs. "I suppose we could be worse." She reaches for her mother's hands, taking them in hers. They are small and rough from years of work.

"Ben and his family aren't even Catholic. Why should I expect him to want to be married in a Catholic ceremony?"

"If he doesn't have a tradition, fine. But you do. This is your heritage. Have you talked to him about this?"

"Well, no, not in so many words."

"Maybe you should." Maria squeezes Francesca's hands. "I know this is your wedding, but you're our firstborn. Couldn't you at least think about having a church wedding? For us? There's not much tradition left in the world today. Not many things to mark these special occasions in someone's life. If you're dead set on having this wedding so far away, can't you at least think about having the ceremony in a church?"

Francesca looks at her mother. There is an invisible boundary that both women sense and neither, wisely, dares to cross. They understand this instinctively, as they always have, for they are two sides of the same fragile but unyielding cloth: warm, open and affectionate, innocent really, but very principled and brutally hard on themselves and on anyone who dares to breach the line. Both can be very unforgiving when hurt.

There are so many things Francesca admires about her mother and hopes to emulate—her tenacity in challenging situations, her skill in providing a beautiful, comforting home for them while working long hours at the restaurant, her ability to sustain deep friendships and close family ties on a harried schedule, her striving for perfection and her refusal to accept failure or defeat, a lesson she repeatedly imparted to Francesca throughout her life. She values her relationship with Maria and hopes her mother will be there too when she has children, to share in the joy, and to pass on her wisdom. This is, in fact, their only disagreement. Yet it is such a fundamental one and Francesca senses this is something that could put a rift between them for a long time.

"I'll talk to Ben," she says. "Maybe we can work something out."

Maria, grateful, looks at her and nods.

Later that night, Francesca lies in bed with Ben in the small apartment they rent together a few towns east of her childhood home.

"My mother's upset that we're having the wedding so far away."

Ben laughs. "Vermont isn't that far away. Only a few hours. Less without traffic."

"Well, *she* thinks it's far away. And there *is* always traffic."

Ben repositions the pillow and, leaning over, sets the alarm clock on the night table next to him.

"More than that, my parents are upset we're not having a church wedding."

"Do you want a church wedding?" he asks, turning the pillow over one more time then, leaning back, looks up at the ceiling. Francesca observes his outline as the soft light from the living room seeps into the darkened bedroom.

"I don't know. I'm not religious." Francesca turns on her side, facing him. "Do you?"

"I'm not even Catholic. And the only time my family seems to go to church anymore is for—" he pauses "—is for funerals." A long silence follows. Francesca strains through the shadows to see him. He continues. "But there *are* some beautiful churches in Vermont. Some that are pretty interesting. Architecturally speaking. I wouldn't have a problem being married in one if that's what you want. It might give us some great photographic opportunities."

Francesca smiles through the darkness and reaches out her hand to him. He takes it, pulling her toward him, and gathers her in his arms. For a moment, they lie together, her head on his chest, rising and falling with each breath he takes. It is she who breaks the silence.

"Do you ever wonder?"

Ben laughs softly. "Never."

"No, I'm serious. . . ."

"Of course, I wonder. About what?"

"About all of this. Life. Death. The universe. If this is all there is."

"This *is* all there is."

"You're so sure?" She doesn't give him a chance to reply. "We had a meeting this morning at school. The mother of one of my students asked to speak with all his teachers." A tear slips down her cheek. Francesca wipes it away before Ben feels it. "The reason she asked for the meeting is because she's in the last stages of cancer. She wanted to discuss her son's future at the school, to make sure we would take care of him. Soon she won't be here to take care of him herself. She won't be here to see him through the rest of his school years." Francesca pauses. "He's not even seven."

The only sound she hears is the beating of her own heart. And his.

"She's not much older than me. Thirty, maybe. I stopped believing in a god and an afterlife when I was in college. Too many science courses, I guess. But my mother, she very much believes in a god and an afterlife. Her faith is so strong. She just seems so, so—certain. I envy her certainty. I wish I could be like her. Sometimes, I wish I could believe."

"Wishing there's something more than this won't make it true," Ben whispers.

"How are you so certain that this is all there is?"

Ben tenses; he remains silent as if retreating far into himself away from her thoughts and words which seem to disturb him. After a long moment, he replies, "Because of Lucy."

Ben rarely speaks of his sister, nor does his family. There are no photographs of her displayed anywhere in their home; all evidence of her physical existence remains hidden, packed away, stored only in the minds and hearts of the remaining family members. Francesca has never had the courage to question him about his sister's untimely death or her life among them. She listens intently now for anything he might offer about her.

"People try to find meaning in all these stupid, random events. But that's all they are. Random. Senseless incidents without any meaning. Things just happen. Good things. And bad. There's no grand plan, no 'prime mover unmoved' dictating that this or that should or shouldn't happen. It just happens. Or doesn't happen. It's all just a matter of luck. Things could always happen different than they do. It could've been different for her."

Francesca speaks, softly. Hesitantly. "Tell me."

"There's nothing to tell," he snaps. "She's dead. And when you're dead, you're dead."

She sighs, sensing her one opportunity to learn more about his deceased sister has slipped away. She sits up and looks around the darkened room. "Then why is all this here? How did it all come to be? Why am I here? Or you? If it's all random?"

"You're trying to find meaning where there is none." He sighs. "There's nothing special about us or our lives here on earth. If that was the case, what about all these other creatures? The birds of the air, the fish we eat, the insects we crush under our feet? What happens to them? Do they get to live on, too? Is there some grand meaning in a cockroach's existence?"

Francesca whispers. "I've asked myself this. Many times. Maybe all this really did come together just by chance. Maybe it really is just a fluke. A meaningless, random event that led to all this. To us. Then other times I think, how do we really know there isn't something more out there? That there might not be some other reality we can't or won't perceive?"

"There isn't," Ben says. "I know."

"Isn't it a little presumptuous of us to think we know everything there is to know? That we really have all the answers?"

Francesca feels the subtle twitching of Ben's arm against her, a signal that he is drifting off to sleep. She continues anyway. "What about all those near-death experiences that have been documented? These people are convinced there's something else beyond this life. What if they're right?"

Ben stirs. "They're not right. Once you're dead, you're dead. If there really is life after death, Lucy would've contacted me. I'm sure of it. But all I've heard these years is silence."

"Then what do you think these experiences are? Everyone who's been revived seems to have them, and they all say the same thing."

"They're nothing but hallucinations. It's their dream while dying."

Francesca leans close to him, propping herself up on her elbow as she absentmindedly strokes his chest hairs.

"Well, what if—" she pauses; her arm slices through the darkness like a well-tempered blade. "What if—*this*—is the dream?"

Francesca shook her head and blinked into the darkening sky. She was quickly losing her ability to determine what was real and what was not. Her body was no longer there; it had gone missing, as if she had already shed this heavy cocoon that kept her pinned to life. She tried to stay afloat by moving her arms and legs, but she no longer felt them. Her head bobbed just above the surface, and with each labored breath she took, she inadvertently swallowed freezing water.

Had this truly happened to them? In a split second, their lives unraveled. She looked around again. She couldn't see or hear Addie and yet just this morning she was showing her photographs from their wedding as she drank her tea by the fire while the child sat safely on her lap, turning the stiff pages of the photo album and asking questions like, "Who is this? Where was I?" Just this morning, her beloved daughter smiled up at her with approval and concluded that their wedding was, "Butiful!"

Was any of this real?

The second Saturday of October, the year that Francesca turns twenty-six, dawns bright and beautiful. The sun ascends into a cloudless deep blue sky, banishing the chilly night air and blotting away the near frost that veils fields and forests, mountains and meadows. It seems as if overnight, late summer surged into fall. When Francesca awakens on this, her wedding day, and pulls up the window shade, she gazes out on a world that is aflame with dazzling oranges and vivid yellows, deep reds and rich purples. She smiles then; she laughs.

She couldn't have asked for anything better than to be married on a day such as this.

"Francesca!" Maria calls from downstairs. "Christi's here."

"Send her up," Francesca, torn from her reverie, answers. Maria leads the photographer up to the second floor where the bride and her bridesmaids, along with Laura, gather. The morning is aflutter with preparations; the women have taken over the Vermont house, the men, including the bridegroom, have been relegated to his best man's residence in another part of town.

Christi, a young woman in her late thirties, lays her camera and equipment down on a nearby chair. "You guys just continue doing what you were doing. I've got to set things up and make sure the lighting is correct. But don't get dressed yet. That's what I want to document. The transformation of an ordinary, everyday woman into an elegant bride."

"Well, I certainly look like an ordinary woman right now," Francesca laughs as she gazes into the nearby mirror and ties her bathrobe tight around her waist.

Maria, also in her bathrobe, remarks, "She hasn't even combed her hair!"

"None of us have," Danielle laughs. "We can't get dressed until we've had our five cups of coffee, and we're only on our third!"

Laura, who was up before anyone, sleepless since the wee hours of the morning, has dressed in an elegant gray satin sheath with a matching buttonless, gray satin jacket. Her straight hair is neat as usual, turning under as it touches her shoulders. She looks too perfect for so early in the day. But her eyes betray her. They are puffy, swollen and shadowed. Even the makeup she applied can't hide what they reveal.

Christi tests the lighting, gages the meter and the flash. She frowns as she adjusts it, then tests it again. When the results satisfy her, she looks up and smiles. "Ok, so who's doing the bride's hair?"

"I am," Teresa says. "But Angela and Danielle are helping me."

"So, I guess you could say, all of us are," Danielle chuckles.

"Fine, let's start getting her ready, and I'll just keep shooting."

Teresa, Angela and Danielle dart around like the ladies-in-waiting they are, giggling and chatting as they help Francesca prepare for this momentous event. It takes the three of them, with firm instructions from the bride and direction from a few YouTube videos, to gather her long hair into an elegant and intricately woven updo. They help Francesca apply her makeup, which enhances her natural beauty without making her look false. Together with Maria and Laura, who alternately laugh and sob, they help her into her dress, an elegant strapless sheath with a long train that spreads out behind her like a field of white phlox and a small, long-sleeved, high collared lace jacket that will provide just a minimum of warmth should the day turn cooler. Maria, who is now dressed in a pink satin dress and matching jacket and shoes, places the flowing veil with trembling hands on her daughter's head. Together they gaze into the mirror as Maria cries. All the while, Christi documents every move, creating a pictorial and video chronicle of the transformation of an attractive young woman into a beautiful, glowing bride.

"Mama," Francesca says as her mother's tears flow unabated, "be happy for me, not sad." Maria nods as she covers her face with her hands. Laura stands next to her, her arm around Maria's shoulder.

"She *is* happy for you," Laura tells her in her usual quiet way. "But you are her firstborn." She looks down and closes her eyes, then takes a deep breath and continues. "Wait until Danielle gets married." She looks across the room at her only living daughter as the young woman laughs. "Don't worry, Mom, I'm going to elope, so you won't have to deal with any of this!"

"Such a beautiful young woman," Maria gushes, cradling her oldest daughter's face in her hands. "I only wish the best for you."

Francesca smiles and leans forward, hugging her mother. Her movements are slow and ungainly for the heavy and restricting garments weigh her down. "Don't worry. I have the best!"

Laura looks out the bedroom window and says, "Your father's here with the limo. Looks like it's time to go."

The church they selected for the occasion of their marriage is in the town just south of the Bodin's house. St. Charles is a stately, gothic rendition, well over a hundred years old, and stands high on a hill, flanked by a row of large pine trees. A golden cross sits atop its spire, rising high into the cloudless blue sky. The red and gold stone façade sports three arched doorways with one large and several lancet stained-glass windows. A series of broad stone steps lead up to the central doorway where the wedding party gathers.

When the music begins to play, drifting out to them from within, Dominic, blinking away a tear, extends his arm to his daughter. "Ready?"

Francesca smiles and nods. So, the procession begins. The church is full; her parent's fears are unfounded as almost everyone they invited has come. She enters, gripping her father's steady arm. Everything else falls away—the bridal party which proceeds her, the music that fills the air, the guests who stand to face her and even her father as they glide down the aisle together. The only thing she is mindful of now is Ben, who awaits her at the altar. He stands tall and handsome as ever in his dark suit, his hands clasped in front of him. A wisp of his light hair brushes his forehead, as a gentle smile wavers on his lips and a tender glint flashes in his eyes.

And when her father lifts her veil, kissing her long and hard on the cheek, a tear falls from her eyes. She hugs him close, then turns to Ben and, taking his hand in hers, stands solemnly next to him. And there before friends and family, they make an unbreakable promise to one another, a lifelong bond which no one and nothing can shatter.

Back at the house, tents are set up by the lake where the bride and groom and their party join the two hundred or so family and friends who have gathered there to celebrate the young couple's union.

As a wedding present to them, the members of Francesca's chamber group provide continuous music during the afternoon and as the festivities continue, well into the evening. Likewise, the employees of the restaurant cater a sumptuous banquet. It is a grand gala; people talk and dance and sing; children play at the lake's edge and romp through the bright forest.

"What are you guys doing in there?" Ben demands of a group of giggling children he sees running in and out of the woods. He frowns, but they are having too much fun to notice.

They halt before him and one boy whispers, "Playing."

"What are you playing?"

"I don't know."

A little girl in a red lace sequined dress with matching red shoes answers. "Pretending we're being chased by tigers." She twists from side to side, swinging her arms as the tiered skirt of her dress billows back and forth.

"Well, maybe you guys should stay out of the forest," Ben cautions them, "because there really are wild animals in there."

"Really?" a small, dark-haired boy in a white tuxedo jacket says, his smile fading as his eyes grow wide.

"Yes, really. There are coyotes and bears and bobcats too."

Their smiles and laughter evaporate as a quiet dread replaces their joy.

"A few years ago, I came face to face with a coyote. He was so big, he looked like a wolf. He wouldn't back down. I saw him right over there."

The once happy children grow fearful and somber and glance hesitantly in the direction he points.

Francesca, overhearing Ben, comes up behind him and places her hand on his arm. "Ben, don't go scaring them like that."

"It's true." He turns to her. "I don't want them going off by themselves into the woods."

"The woods are beautiful! It's paradise in there. If I had access to this when I was their age, I would've never come out. I would've taken up residence in there. Permanently." Francesca is lighthearted as she laughs and looks toward the tree line.

"No, you wouldn't've," Ben says gravely. "The forest can be very dangerous. The growth is deep and thick. They could get lost or hurt. If they went in too far, they might not find their way out again. Unless you're familiar with it, it's hard to find the trails. And they might accidentally step on or uncover a coyote or bear den and wake a sleeping predator. It's safer for them to stay out of the woods."

"But you take me in there."

"Of course, I do. But I know the woods. They don't. I wouldn't want you going in on your own either." He puts his arm around his wife. "I certainly wouldn't want you getting lost or hurt."

While Ben's protectiveness flatters her, she is quite certain she could take care of herself.

She reaches up and touches his forehead. "Stop frowning. It's our wedding day. And it's a beautiful day. Smile!"

He bends down and kisses her. Suddenly they are mindful of their guests clapping as the music swirls around them. Francesca takes his hand and leads him into the center of the gathering near the tents at the edge of the lake which glistens and ripples in the clear autumn air. There they dance and eat and drink and visit with each of their guests.

In the evening, after everyone departs, as Ben and Francesca pack the car to prepare for their week-long stay by the ocean in Maine, Ben's parents approach them.

"We'd like to talk to you about the wedding gift we want you to have." Dan takes a large envelope from the nearby table.

"Dad," Ben says, flustered, "You don't have to—"

Laura raises her hand to silence her son's objections. "We've been planning this for years. Your father and I knew we would give this to you as a gift whenever you got married."

Dan hands the envelope to Ben, who opens it and withdraws some papers. Francesca peers at them, then looks at Ben and shrugs. Ben eyes his father, perplexed.

"We're ceding a thirty-acre parcel of land to you and Francesca on the other side of the property so you can build a house. Or a camp. Whatever you would like to do with it."

Noting the young people's stunned expression, Laura explains. "It's the part of the property that goes up to the other road. That'll be where you can access it from." She points east of them. "It would be far enough away from this house to give you the feeling you're in the area but not right on top of us. You'll have your privacy, and we'll have ours.

"You'll still have access to the lake and the trails we've built," Dan adds. "You'll have to log it, of course, if you want to build a house. "

"Wow," Ben says, gazing down in awe at the legal paper he holds before him.

"What a wonderful gift!" Francesca says, truly touched. That they now have land and a place to build their future home moves her.

The next day, Ben and Francesca stroll along the Maine beach, hand in hand, still wrapped in the aura of their wedding and the excitement of their new life together. "I can't believe my parents gave us that land," Ben says as he zips up his jacket and pulls up the collar to shield his neck from the rising gusts.

"That was very generous of them." Francesca looks out over the ocean as a chilly breeze stirs.

"Yes, it is. I think they've always suspected that this is where I'd like to live, just as they've always known that Danielle would never live here. That's why it didn't surprise them when she applied to colleges in the south and in Southern California. My opinion is, she's out there to stay."

Francesca stops, picks up a half-buried stone and tosses it into the choppy waters. The waves come crashing onto the shore as the wind whips up around them. She pushes her hair out of her face.

"So, you want to move up here permanently? What would you do for work?"

"My father and I have talked about this for a while. Starting a Vermont—actually, a New England—part of the company, I mean. He has enough contacts up here that could certainly get me started. It would be a risk, and I'm sure I'd have to put in a lot of hours and maybe travel too. It's a real challenge, but I'd like to try it. Sometimes I feel like he's done everything for me. I'm part of *his* business. Now he's giving us some of *his* land. This would be a great opportunity to prove to him—and myself—that I can do this on my own."

"What about me?" she asks quietly. Too quietly. The squall carries her words off and out to sea like a stray piece of debris.

"What?" Ben shouts into the forceful gust and adjusts the collar again, shuddering from a sudden chill.

She stops and turns her back to the intensifying gale. It blows through her and around her as she faces him. "Me. What about me?"

He smiles then and winks. "Oh, you can come too."

"Be serious," she chides. "My job is on Long Island."

"I am being serious." He puts his arm around her shoulders as they continued their stroll on the beach. "There are schools up here. I'm sure you could get a job in one of them."

"These positions don't come up that often, even in schools near a big city. Might not be as easy as you think to get one. And what about my chamber group? I love performing with them. I don't want to leave them."

"Then I guess you'd have to travel down to New York. It takes you three hours to get on and off Long Island anyway with all that traffic. In the same amount of time, you could travel from Vermont to the City."

There was some logic to his arguments. She admits this only to herself, however, and not to him.

"What about my parents? I can't imagine having children and not having my mother close by."

"With thirty acres of land, we'll have room to build a small cottage for them." Ben looks at her and smiles, hugging his new wife to him. "They'd have no excuse not to come."

Francesca had often wondered what it would be like to live in Vermont full time. Their frequent weekend jaunts and longer summer stays in the middle of such a beautiful countryside always felt like visits to Shangri-La. It was perfection. Would living here all year round be as perfect and as peaceful? She is at the very least intrigued by the possibility.

"This is a great opportunity for us to try something like this. What've we got on Long Island?"

She hesitates, gazing out over the rough ocean. "My family, my job, my friends."

"You can get another job and make other friends. And your family will come. It's not that far away. Only about three hours. Well, four with traffic . . ."

"And there *is* always traffic."

He stares at her, expectantly.

She sighs. "It would be a big change for me. I'd miss them being so close. I'd miss all those good New York restaurants and all the things there are to do down there." She looks at Ben askance. "This is really important to you, isn't it?"

Ben halts and, turning to her, puts his hands on her shoulders. "This is a wonderful place to raise a family. It's an opportunity we should take. We won't regret it. I promise."

She moves away from him, sidestepping the shifting sand as the waves lap at the beach. "Then I guess we should do it."

Ben goes to her and hugs her. "You won't regret it. You'll be very happy here. I promise. Who wouldn't be?"

"Well, I'll be happy here so long as we're together."

"We will be. Always." And he kisses her.

Francesca smiles. She has no reason to doubt this.

None at all.

Francesca sobbed and gazed longingly toward the shore and the surrounding forest as the gray sky deepened into twilight and the clouds boiled and thickened overhead. She had come to love this place as much, if not more, than Ben; the life they had built for themselves over the past years had inched its way into her soul, it melded with her being; it was paradise found. She wiped her cheeks with her cold, wet glove and shivered again. How could paradise so quickly turn to hell? She closed her eyes and thought of her beautiful, warm, and comforting home that lay just beyond the forest. If she could will herself and Addie out of the lake and into the living room, things would be all right again. The soothing fire, her daughter's infectious laughter as she ran through the rooms chasing and being chased by Cruz, whose tail never stopped wagging, the smell of Sunday dinner filling the air, as Ben tinkered with whatever project he was working on that day. They had not only built themselves a house, they had forged a home. It seemed to have taken so long with obstacles they never anticipated. But they did it. Now it had all come undone.

Ben places his laptop on the long counter in the kitchen of the family restaurant and opens it. Dominic looks over his son-in-law's shoulder at the screen with great interest. Maria resumes putting the silverware away, a frown furrowing her brow.

"We think this is the final design," Francesca says. "Mama, come and see."

Maria grudgingly moves toward the counter and, after a cursory look at the screen, she pouts and moves back to the drawer across the kitchen. "It'll be a lovely house, I'm sure, even if it's so far away."

"Mama . . ." Francesca looks at Ben, then rolls her eyes and shaking her head, exasperated, sighs.

"Here, look at these plans." Ben motions for his reluctant mother-in-law to come closer. "We're going to build a small cottage, not too far from the house. On this side of the property, right about here. It'll have two bedrooms, one and a half baths, and a living room/kitchenette combo."

"Nice," Dominic says, inspecting the screen with great interest. "Are you going to rent it out?"

"No," Francesca says. "It's for you, when you come to stay, which I hope you do. Often."

Dominic's eyes light up. "Certainly, during fishing season!"

"We won't be able to," Maria snaps, amid the sound of the cutlery clanking into place. "This restaurant takes all our time. And all our energy. We can't just up and leave it for weeks on end. We need to be here."

"I don't know about that," Dominic answers, still eyeing the screen and the plans of the house and grounds. "Maybe it's time we cut back on our workload and take small vacations now and then. Ernesto's capable of running this restaurant. This'll be the perfect excuse, for us to visit our daughter. And our son-in-law."

"And at some point, grandchildren," Francesca adds as she puts her arm around her mother's shoulders. "We're doing this for you, Mama. Vermont's a beautiful place. This is where our home will be, but I want the both of you to be part of our lives. You work too hard. We want you to visit as much as you can." She kisses her mother on the cheek. "And besides, the cottage was Ben's idea." She beams at her husband. "He wants you to spend as much time with us as I do!"

Maria looks down, suppressing a smile, and wipes her hands on her apron. "Well, maybe we can get away more than we think. Maybe you won't seem so far away then. My oldest daughter." And she hugs Francesca who laughs, then holds out her arms to Ben who leans down and embraces his mother-in-law. "And my *son*!"

The young couple's lives enter a period of frenzied activity. Ben and Francesca struggle to balance their jobs and their lives while designing and building their house. They are overwhelmed. They are obsessed. But they are happy. Ben stays primarily in Vermont, working hard to establish his business in that state, and only returns to Long Island when necessary. Francesca, on the other hand, spends most of her time on Long Island, teaching and giving performances with her chamber group in and around the City. She heads up to Vermont, usually for the weekends. They communicate by phone, by texting and by video chatting. When they are together, they continue to craft the design of the house and the grounds.

Sitting on the couch one evening in their Long Island apartment, Ben brings up a satellite view of their property on his tablet.

"This is where the septic system will be." He points to the screen that shows nothing but a thick forest. "This is the area where I hope the well will be drilled. Here's the alternate spot for it, just in case they can't go deep enough here."

"How deep are they going to go?"

"A hundred feet. There's water down there, but there's a lot of rocks and stone, too." He points to another area on the screen. "And this is where the house will sit."

"What's this?" Francesca points to a lighter area in the middle of the dark woods.

"I don't know," Ben says squinting at the screen. "Probably just the way the sun is hitting the forest when this photo was taken."

"We're not going to clear too many trees, are we? I want to live in a house that's truly in the woods."

"Don't worry, there'll be plenty of forest left after we clear what we need to. That'll, of course, include a large enough yard in the back for the children to play."

"What children?" Francesca laughs and snuggles closer to him.

"The ones we're going to have." He gives her a quick kiss on the cheek and drapes his long arm around her. "Since we're doing all this work now, we should plan for the future. While we're making way for the house and the yard, I thought we should also create trails all around the grounds."

"Well, yes, we said we wanted to do that eventually, so we might as well do it now. Will it fit in our budget, though?"

"I think it can. I've gone over the numbers several times, and I believe we'll be able to afford this." He taps the screen with his finger, then traces a pattern as he talks. "Here's where the trail will begin. From here, near where the house will be, it will run through our property, crossing over onto my parents' land, and go right down to the lake. Then it'll join up with the trails my father and I've already made and circle back through their land, up through ours and end back here."

Francesca smiles as she imagines their finished house and the park-like setting that will be all theirs. "So, we'll be able to use the trails in the spring and summer and fall for hiking?"

"Yes. It'll be like our own private resort. And in the winter, we'll ride."

Francesca can't take her eyes off the screen. "It seems like a fairytale."

"Maybe it is."

She throws her head back and laughs.

Like a dream.

She tried to crush the rising terror within her. This was nothing more than a nightmare, she was sure of that now. She wasn't really trapped in this icy prison, unable to see or hear Addie. That's why Ben wouldn't answer her. She was merely asleep, while in reality, her daughter was safely sitting on the couch by the fire, reading her favorite book as she often did before dinner. And Ben was in his basement workshop tinkering with his various weekend projects.

She looked around as the cries of the barred owls echoed over the lake. Francesca often heard them calling to one another at this time of day whenever she was outside with Cruz, a bonded pair who, though separated across the vastness, were inseparable. She closed her eyes and smiled. No, this couldn't be anything other than a terrible dream.

Slowly, reluctantly, she opened her eyes, expecting to see Cruz close to her, to hear Addie's laughter nearby. Her smile faded; her fear mounted. The only thing she heard was the grim sloshing of the water as she struggled to keep herself afloat; all she saw was the expanse of ice that trapped her and the dark, foreboding woods that surrounded her, leaning in toward her, accusing her. No, this was real. She and Ben had been responsible for defiling this beautiful piece of land by carving up the forest to build their home. They had hacked their way through the woods to make trails. Perhaps this was their punishment.

In late fall, when the trees drop their leaves and the forest loses its lush barrier, Ben decides it is time to begin the task of clearing the land to make way for their house and the sculpting of the grounds they have spent the previous year designing. With the help of Ben's father, they clear away as much of the small brush and debris as possible. But felling the many larger trees is beyond them, so they hire professionals. First comes the forester who advises them which trees to keep and which to cut down. His recommendations are in keeping with the natural landscape they wish to preserve while maintaining the overall design of the grounds. This includes not only carving out an area for the house which will be amply set back from the road and surrounded by woods, but also creating a substantial area for a large backyard and extensive gardens. And of course, the trails, which will weave through the trees like a savage serpent.

When winter comes, so do the loggers.

On this gray morning in mid-February, the contractors arrive with skidders, excavators, chippers, bulldozers, cranes, and log trailers.

Francesca watches with consternation as one by one the heavy machines roll past them, cutting wide swaths in the snow. They come to a halt in formation, facing the woods. "Oh, my god," she shouts to Ben, "this looks like the Omaha Beach invasion!"

When she has recovered sufficiently from the shock of seeing so many powerful machines taking their place on the property preparing to do battle with the challenging terrain, she wraps her arms around her body, shielding herself from the early morning chill. Though the forecast calls for no new snow, the air is damp and biting. "Tell me this isn't going to cost a fortune to do," she laments and shivers.

"We'll be able to stay within budget," Ben says. His words are meant to reassure himself as much as her. He looks toward the forest and the myriad workmen who hover around the machines. "I'm going to let some hardwoods go, so we should get some good money for them. That'll reduce the overall expense. The pines aren't worth much, but some of the maples, beech, and yellow birch are."

"Don't let too many of them go," Francesca pleads. "They're the ones that are so beautiful, especially in the fall. Let's keep as many of them as we can." Her eyes sweep over the surrounding trees wistfully. "Remember what we agreed to. We said we didn't want to change the look too drastically, only as little as we had to." She pauses. "Right now, it's such a gorgeous mixture—the maples, the pines, the firs, the spruces. It's too bad we even have to touch any of it."

He sighs, exasperated. "Francesca . . . we have to cut down *some* of these trees to build the house. That's what we paid Wayne Watkins for. Remember that guy who spent a whole day here in September and who walked the property with me, tagging the trees, pointing out which could go and which should stay?"

"I wasn't up here that weekend, but, yes, I remember you talking to me about him."

"Well, he understood exactly what we wanted, that we want to preserve as many of the trees as possible and keep the landscape as natural as it looks now. He was on board with that plan. So don't worry."

She nods. "I just want it to be perfect. Like it is now."

Ben sighs again. "We have to change it. Can't do anything about that. But I promise you, it'll be beautiful. It'll be what we want. It may not be 100 percent perfect, but it'll be *almost* perfect. Think you can live with that?"

"If it isn't, then I'll find a way to make it so." She gazes stubbornly toward the forest.

"When we walked the property in the fall," Ben says, changing the subject, "we discovered something else. Something I didn't mention to you before."

"What?" She cocks her head and looks at him. "Tell me."

"I thought I saw it on the Satellite image of the property, but I wasn't sure."

"What?" She asks again, impatiently dragging out the word.

"In the middle of the forest, we found a meadow."

"A real meadow? Wow! How cool is that?"

"Very cool, especially since it's not man-made. Seems to have occurred naturally. Watkins was pretty surprised, too. He said it happens sometimes, but it's rare." He looks at her as her eyes grow wide with wonder, then he turns his gaze to the woods and points. "It's back there, just beyond these trees. When they take them down, you'll see where it is. Of course, you'll have to wait till Spring to see it in all its glory. We might have to clean up the debris a bit, but last I saw, in early fall, it came with wildflowers and green grass."

"You're not kidding? You're serious?"

"Very serious."

"Like a hidden gem you just happened to stumble upon?"

"Exactly."

She throws back her head and laughs. "Then let the demolition begin! Spring can't come soon enough."

Over the next few weeks, the machines and their workmen labor to make the necessary modifications to the property, pulling down trees, laying bare the land, opening up the forest and exposing the secret meadow. On weekends, when Francesca returns, she sees the progress firsthand. Initially, the grounds look like a killing field, with trees, once standing tall and grand, now laying scattered—nude, emaciated soldiers, pathetic casualties of an unnamed war. But by the time she visits again, the trees have been turned into logs, precisely cut and neatly stacked in a few immense piles that line the perimeter of the forest. These wooden heaps disappear at the start of each week and are replaced by others in time for the next weekend. The snow on the ground grows and buries the mounds of logs, but just as the days grow longer and the sun warmer, just before the ice melts and the frost beneath the earth heaves up from the depths, softening the grounds and the roads, turning them to thick mud, the heavy equipment and the logs disappear for good, leaving a large area of the property bare and brown and ready for building. And there, in the distance from where the house will sit, surrounded on three sides by the forest that once housed it, is the meadow.

Francesca arrives in early April to spend her week-long spring vacation in Vermont. When she emerges from the car and surveys the muddy expanse and the barren, colorless land, she is saddened. She can't imagine how they can ever recreate the natural beauty they spent all winter destroying. But then she sees it in the distance—the secret meadow, once hidden, now exposed and fully visible. It stands like a bright oasis in the middle of the sea of mud, already green and budding with life. As the morning sun creeps over the nearby mountain, it spills its light onto this parcel, turning it to gold, while the surrounding terrain remains shadowed and dim.

"Hope you brought your Wellies," Ben says as he comes up behind his wife and, placing his hands on her shoulders, leans down and kisses her.

Laughing, she turns and faces him. "I've got them on," she says as she kicks up one leg, holding it out in front of them for him to see that indeed she has on her knee-high, army green boots.

"Good," he says, "because you're going to need them. This place's a mess."

"It certainly looks that way. Except for the meadow. Which I want to see. Now. I've been waiting a long time."

"That's where we're headed." He takes her hand in his. "But first we have to cross this slimy sea!"

"Ugh!" she groans as she steps gingerly over the swamp-like grounds.

"Be careful. If you fall, it'll suck you down like quicksand, and you'll have to wait 'til June when everything's dry for me to dig you out!"

She grips his steadying hand. "Oh, don't worry about that. I'll just take you down with me!"

Their hike to the meadow is slow and arduous as they plant one leg then the other and lean forward, steadying themselves as they sink to their knees in the soft, moist soil which tries to pull them in and draw them under. They fight to keep themselves upright and out of earth's grasp, begging for the muck to release them from its slippery hold and laugh and moan as they move to a symphony of squishing and gurgling.

Finally, they reach their destination, emerging out of the slime and onto firmer, drier land. Francesca looks up and around with awe and wonder. "It's like another world here!" She bends down and runs her hand through the fledgling wildflowers and nascent grass.

"There's still snow on the mountain," Ben says as he points into the distance, "and there's still snow by the edge of the woods, over there."

She stands, turning her face upward. "The sun is so warm here, too!" She circles slowly, taking in the view from every angle, then stops and faces Ben. She slips into his arms and leans her head on his chest. "This is home."

And he smiles down at her. "It certainly is."

While Vermont's beauty is unparalleled, Francesca, who is drawn in and seduced by it, isn't quite aware yet that it comes at a significant cost.

It is Friday in late March, five months after their first anniversary; it has rained all day with the temperature hovering just above forty degrees. An after school meeting that Francesca scheduled with a parent lasts longer than she anticipates. This delays their departure from Long Island. However, despite the bad weather and the later starting time, she and Ben decide to head up to Vermont anyway. During their ride north, the rain pursues them, dropping in torrents around them. As the temperature plummets, an icy glare coats the roads. Throughout the winter, Francesca learns to cope with—and even enjoy—the snow, but she hates and fears the ice.

They are almost to the house when, in the distance, they see the taillights of the car up ahead of them turn bright red. They hear a thunderous crash, and the car disappears into the night. Ben slows their vehicle to a crawl.

"What was that?" he asks Francesca, his eyes darting back and forth over the road. "Did you hear that? Did you see what happened?"

She strains as she searches the darkness before them. "No, they were too far ahead of us. I can't see a thing."

Ben maneuvers their car over the slick, indistinct roadway. Streetlights are rare in this area and what houses exist are set back in the woods, their light barely permeating the shadows. There is little other than the headlights to guide their way.

They soon come upon the vehicle that proceeded them. It is rolled over on its roof, facing the opposite direction. The driver's side is crushed and pressed up against the metal railing. In the road, at some distance from the wreckage, lies a person on his back, arms flung out to each side.

Ben brings their car to a halt, aiming the headlights on the wreckage and the old man in the roadway. Francesca leaps from their vehicle and goes to the unconscious man, cautiously navigating the icy blacktop. Ben follows. She kneels beside the stranger amid a fine sleet as a lake of blood pools around him. His eyes stare up, wide open.

As she leans closer to him, his eyes flicker. He gasps once, then expels a terrible, gurgling sound. His body twitches and shakes, then becomes still.

"Oh, my god," Francesca shouts, drawing her hand to her heart. "I think he just died!"

Ben, who has been standing close to them, suddenly realizes that death has indeed overtaken the man in the road. He jumps back, letting out a yelp.

"Are you all right?" She turns to her husband.

"He's, he's dead!"

Francesca reaches out a trembling hand toward Ben, seeking both comfort for herself and to comfort him, but he recoils from her as if she, too, is infected with death. He steps away, eyes wide, and says again, "He's dead!"

A cry rises, emanating from within the mangled automobile. They realize there is a passenger trapped inside. Francesca stands, and almost slips, but she regains her footing as she nears the overturned car. A gray-haired woman is bleeding and crying.

"It's all right," Francesca says as she bends down, leaning close to the shattered window. The woman's cries mount toward hysteria. "We're going to get you some help." Francesca takes her cell phone from her pocket and peers at it as it sways in her unsteady hand. She closes her eyes and exhales. "Damn. No service."

"Please, get me out of here," the woman begs.

"We will," Francesca says, trying to comfort her. She checks her phone again, this time shaking it as if that will help bring on the required bars. "Ben, check your phone. Do you have service?"

He doesn't answer.

"Ben?" She turns around; he is nowhere in sight. "What the—"

"Please, help me, please!" The injured woman emits labored, frightened sobs.

Francesca, shivering, tries to soothe her. "I'm going to help you. I promise. We don't have cell service here. But we're close to our house; we have service there. I'll call the police and an ambulance when I get home."

"No, no! Please don't leave me, please. . . ." The woman's sobs turn to wails.

Francesca speaks kindly, but firmly. "Listen to me. I know you're hurt and scared. In order for me to help you, I need to get where there is service, which means I need to leave you. I won't abandon you, I won't let you down. I promise."

"Okay," the woman mutters, struggling to breathe. "But hurry, please hurry."

Francesca makes her way back to the car. Ben sits erect in the driver's seat clutching onto the steering wheel, staring ahead without blinking. "He's dead!"

"Yes, and she will be too, if we don't get her some help. Let me drive."

"Just like Lucy."

The mention of his sister's name takes Francesca up short.

"Here, let me drive." She pulls Ben from the driver's seat, helps him around the car and forces him through the passenger side door. He trembles and is rigid to her touch.

She gets behind the wheel, brushes the strands of wet hair from her eyes and drives away. She wants to get to the house quickly but is mindful of how treacherous the blacktop has become. It takes seven minutes before she turns onto their dirt road where she finally gets a signal, but those seven minutes seem long and torturous. Still at a distance from the house, she stops the car and calls 911. She tells the dispatcher what has happened, gives her name, address and number and why she left the scene. The dispatcher tells her to go home, as there have been many accidents in the area due to the treacherous road conditions. If they need any more information, they will contact her.

She lets the car idle but doesn't move it.

"Let's go," Ben whispers.

"We will in a minute. I want to wait at least until I see the ambulance."

"I just want to get to the house," he says more firmly.

She is about to answer him, when in the distance they hear the siren's wail. It draws closer and closer. Then they see flashing lights rush by, down on the main road.

"They'll handle it from here," Ben says. "Let's just go."

Francesca puts the car in drive and crawls up the road toward the house. Once there, Ben, without a word, gets out of the car, goes inside, lights a fire, and brings their suitcases in.

"I hope she lives," Francesca says when she settles herself on the couch, the glass of wine wobbling in her unsteady hand.

Ben sits stiffly, solemnly, in the chair across from his wife as he gazes blankly into his glass. He says nothing.

"I'm guessing that was her husband. Even if she'll heal physically, she'll have to deal with that loss. Now she's alone. How happy is that?"

Again, Ben says nothing but continues staring into his wine.

He has withdrawn into himself, retreating to a dark place beyond anyone's grasp. Even hers. A sudden sadness overwhelms her. She desperately wants to help her husband, to reach in and snatch him back from the sunless depths into which he has unexpectedly tumbled. She wants to pull back the black shroud that covers him and help him live again in the light but has no idea how to do this.

Instead, Francesca rises, goes to Ben and, bending down, kisses him. "Let's go to bed now." She takes his hand. "Let's say goodnight to this terrible day. Tomorrow will be better. I promise."

And it was.

And so was the next day. And the day after that. So many of the days that followed were happy for them again and full of light and warmth.

But it was their fate that not all their tomorrows would be good.

Francesca gazed wearily around the lake. A sense of despair and doom crept over her with each passing moment. She had always been so lucky; her life had progressed seamlessly, moving along as if in accordance with some flawless, pre-ordained script. How could one instant change everything? Maybe that was the problem, she thought bitterly as she forced herself to take a breath and exhale. Maybe her life hadn't been as perfect as it seemed. Maybe it was all just a false dream. Francesca shook her head, growing dizzy. No. There was a time when her life truly *was* perfect. She knew it. She felt it. It was real.

It is remarkable how blessed Francesca is, how the light of good fortune shines steadily down upon her, tapping the pieces of her life into place like some well-ordered and easily assembled puzzle. She secretly thanks a god she doesn't quite believe in for all she has; she praises the stars above, the earth below and whatever spirits that might be around her for her continued good luck and prosperity.

The following spring sees the completion of their house, the culmination of all their hard work and planning. Francesca is determined to make everything perfect. Like the color for the clapboard. Out of all the many shades of beige, she finds just the right one. Not a beige tinged with yellow, or a beige tinged with gray, not the too dark or the too light one. But that perfect color—of chocolate mousse. None of the existing paints come close, so the desired color—the one she sees in her mind's eye—is mixed by the skillful paint department manager at the local hardware store. And at her request he also mixes that most perfect shade of red for the shutters and the doors. Not that loud, fire-engine red, nor the dark barn red that people often see in Vermont. Not the one that has a tinge of orange or a tinge of brown or a tinge of pink. Not the one that's too murky like mahogany or too muted like wine. Rather that perfect red—the almost, not quite rust-red she sees in her head. Likewise, she finds the perfect colors for the interior of the house, subtle apricots, ivories, greens and blues. Her images come to life; she makes real what she envisions.

Francesca hunts down the perfect furniture, determined to purchase the perfect couches and wingback chairs, the perfect tables and lamps. When the material and colors she visualizes are unavailable, she searches the internet and orders them from afar or convinces the local stores to miraculously obtain them. Thus, she recreates what she imagines. When they see her coming, the sales staff in the local stores sigh heavily, roll their eyes, and flee to the back room for a break.

All winter long Francesca searches for teaching jobs near their new home in Vermont. Just in time for their scheduled move, she interviews for and is hired at an elementary school sixteen miles south of their house. The school is small and quaint, but it is well-funded, specifically the music program, which is one of the best in the state. She can hardly believe her good fortune. Not only to find a job in an already tight market, but an excellent one at that. And so close to home. Her commute will now be down a beautiful country road that runs alongside the Connecticut River. Gone are the days of her hour-long morning and evening journey in stop and go traffic on the Long Island Expressway. Now Francesca will have the privilege, when driving to and from work, of looking across the river at the steeple of the church and the small, quintessential New England town that graces its banks.

The head of her chamber group decides that the following year's concerts will include a few appearances in Vermont. Francesca is ecstatic; she thrills at the possibility of performing with them in her newly adopted state. There is even talk of a joint venture with them and the Vermont Symphony Orchestra in coming seasons.

And Ben's hard work is paying off as well. His client list is growing. He recently bid for and received a contract to do a major renovation of the library in the same town where Francesca's school is located.

Life for them is better than either of them could have hoped for or dreamed of.

So it is, on the last day of June in the year when she turns twenty-eight that her husband gathers her up in his arms and carries her ceremoniously over the threshold of their completed home. They kiss and caress and speak tender endearments to one another. Hand in hand they run through the rooms in wonderment, like children discovering a king's palace. They laugh and dance to whatever song fills the air from the radio; they open housewarming gifts sent by their families and friends, and they toast their future life within these walls with tall glasses of expensive red wine. They are giddy with hope and possibility.

In between the rigors of unpacking and setting up their household, Francesca pauses often, stealing long moments from the tedious and exhausting task to look out of the multitude of windows that run across the rear of the house. From the glass alcove above the kitchen sink, to the French doors near the table in the breakfast area, to the bow windows in the living room and adjoining family room, her view of the forest, the meadow and the mountain beyond is unobstructed. She is fascinated by the bright white wisps that hover above the treetops, punctuating the deep blue sky at irregular intervals as if they are nothing more than splatters from an artist's brush. She is in awe of the multicolored wildflowers swarming the meadow.

"Beautiful day, isn't it," Ben says, and coming up behind her, puts his large hands on her shoulders as she stands at the French doors, gazing out at a world in full bloom.

"It is. What a beautiful sight. How green everything is. And look at all those wildflowers. So many colors." They ripple in the soft breeze, in tandem with her speech.

"I told you you'd like it here." He leans down and kisses her.

"I used to dream of something like this, when I was a little girl."

"Like what?" He envelops her in his long arms as they gaze out at the scenery together.

"Being surrounded by forests and mountains. In a place so lush and private that I could dance naked in a meadow and no one would ever see me!"

Ben throws his head back and laughs. "So, let's do it."

"Do what?"

"Dance naked in the meadow. It's our house, our property. We can do what we want."

He leaves her, gathers a bottle of wine, two glasses, his phone and the portable Bluetooth speaker his sister gave them as a housewarming present. "C'mon."

Giggling like an embarrassed teen, she follows him to the meadow. "So, what are we going to dance to?" she asks him, tilting her head and giving him a seductive sidelong glance as he uncorks the bottle and pours the wine.

"To that new recording you and your group just made." He sets up the speaker near to them, then flips through his phone.

"Haydn's Notturno?"

"Why not?"

"Well, it *is* a fun piece which is why we chose to record it. Definitely one of my favorites."

"Ah, championing the neglected younger brother, are you." He hands her an overly full glass.

Some of the wine spills as she brings it to her lips. She brushes the red drops from her tee shirt. "Yes, of course. Always. Especially since poor Michael is destined to live in Franz Joseph's shadow forever." She raises her glass to her husband's in a toast. "Here's to Michael Haydn. Siblings shouldn't have to live in each other's shadow. It creates self-esteem and dependency problems."

Ben flinches. Francesca looks away and pauses. Then she turns, facing the forest and the mountain beyond, stretching out her arms and smiles. "If I had one wish, it would be to live here forever!"

"You can do that if you want."

"Maybe I will!"

As the music plays, Ben takes her hand in his, swings her around to face him and bows low.

"Madam."

She laughs and curtsies. "Sir."

And to this old song of the night, hand in hand, arm in arm they whirl unseen over the meadow, through the wildflowers that seem to make way for them, parting in the breeze like the red sea once parted for Moses. Little by little, amid laughter and flirtatious pantomime, they discard bits of clothing until finally at music's end, they stand naked in the sunlight. There they lay down among the blossoms, wrapping themselves around one another. And with only the trees of the forest and the birds of the air as witness to their love and passion, they affirm their undying promise to one another.

As the weeks fly by, they are aware that while they have so much, there are still two things they lack. A dog and a child.

So, on a beautiful, cloudless Saturday morning in late August, Ben turns the car into the driveway of Linda Clark's Connecticut home. The house, a plain but well-kept blue Cape Cod with white shutters, white doors, and a gray roof, is set back on a couple of acres and shields the several outbuildings hidden behind it.

"I don't know why we had to come all the way to Connecticut to buy a dog," Ben complains as he shuts off the engine. "We could've just gotten one from the shelter up in Vermont."

Francesca sighs. "The lake is very important to us. That's why a retriever seems like the best fit for us, the kind of dog that'll be comfortable in and around water."

"There are plenty of labs and lab mixes in shelters these days. They're retrievers, too. And besides, if we rescue a dog, everyone will think we're saints."

"I don't want to be a saint," she says and smirks. "I just want a dog that's healthy and well-tempered. A lot of rescues are older and have problems. I don't know if I can handle that at this point in my life."

"Not all of them are older, and not all of them have problems."

"I want a puppy we can train from the beginning, one who is healthy and has a good temperament. I don't think I can handle some of the possible problems that a rescue might have. Not now. We've got too much on our plate."

She opens the car door. "And a lab or a lab mix isn't a golden retriever. We said we wanted a dog that's great with children. The research I did showed that goldens are better. We *will* have children, at some point. And Linda's a top breeder of goldens. She comes highly recommended."

Ben gets out of the car and shrugs as Francesca, looking askance at him, chides. "And besides, we already had this conversation, didn't we?"

From their vantage point in the front of the house, Ben and

Francesca can only see the fencing that comprises the runs but not the buildings. They hear several dogs barking.

Before they can close the car doors, a large, tanned, masculine looking woman, whose graying blonde hair is pulled back in a ponytail, approaches them.

"Hi, I'm Linda," she greets them with a smile, which deepens the creases around her pale blue eyes. Shifting the metal water bowl to her left hand, she extends her right to them. "Glad you found us. Most people pass Julie Lane, since there's no sign. GPS doesn't help much—the road doesn't exist on maps."

"Telling us to look for the house with the red barn helped us find it." Francesca smiles as she shakes Linda's rugged hand.

"I admit, I hesitated," Ben says as he takes the woman's extended hand, "because it looked like someone's driveway and not a road."

"But you followed my instructions and not GPS. That's why you got here. I always tell everyone you can't take GPS too seriously around here. It usually gets them lost." The water from the dish spills onto her gray tee shirt then drips down onto her faded blue jeans that are fraying at the knees. Linda blots the wet spots on her shirt and jeans with her hand.

"I've put the adult dogs in the runs; the puppies are in the house. That way you can get to play with them without interference from Mama or Papa." She points toward the back. "We can see the adults before going in. They're all related to the pups."

Linda leads them around the back to a red kennel building and the five, roomy, shaded runs that jut out from the airy structure. On this day, each run contains an adult golden retriever. The dogs bark as the three of them approach. They stand on their hind legs, tails wagging, tongues lapping, lips curling in what appears to be a grin. Some step in their water dishes as Linda laments, "Oh, crap, I just gave you guys fresh water. Step *around* the bowls, not *in* them!"

Francesca shouts above the din, "Do they actually understand what you're saying?"

Linda smiles. "Of course, all the time. But they don't always listen!"

She leads them to the first run closest to the house. "They're excited because they're not usually confined. I let them run free most of the time. The property is fully fenced. But occasionally, they need to be put in here. Like when company comes. Otherwise, they'd mob you." She pokes her hand through the fencing and scratches one dog's head. "Yes, I know, you never get any attention, none at all, poor babies."

Ben looks at Francesca and rolls his eyes. She shakes her head and gestures, bidding him to behave.

"And here we have the mama of the litter," Linda points to the first run. "This is Lacey, Champion Glenndon's Finer Than Lace, CD, AFC, RN. She's my pride and joy. She finished her championship easily. She's a very typey golden, beautiful movement, great hips—I've got the paperwork in the house—great temperament too." Linda bends down, her face touching the fencing and purses her lips. The enthusiastic dog whimpers and licks Linda's mouth. "Aren't you Lacey, Gracey," she coos to the dog who barks in response.

"She's beautiful," Francesca says in awe.

Ben clears his throat and looks away.

"What do the letters after her name mean?" Francesca asks.

"Obedience and field titles she's earned—CD is the first level obedience called novice, the RN stands for Rally Novice, kind of a fun, but watered-down obedience competition. The AFC is what I'm most proud of—Amateur Field Champion. I try to do basic obedience as well as field trials with all my breed champions. I like titles on both ends. I think dogs should do what they are bred to do, not just prance around the ring and look pretty. She's easy because she's so much fun to work with. Very responsive. You'll see that same temperament in the female puppy I've selected for you."

She points to the other, quieter dog. "And this is her half-sister, Mona. Just as beautiful, but she never much cared for the show ring. She likes field trials though. I'm hoping to get her title next year."

"Impressive," Francesca says, as she looks with admiration at the dogs. Smiling, she glances up at Ben, who is gazing absent-mindedly toward the distant trees and yawns. She frowns at him.

"Sorry," he whispers. "Had a hard week at work."

Linda moves to the end run. "And here's my real pride and joy. Papa. Grand Champion Silver Glenndon's Deck the Halls, CD, CDX, AFC, FC, MH, HRCH. Call name is Dexter. He's got two obedience titles, he's an Amateur Field Champion, Field Champion, Master Hunter, Hunting Retriever Champion. Hips are still good, he's nine. This is his last litter. He's produced many field and breed champions. He is truly the best dog I've ever bred. You're lucky to be getting one of his puppies." She opens the gate to the run, extends her arms and Dexter jumps up and placing his front paws on her shoulders, licks her face as she strokes his back, cooing, "aren't you, Dexter Wexter, you're such a good boy, the best big boy anyone could ever have." He answers, barking three times, and wags his tail like an unstoppable rudder.

Ben looks at Francesca and sneers, then looks at his watch. "So, can we see the puppies now?"

"That's where we're going next," Linda says and puts Dexter back in his run. She leads them into the house and into a large clean kitchen whose entrances to the living room and dining room are closed off with baby gates. The room seems larger because the normal kitchen table and chairs and island are missing. Instead, in two corners are a series of white puppy pads. In the opposite corner is a bowl of water and a bowl of kibble. In the middle of this space are a myriad of toys: balls, stuffed animals that squeak, chew hooves which give off the aroma of a barn and visually unappealing half-chewed smoked pigs' ears. When Linda opens the door and ushers Ben and Francesca in, ten eight-week old, squirming, playful, squealing puppies come charging at them. "Oh my goodness," Francesca says and grins ear to ear at the sight of all these squiggly puppies crowding to get near her, their tails wagging so fast she can feel the air stirring around them. "How precious! How adorable!"

"Yes, I have to admit, golden puppies are the cutest puppies around," Linda says proudly. "You can sit down and play with them. That's what they want."

Francesca laughs and drops to the floor, sitting cross-legged as the puppies scurry toward her, tumbling into her lap, tugging at her shirt, her jeans, her wristwatch, her sneakers. "Oh my goodness," she says again, "I'm in heaven!" She picks up one after the other, brings them to her face as they lick her and yelp with joy.

"You can sit down too," Linda says to Ben, who standing, hovers on the edge of the kitchen.

"Nah, it's okay. I'll let my wife have all the fun." As he moves nearer to the door, he steps on a stuffed hedgehog that emits a loud squeak. A few of the puppies run toward him. He looks down at the flattened hedgehog and grimaces.

Linda turns her attention to Francesca. "You said when we spoke on the phone you definitely wanted a girl. So, I've picked out the red girl for you. I think she'll be great with your lifestyle, and I think her temperament will be a good fit for you. All the puppies have been exposed to children. My daughter comes every few days. She has a toddler and a five-year-old. Keep that in mind when you have a family." She laughs and looks at Ben, who forces a smile.

She looks around the kitchen for the red girl. "Hmm, she's usually the first to greet people when they come in."

Francesca looks around and reaching behind her, pulls out a puppy who has been tugging on the back of her tee shirt. "Is this the one?

"No, that's Green Girl. Oh, here she is." Linda reaches into the middle of the mass of puppies and picks up one with a red collar, then peers underneath. "Oops, this is the red boy," she says as she puts him back with the others. She surveys the kitchen, spotting another puppy with a red collar behind the water dish in the opposite corner and picks her up. "Here she is. This is your girl."

Francesca takes her and brings her up to her face. "Oh, what a cute little girl!" The puppy cries and squirms and struggles in her grasp. Several other puppies, however, tug at Francesca. Some have found their way onto her lap, but one, sporting a blue collar, wiggles his way in between her and the other puppies and, pushing them from her, stands on his hind legs, and draws his face close to hers. Francesca looks down. "Well, who are you?" she says as he licks her nose vigorously and wags his tail, emitting soft, happy bleats. She puts Red Girl down who scampers off to the opposite corner as the boy with the blue collar continues to kiss her.

"That's Blue Boy," Linda says as she reaches down and peels him from Francesca. "He's reserved for my grandchildren." She puts him in the opposite corner of the kitchen where Red Girl plays with two of her littermates, and picking her up again, returns her to Francesca's hands. "Here's your puppy."

But the same thing happens over and over. Red Girl squirms and cries until Francesca releases her and when she does, the puppy scurries to the farthest side of the room, where she buries herself behind several of her littermates or the water dish. And no matter how far away Linda places Blue Boy, he worms his way through the crowd, pushes the other puppies out of the way, and takes his place on Francesca's lap. Then he curls up close to her, facing his brothers and sisters and emits little barks when any of them approach. Francesca smiles, but Linda is flustered. She picks up Red Girl and caresses her.

"I don't know what's the matter with her," she says. "Red Girl is one of the friendliest of the litter. She never acts like this. And Blue Boy has always been stand-offish."

"Well it looks like Blue Boy has fallen in love with my wife." Ben laughs, but Linda is not amused. She puts Red Girl down then picks up Blue Boy and stroking him, places him down at the opposite side of the pen, as far away from Francesca as she can put him. "Blue Boy's my daughter's, he's already reserved, the kids have already named him," she says bluntly. "He's not for sale."

It is noon when they bid Linda and her dogs goodbye and head back to Vermont, puppy and paperwork in hand.

"So, what should we name it?" Ben asks as he turns the car north toward home. Francesca strokes the sleeping puppy, who is curled up on her lap, clearly exhausted from the morning's activities. "We can't keep calling him Blue Boy."

Francesca says as she looks tenderly down on the pup. "Yeah, he kind of just cruised into our lives, didn't he? I hope her daughter isn't too mad. I hope her grandchildren aren't crushed."

Francesca loves Cruz with all her heart. He is soft and plump and sweet; he is obedient and playful and thoroughly irresistible. And he amuses them continuously. They love the way he falls all over himself whenever he comes running. His back end moving faster than his front end, he tumbles and rolls whenever he stops suddenly, after which he stands up and shakes himself off, looking at them with intense brown eyes and a silly smile. He flies into the lake, doing belly flops onto the water, then paddles his way back to them with his favorite ball or stick, placing it gently at Francesca's feet as if he wants to share everything with her. He sleeps on the floor of their bedroom beside her. She calls him her little shadow, for he always wants to be near her. Even as a puppy, he places himself between her and whatever he perceives as a threat. As young as he is, he takes on the role of her protector. Naturally, she loves him intensely.

But a baby comes harder for them. They try for almost a year, and at one point she believes she is pregnant only to learn this is not the case. Her doctor, listening to their concerns, assures them they are both young and healthy, and there is no reason they wouldn't be able to have a child. He counsels them to stop worrying and let things happen in their own time.

In late August of that year, Francesca puts the disappointment and anxiety from her mind and turns her attention to her new job, which she loves from the moment she steps into her classroom. Her life is full now, as she puts in long hours getting to know her colleagues as well as her students for whom she is determined to prepare valuable and interesting lessons. She devotes a lot of her time to restructuring the music program at the school, a task that was given her as a condition of her employment. Francesca continues to meet up with her chamber group and give performances in and around the City. She is so preoccupied with the sudden demands of her new life, that she doesn't notice she has missed her period or she is unusually tired to the point of exhaustion most days.

As the second anniversary of their marriage nears, a test reveals she is indeed pregnant; their longing for a child and a family will now be fulfilled. Her due date is the first day of summer of the following year.

They are ecstatic and so are their families, as this will be the first grandchild for both her parents and Ben's. They anticipate the far-off event with much hope and joy and look forward to welcoming into their midst the first member of the new generation. Francesca marks every change in her body, even the most subtle, as supremely important, worthy of research and lengthy discussions with her mother and mother-in-law. Both women have many stories to tell her and much advice to give about their own experiences as first-time mothers. In this way, she is received with opened arms into this exclusive group; she too is now linked inextricably to the future. She bears her initiation into this privileged society well. Every morning, before showering, she stands naked before the mirror, looking at her body first head on, then sideways, trying to see if she can notice the smallest growth of the life within. She doesn't object when her slender figure gives way to a more matronly one. Her belly takes on a round and hardened appearance as it protrudes month by month, throwing off her posture and causing her back to ache and her legs to hurt after standing for any length of time. Her small breasts swell and grow at least two sizes. They are painful to the touch and uncomfortable most of the time. The queasiness she feels like clockwork at 4 p.m. isn't some virus she has contracted from her students. Rather it is the distress of morning sickness, albeit in the afternoon. But she endures these pains and discomforts readily, knowing they are little sacrifices for a far greater gift. One day, soon, she will hold in her arms a baby. Her firstborn. She feels a special bond with her mother. Is this how Maria felt when she was expecting her? Excitement? Unbearable love? Elemental fear?

On the day of the ultrasound, Ben takes the afternoon off from work and accompanies her to the appointment. She sits on the table, dressed in a skimpy hospital gown.

"I hope everything is all right," she says.

Ben smiles. "I'm sure it is. According to both your mother and mine, everything has progressed normally so far."

Francesca laughs. "Yes, they're the experts, aren't they." Her fingers tap the metal table. "I want to know whether it's a boy or a girl. I don't really want to wait."

"It figures, since you hate surprises." His eyes dart around the room.

She nods. "Yes, I hate being blindsided."

He shrugs. "Fine with me."

The technician enters and extends her hand to them. "Hi, I'm Amber, I'll be doing the ultrasound today. You're far enough along so we can determine the baby's gender if you're interested."

"Yes, we'd like that very much." Francesca smiles apprehensively.

"You can lay back now. Here's a pillow. Are you comfortable?"

"I'm fine."

"It'll really depend on the baby's position. We may or may not be able to tell. We'll give it a shot, though." She slathers Francesca's abdomen with a cold gel which makes her shiver.

"I know it's cold, sorry."

Amber then takes the wand and presses it to Francesca's belly.

Ben holds his wife's hand, and together they peer at the screen and the murky image of the life that has taken root inside her.

Amber glides the wand over her abdomen, then stops. She presses buttons on the monitor and points to the image. "This is a leg, and here's the foot." She turns the volume up on the monitor. "The heart sounds good and strong."

Ben and Francesca say nothing but stare mesmerized at the screen. He squeezes her hand.

Amber moves the wand again, trying to find the right position, then she smiles and taps her finger on the screen. "See this? This is the umbilical cord. And look here. It's definitely a girl."

As if they have been washed ashore in a foreign land, Ben and Francesca clutch onto one another, holding each other close. They stare at the screen, eyeing this nascent creature whose heart beats strong and rapid, the sound of which rushes through the room like the wind and thunder of a rising storm. The baby now has a reality that overwhelms them both.

Later in the evening, after dinner, Francesca sits on the loveseat across from Ben, smiling and softly stroking her belly as he talks about a client he met with earlier in the week.

"There's one more thing she needs in order to make her real," Francesca interrupts his story.

"Which is?" Ben realizes she hasn't heard a word he said.

"A name."

He chuckles. "'What's in a name?'"

"Everything. Shakespeare was wrong. But it's got to be the right name."

Francesca gets up and joins her husband on the couch. He puts his arm around her. "Any suggestions?"

She hesitates. "Yes, actually. What if we named her after your sister?"

"Danielle?"

"No—Lucy. . . ."

He stiffens and sits upright, removing his arm from her and stares ahead. "No."

"Why not?" She persists. "It would be a nice tribute to her."

"No. There was only one Lucy. She didn't make it past seventeen. Let her be."

"But I'm sure your parents—"

"Please, Francesca, let it go. We'll give our baby her own name. A good name. But not Lucy's." Ben leans forward and away from her, takes the remote and turns on the television, concentrating on finding the right channel.

Francesca sighs, gazing long at her husband. She desperately wants to ask him about Lucy, but he is unapproachable now. Instead, she rises from the couch and goes upstairs to get ready for bed. As she lies alone in the dark, the television blaring beneath her, she rubs her belly, trying to comfort and soothe the child who moves within her. "It's all right, my love," she whispers. "You'll have your own name. A good name."

That night she sleeps fitfully. And she dreams a strange dream. She is in a classroom with many young children, but only as an observer. The teacher is an attractive, tall young woman, with blonde hair neatly tied in an elaborate braid which falls behind her to her waist. She wears a gray skirted suit. The jacket sports a large Peter Pan collar and large gray buttons. She stands, dignified and genteel, in a pair of gray, low-heeled pumps before an old-fashioned blackboard which runs the length and width of the wall. Written all over it in bright white chalk is only one word repeated countless times and in countless ways: in capital and in small letters, in bold and italics, in calligraphy, in script and in large block letters. That word is adieu.

The children, who wear gray uniforms, sit at wooden desks in rows facing the front of the room. They sing out the word over and over, a lilting melody, as the pretty young teacher smiles and nods with approval. Her arms, stretched out in front of her, move to the beat of this rhythmic symphony. She gazes lovingly upon them with blue eyes that are as clear as the sea and as bottomless. There is something peaceful about this scene but also something disturbing. However, as Francesca stirs and consciousness crowds out the images, banishing the voices and blotting out the word, the dream ebbs like the ocean retreating from the shore during low tide, leaving behind no remembrance of it, but only an impression. Only an unsettled feeling. And like a fading footprint in the sand, only a child's name.

Addie.

Oh, Addie. Addie. Why? Why has this happened? And how? How could this have happened to you? Again, Francesca strained through the creeping darkness to see if she could spot her daughter, but she could see nothing except the vastness of the lake and the tall trees, crowding like dark predators around the perimeter.

"Ben!" she screamed, desperate to get his attention. "Please, you have to help Addie!" Her strained voice echoed over the lake, expanding into the surrounding space, rising to the sky, snaking through the forest until the sounds vibrated over and around her. Just as suddenly, her words fell back on themselves, tumbling down into an eerie void, vanishing as if they had never been. All she could hear, then, was the sound of her own rapid breathing. All she could feel was the fluttering of her own drowned heart. Ben never looked back. He never responded.

"Please, Ben," her voice faltered, fading to a whisper. "I know you love Addie. I know it. Please. . . ."

On this first day of summer, which dawns bright and sweltering, they welcome their daughter into the world.

In recent weeks, Francesca's body has swollen beyond anything she thought possible. It aches continuously, inside and out, preventing her from getting comfortable enough to sleep well, though she surrounds herself with so many pillows that Ben quips it looks like a fort has been built in their bed.

When she does manage to fall asleep, it is merely out of exhaustion and never for more than a few hours at a time. Walking, bending, stretching, turning have long since ceased to be instinctive. Every movement, every motion must be well thought out and purposefully executed. Otherwise she fears she will stumble or fall. She has always been agile and nimble but now feels awkward and graceless.

Maria takes a leave from the restaurant and moves into the newly completed guest cottage. Teresa and Angela join her a few days later. Dan and Laura begin spending long weekends at the Vermont house, with Laura staying on while Dan goes back to Long Island to tend to his company. But as the day approaches, Dan and Dominic put aside their work, leave their businesses and head north. Everyone wants to be there for this momentous event.

Francesca is glad to have the support of both families, because as the day of Addie's birth draws near, her anxiety increases. Her doctor tells her all is normal. She is proceeding on schedule. The baby is in the proper position. There is nothing to worry about. Everyone reassures her. Despite these words of comfort, however, she grows concerned about what awaits her. How will the delivery go? How much pain will she have? Will it be one of those long, hard deliveries that will wrack her body and deform—or even worse kill—her child? Or will it be easy and painless for both of them? Her doctor and nurses have assured her that everything is fine, but what if they are wrong? What if they have overlooked something? What if there's something wrong with the baby, and the tests haven't picked it up? Some physical defect or genetic problem? And what if she never makes it to the hospital and is forced to give birth in the car? What if, what if, what if?

To all these concerns, both Maria and Laura reassure her things will be just fine.

By the time June 21st dawns, she is ready.

It begins in the early hours of the morning. A severe pain in her lower back which doesn't cease even when she changes positions abruptly awakens her. Her abdomen tightens and feels hard to the touch as a terrible cramp ripples from top to bottom. This isn't just Addie jostling around during her usual morning activities which have become routine. This is different. The cramping seems to last forever, but when it stops, she breathes again, relieved, and looks over at her husband who is sleeping soundly. Rubbing her belly, she whispers, "It's all right, Addie. It's just you and me now. Everything's going to be okay."

Francesca lies awake as the contractions which last less than a minute come at irregular intervals. There is no need to wake Ben just yet. Instead, she soothes the restless and determined child within, comforting herself as much as she is comforting Addie. She watches the sun rise on what will be a very special day, a day that will change her life forever.

When Ben awakens and turns off his alarm, one look at his wife tells him he will not be going to work this day.

It is close to noon when, as the young couple's families gather at their house, Francesca's doctor advises her it is time to go to the hospital, for the contractions are now fierce and regular, coming closer and closer together. He tells her he will meet her there.

Ben, who seems more and more dazed as her contractions grow stronger, stumbles around the house, trying to make last-minute preparations. Just past noon, the entourage pulls out of the driveway, heading toward the hospital like a circus caravan, one car following the other almost bumper to bumper.

"Are you sure you're okay to drive?" Francesca asks her husband as they head down their dirt road, leading the way.

"Yes, yes, I'm fine," he assures her.

"Then what's beeping?"

Ben looks down at the dashboard and the flashing red light. A rhythmic tone rings out. He looks in the mirror and sighs, then steps on the brake. Dominic, who is driving behind him, comes to an abrupt halt, almost hitting him. Ben gets out, goes around to the back and smiles weakly at his in-laws. "I forgot to close the trunk," he shouts toward their open window as he slams the rear of the car closed with such force that the entire vehicle bounces.

Dan pulls up behind Dominic. Laura opens her window and calls to her son, "You left the garage doors open."

Ben lowers his eyes, his shoulders drooping.

"It's all right," Danielle tells him as she rolls down her window. "We closed them for you. Don't worry. It's all good."

He motions his gratitude to them with a raised palm then slips back behind the wheel, and they continue on their way.

Soon Francesca settles into her bed at the hospital's birthing unit, as several nurses dart about, while her doctor examines her and Ben holds her hand. Teresa, Angela, and Danielle, who sit huddled together on a nearby couch, look through some baby and parenting magazines that are scattered around the room. Laura scurries about, helping Maria unpack Francesca's suitcase, organizing her things in the closet and in nearby drawers. The men stand in the doorway, hands in pockets, talking business.

"Nothing to worry about," the doctor says, addressing not only her and Ben but their families as well. "You're right on schedule. The baby's heart rate is just what it should be. Everything is fine." He places a comforting hand on her shoulder as he stands over her. "Did you decide about pain meds?"

"Well," she says, biting her lip and squeezing Ben's hand, "I wanted to try to do this without meds, but—" she hesitates "—so far it's been pretty painful, and I'm just getting into it. I don't want an epidural though."

"We'll set you up with an IV, and you can decide later if you need something." He turns to the nurse, giving her some instructions. Francesca pulls the sheet to her neck and shivers. "I'll be back in a little bit." The doctor smiles and pats Francesca's leg.

Maria, touching her daughter's cheek gently, affectionately says after the doctor leaves, "Don't force yourself to be brave, Francesca. Take whatever help they offer you."

The nurse motions for Ben to move away from the bed as she applies a tourniquet to Francesca's upper arm. No one notices how pale he grows as he looks on with glazed eyes.

"Yes, listen to your mother." Laura draws close to her daughter-in-law. "This isn't a contest about bravery. Don't turn down any help."

The nurse unwraps a large butterfly needle, and probing for the vein with her gloved finger, maneuvers the sharp instrument through the skin until it finds its way into the blood vessel. The nurse then hooks up a long tube to the needle and connects it to a bag hanging from a pole above her. As another nurse tapes the needle and the tubing to Francesca's arm, the sound of a thunderous crash fills the room. For an instant, everything stops, even the contractions. Then chaos ensues. Francesca looks over the side of the bed, clenching her teeth as another contraction surges through her. Ben is sprawled on the floor, his head in a pool of blood. A metal hospital stand lies on its side, its contents scattered throughout the room.

Everyone rushes to the injured man. The nurse calls into the inter-com for a doctor, shouting, "Stat, stat!"

Ben, dazed, sits up slowly, clutching his head in his hands. Maria supports him as Laura holds a towel to his bleeding head.

"Oh, for god's sake," Francesca laments. Another contraction grips her. "Is he all right?"

"I, I'm all right," he mutters, but his glassy eyes never look up at her.

A young resident comes into the room, examines Ben, then calls for a wheelchair. When the orderly arrives with it, the doctor and nurses together lift Ben into the chair.

"I, I can walk," he insists, struggling against their attempt.

"No, you can't," the nurse says firmly.

"Where are you taking him?" Francesca shouts.

"Yes, where are you taking me?" Ben asks at once embarrassed and horrified that he should be leaving his wife at this juncture.

"Sorry," the doctor says. "You fell and have a head injury. You're going to x-ray and then to neurology to be evaluated. Hospital policy."

"But, but I want to see the baby. . . ."

"We'll get you back in time, I promise."

Francesca moans as another contraction courses through her.

"I'll go with him," Dan tells Laura whose eyes have a haunted, anguished look, one he has seen too often during these years. She thanks him with a quiet nod and flicker of a smile.

"Me too," Dominic says, relieved to be away from his daughter's visible pain and weeping.

Francesca cries out again, tears streaming down her cheeks. As the men disappear down the hall, the women—her mother and her mother-in-law, her sisters and her sister-in-law—crowd around her bed, forming a tight wall of protection and comfort.

"He's going to miss this," Francesca sobs.

"No, he won't," Maria says, soothing her daughter. "Your father and Dan are with him. They'll make sure he gets back here in time."

But it is not to be. Addie has other ideas, and as hard as Francesca tries to stop the inevitable, she is unable to do so.

Thus, with only the women as witnesses, amid one long terrifying scream, her daughter struggles out into the world and emerges, crying, into the light.

When Francesca first learned she was pregnant, she worried Cruz might be jealous of the baby, so on the morning of her release from the hospital, she carefully introduces him to Addie.

As they pull up to their house, Francesca feels a vast sense of relief. She is tired, but glad to be home. And, though she hasn't mentioned this to anyone, she missed Cruz terribly.

"I'll go in first," she tells Ben and stepping from the car, she takes the swaddled infant firmly in her arms. "Let me introduce them without any other distractions."

"I'm sure he'll be fine," Ben says as he pops open the trunk. "You worry too much about that dog."

Opening the door cautiously, Francesca enters. Cruz barrels toward her, as is his usual greeting, his tail whipping back and forth like an uncontrolled rudder. He emits soft whimpers as he runs. Every part of his body moves with joy. But as he nears Francesca, instead of leaping up and placing the usual lick on her cheek, he comes to a halt and stands uncertainly before her. His tail is a little lower and sways slowly from side to side.

"Cruz, this is Addie," Francesca says softly, leaning toward him, holding the infant out for him to inspect. With an intensity she has never seen in this laid-back, good-natured animal, he studies the child from head to foot, sniffing her little body, inhaling her scent with great concentration. His nose lingers over some parts of her longer than others, and Francesca notices what appears to be a frown grace his forehead. When Addie moves a little and gurgles, he cranes his head back away from her, and his eyes grow wide. For a moment, Francesca is concerned. But then he relaxes, leaning into her again and continues to sniff until finally, as if satisfied, he sits back and wags his tail. It thumps loudly on the floor.

"You really are a good, good boy!" Francesca says, relieved and happy. She leans forward and plants a long, loud kiss on his head.

The days following Addie's birth are exhausting but joyous. Francesca is grateful for the coterie of women who surround her. Each, in turn, dotes on the newest member of the family. Teresa, Angela, and Danielle continually argue over which one of them will be Addie's favorite aunt, and they pass the baby among them, cuddling her and kissing her until Francesca reminds them the infant needs her rest. Maria and Laura likewise can't get enough of holding, touching, and cradling Addie. Laura, especially, needs to embrace the baby, to kiss her forehead and stroke her cheeks, but whenever she does so even though she is smiling, a single tear inadvertently drops from her eye. Francesca, as she hugs her newborn to her, understands for a first time her mother-in-law's grief, a sorrow that never abates.

But soon everyone's lives, which were in abeyance during this eventful period, call them home and, one by one, they take their leave.

"I can get away from the restaurant in August," Maria sniffs as she hugs her daughter and embraces her granddaughter one last time. "I wish you weren't so far away," she laments.

"Mama . . . we'll see you in a month. I'll take videos and text photos every day. And we can even video chat. You won't even know we're apart."

Dominic leans down and kisses his daughter, his lips brushing her cheek, while tickling the baby's chin. He elicits a smile from the infant. "Maybe you'll come down for a long weekend before you go back to work?"

"I'll try, I promise. But school starts earlier up here—before Labor Day."

Laura is the last to go; she is reluctant to leave behind the grand-daughter she now loves with abandon. It is just after the July 4th weekend. The day is overcast and muggy when Francesca opens her door and invites her in for one last cup of coffee.

"Addie's sleeping," Francesca says as she leads Laura to the kitchen. She pours her mother-in-law a full cup and places it in front of her. "But you'll get to see her before you leave."

"I don't want to wake her," Laura says with her usual concern and consideration for others. Taking the small glass pitcher in hand, she adds a few drops of milk to her coffee. Francesca pours herself a cup of tea and, bringing it to the kitchen table, sits down opposite her. She has grown to love Laura in the years she and Ben have been together and has come to know and appreciate her mother-in-law as a quiet, gentle, kind, and empathetic woman who feels deeply and thinks seriously about many things. They have a special bond, and Francesca believes they can talk about anything.

"You're going to be all right here by yourself with Addie, right?" It is typical of Laura to worry about those she loves.

"Of course." Francesca smiles. "Ben's learning to change diapers and to soothe her. He's been helping me at night. And besides, if I have any questions, I can always text you or my mother!"

Laura nods, and bringing the cup to her lips, takes a sip. Then she places it back on the table, and hovering over it, looks steadily down into it. She draws up the difficult words as if from a well; they dribble out, limp and sodden. "Except for her brown eyes, Addie looks quite a lot like—like—Lucy."

In the years Francesca has been part of this family, she has learned almost nothing about her sister-in-law or the circumstances of her death. She has never seen so much as a photograph of the girl, and except for occasional passing references, Ben and his family never speak of her. Ben rebuffs any attempt Francesca makes at questioning him, and she has never found an appropriate time to ask Laura. But at this moment, she seizes this rare opportunity. Francesca leans forward, placing a gentle hand over her mother-in-law's.

"Tell me. Tell me about Lucy. Ben won't talk about her."

"I know," Laura whispers as she continues to gaze down into her cup. "They were very close, as twins often are." She hesitates. "He was devastated. We all were. We are still." She pauses. "I never realized until Lucy was gone, that she was the glue which held us all together. Maybe it was her spirit. She had such passion. For everything. For life in general. Since then, we've broken apart, we've become more scattered. More separate." Laura pauses again. "Addie seems to be bringing us all back together again. Just like Lucy."

Francesca looked grimly across the table at Laura. "Tell me how it happened."

"There's not much to tell really. Lucy was seventeen. It was a stupid accident. One meaningless moment, wrong place, wrong time." Laura pushes the cup away and stands up. "I'm sorry," she says as she kisses Francesca on the cheek. "I can't. I just can't." She walks out of the kitchen and climbs the stairs to the nursery. Francesca follows her. Laura, smiling, wipes away a tear as she leans over the crib, caressing the sleeping newborn's cheek. "She's beautiful. Just beautiful."

The window onto the family secret closes as suddenly as it opened. Francesca scolds herself for not pushing harder, not insisting Laura tell her more about her deceased sister-in-law. It isn't a morbid curiosity that drives her to wonder; in some inexplicable way, she feels a connection to Lucy, an invisible but enduring bond as if on some level they have known each other and are linked to one another eternally.

Francesca's desperation mounted. She scanned the lake over and over, each time hoping to discern the slightest evidence of her daughter amid the growing shadows—an imperceptible ripple amid calm waters, an unidentifiable object on a distant surface. But all she saw was the barren ice stretching out around her. Trapping her. She wondered then if she would be like Laura, destined to lose a beloved child to an accident. Would her life, too, be forever bound by grief and sorrow?

Shaking her head vigorously, Francesca uttered a determined "no" and "no" again. For the idea of Addie's death was simply unacceptable to her. If Ben wouldn't save them, then she would. Because to live on without her was just not possible. Addie was the reason she got up every morning, the reason she put one foot in front of the other each and every day. Addie was her reason for breathing. Take that away and she would breathe no more. So Francesca rejected what fate had doled out to them, and vowed she would rescue Addie herself.

Again, she gripped the surrounding ice and struggled to haul herself onto it. But again she failed, slipping beneath the surface with a startled cry.

Suddenly, though the darkness of the cloudy water shrouded her, Francesca saw things clearly for a first time. Everything that belonged to her, all she held dear she now saw not as a whole, but in their discrete parts: her home and daughter and dog, her husband, their parents and sisters, her students and colleagues, their house and property. This was it. The sum of her life. The things she valued and loved. Francesca realized at once it was her music which had held all these pieces together. It was the fundamental and vital glue that united such disparate parts, that gave expression to the most important moments of her life when words failed her as they often did. It was the steady, calming, reassuring lyrical undertone pervading her existence. But now, it was gone. She knew then her world was breaking apart, dissolving into its fundamental pieces. Would she ever be able to put it all back together again?

At two months old, Addie has learned how to scream; in her brief life, she has perfected this skill well. It begins with a soft whimper preceded by a gurgle and escalates as a frown wrinkles her smooth forehead. Her lips curl downward, transforming her face into a mask of tragedy. Slowly, her mouth widens as she bellows her anguish, and moves her whole body in tandem with the sounds she emits, arms thrashing like a crazed conductor leading a rebellious orchestra, legs, in synchrony, kicking the air above her. This symphony of infant misery reaches a crescendo and doesn't abate until Francesca has fulfilled whatever need she has. When everything else fails, Francesca has a special way of calming her distraught daughter.

"I don't know, Addie," she says on this morning in August, amid the high pitched, relentless wailing. "You've been fed and burped. You have a clean diaper. You've slept enough. You don't have a fever, you're not sick. What's the matter with you?"

Her daughter's dark eyes follow her and briefly, as Francesca speaks to her, the crying ceases only to resume full throttle when she pauses, taking a breath.

Cruz sits attentively at the foot of the bed in the master bedroom, keeping a close eye on the infant who flails and screams in the middle where her mother has placed her. He looks from her to Francesca and back again, his ears flattened against his head, his mouth slightly opened as if pleading for Francesca to do something.

"Don't worry, Cruz," she says. She leans from the bed and pats his head. "She's just practicing to be an opera singer."

Francesca takes her flute. "I have the perfect antidote to her misery." Cruz, still sitting, scoots closer and wags his tail.

She lies down next to her baby and whispers into her ear. "I know someone who wrote a lovely lullaby just for unhappy babies like you." She kisses Addie on the cheek and gently rubs her stomach. Addie's screams cease momentarily, she sniffs and turns her head and looks into her mother's eyes as her hand reflexively clutches her mother's hair. Francesca sits up, freeing her hair from her daughter's vice-like grasp. "This will soothe you, I guarantee." She brings the flute to her lips and plays Brahms' song. Addie's cries soften to whimpers, then to pleasant gurgles. Soon her eyebrows lift, and her down-turned mouth adjusts itself into a smile; her arms and legs move now, not in tandem to her screams, but to the sound of the flute. When Francesca finishes playing, a hush falls over the room, as if none of them wants to break the spell, not Addie whose hands move through the air, reaching for her mother, nor Cruz who tilts his head to one side, then another, looking intently at the flute. Francesca smiles and leans down, kissing her baby again, this time on her head, her cheek, her stomach. "See?" she tells her softly. "I told you I could take away your sadness. That's what music does. It takes us away from all our troubles and brings us to a better place."

Francesca is taken aback by the overwhelming love she has for her daughter. She has never experienced emotion this deep or this profound, not even toward Ben. Like a mad torrent, it swells and overflows, a raging river of joy and hope that floods every moment and every deed. It bursts forth from the deepest part of her, surging down through morning and evening, washing over and around this perfect little creature.

Exhausted though she is, she delights in being a mother: she rocks the child in her arms, stroking her soft cheeks, talking, singing or reading to her, watching her smile. Or laugh. Or cry.

Francesca loves those large dark eyes that follow her everywhere as she moves about the room or the house, the tiny, soft hands that always reach out longingly toward her; the gurgling and insensible attempts at language, the laughter, and even the tears. She feels a profound connection to this child that she feels toward no one else. Not even Ben.

It is torture when she returns to work and places Addie in the care of a nanny. Every day is a struggle to leave her baby, as if she is surrendering a severed limb.

But her work, both with her students and her chamber group, is good for her as it provides her with a distraction from her unending longing to be with her daughter. Her music especially calms her; it soothes her sore spirit and gives clarity to all the elements of her life, the fertile ground where hope and joy take root and grow. She hides the extent to which she misses Addie; even Ben is unaware. She structures her life so she is away only as needed. Where once she stayed for an hour or two beyond the school day, now she leaves work after the last bell, arriving home by four. If weather permits, she swaddles the infant, puts her in the stroller and calls to Cruz. The three of them walk down to the meadow where Addie gurgles and laughs, taking in the beautiful sight of the wildflowers which seem to grow without end, and the sounds of the birds as they sing and warble, an unseen, lilting chorus seeping out to them from the surrounding woods. Cruz chases his favorite ball which Francesca throws for him. He returns over and over with it, but instead of giving it to her, he rather places it delicately, like a beloved offering, into Addie's lap.

Francesca's only comfort when she leaves her daughter in the nanny's care, a woman who came highly recommended to them and whose background they scrutinized with every available resource, is that Cruz is there to watch over and protect the child.

Cruz's connection to Addie is apparent from the outset; he extends his protectiveness to her from the moment she appears in their house. Instead of lying next to Francesca's side of the bed, he now takes up a position at the foot of the crib in the adjoining nursery and alerts her to the baby's every whimper and wail. He follows them dutifully around the house, watching intently as Francesca changes the baby's diapers, bathes her, cuddles her, feeds her. When Addie is old enough to crawl, Cruz is the one who teaches her how to do it.

On an evening, just after the New Year, Ben drops to the floor at one end of the living room, and Francesca sits opposite him at the other end. She places the baby on her stomach, facing him.

"There you go, Addie, let's see if you'll go to Daddy."

Ben claps his hands together to get her attention. "Hi, Sweetie, over here. Come to Daddy! C'mon." Her head bobs up and down and she laughs and coos. Suddenly, without direction from either of them, Cruz drops beside her and begins inching along. Addie, intrigued, tries to imitate him, but she can't quite get the hang of it. As if aware of her struggle, Cruz gets up, goes behind her and nudges her forward, then returns to his position next to her, again attempting to show her the way. He does this until Addie is almost across the floor.

"Wow," Francesca laughs. "He's a better parent than we are!"

It isn't long before the two of them are crawling around the house together. And soon he teaches Addie to walk. When Ben and Francesca hold her hands, placing her in a standing position as she laughs and mutters, Cruz worms his way in between them, as if to say to all of them, "Here, like this. . . ." He encourages Addie to hold on to him for support. When she falls, he nudges her and allows her to pull herself up by holding on to him. He comforts her, too. When she sits, dazed from a fall, about to cry, he goes to her, licks her face briskly until she is distracted and laughing.

It is natural then that Cruz also teaches Addie to swim.

The lake stands at the center of their lives. Their house and property have become an Eden of sorts, a private sanctuary away from the busyness of their careers and the stress and flurry of the world—a quiet, beautiful haven full of natural wonders where they retreat when life overwhelms them.

Therefore, they spend most of their free time by the lake. In summer, they take their kayaks and paddle around the perimeter. Sometimes Ben and Francesca disembark at the deepest point and race each other back to shore. In winter, they snowmobile and skate on and across the ice. Ben and his father keep the lake well stocked with rainbow trout, which they catch either from the boat or from shore. When the lake freezes, Ben and Dan pull their little shanty out into the middle where they spend long weekends fishing. They feed their lines through the small holes they bore in the hard surface as they sit on stools around the fire and talk sports or business.

The summer following Addie's first birthday, Francesca introduces her to the water, often taking her and Cruz to the lake for the afternoon. After spreading out a blanket on the bank, she enters the shallow part while holding the child protectively in her arms. Addie squeals as the water laps against her feet, her legs, her back. She leans away from her mother, plunging her hand into its coolness.

"You like this, huh?" Francesca smiles at her daughter.

"Pretty!" Addie shouts. Her laughter echoes through the mountains.

"Yes, pretty water it is. Beautiful water." And she kisses her.

Cruz paddles around them in a circle, keeping a watchful eye on both while Addie gleefully tries to splash him.

When Addie is three, Francesca teaches her to float and hold her head under water.

"Breathe in deep, don't let it out. Hold it. Like this." She demonstrates, drawing in the deepest breath she can take and pressing her lips tightly together, she counts off the seconds by raising each finger of her hand in sequence. When Francesca holds up the last finger, she exhales with such a force that Addie laughs. "See how it's done? Now you try it, and I'll count."

Addie takes a deep breath but giggles and doesn't hold it.

"You'll never do this if you laugh, you silly girl!" Francesca pretends to scold.

Addie adopts a more serious demeanor. "I can do it. Watch. I can do it longer than you."

"Maybe you can. Let's see."

Again, the child opens her mouth wide, but this time she draws in so much air and with such a force Francesca thinks she sees the surrounding trees lean toward them. Addie holds her nose then plunges beneath the surface as her mother counts the seconds out loud. Cruz, who has been circling nearby, glides over to them when he sees Addie sink out of sight. He cocks his head and looks at the spot where he last saw her. When Francesca reaches the count of twelve, as if it is a signal, Cruz dives head-first and disappears. Seconds later, Addie emerges like a synchronized swimmer lifted high on the dog's back. She falls into the water, thrashing her fists in the air, then turns to Cruz and shouts, "You ruined it! Bad dog! I could've stayed under longer!" She splashes water in his face. He looks from one to the other, his tongue dangling from his open mouth, his lips curling into a grin.

"Addie," Francesca says sternly, "Don't be mad at Cruz. He only thought you were in trouble and tried to help." She leans over and pats the panting dog's head. "Be grateful you have such a loyal friend. He's a good dog, not a bad dog."

Addie thinks for a moment, then glides over to him, puts her arms around his neck and kisses him. "Thank you, Cruz, I love you."

Cruz is always there to buoy her, so she learns to float and later, to swim with his aid. Like a worried nursemaid, he keeps a watchful eye on her and helps her as she learns in increments. After she has mastered holding her breath for long periods of time, the patient dog allows her to straddle him as she leans back until she grazes the water while he keeps her floating and level by paddling in place beneath her. Soon, she floats on her own.

By the end of the summer, Addie fearlessly jumps into the lake beside her beloved dog, who still enters it with his usual passionate belly flop he perfected as a puppy. He swims happily, his head held high, his tongue lapping at the water. Together they wade and swim, splashing each other and racing one another toward shore. Francesca marvels at how often Cruz lets Addie win these races.

When winter comes, and the lake is overlaid with thick and sturdy ice, Francesca and Ben take their daughter there, hold her up between them, teaching her to balance on her new skates. As much as Cruz loves the water, he dislikes the ice. The few times he ventures out onto it, longing to stay close to his family as they whirl around the lake, he is unable to maintain his footing. He steps out, one paw at a time, attempting to keep his balance, but sooner or later, his legs fly out from under him; he lands on his belly with a thunderous whop as all four limbs splay outward. He then slides helplessly with a miserable look on his face. Ben and Addie laugh as he, frantically and not very gracefully, tries to get up. Francesca feels for the poor dog; she goes to him and helps her friend back up onto his feet and off the ice. With a lick on the nose and a wave of the tail, he expresses his gratitude to her while remaining sure-footed in the snow. There he trots back and forth, barking happily as he follows them around the perimeter, his tail wagging like a rudder, whipping the air up as he goes.

But his love for his family and his desire to protect them is greater than his fear and loathing of the ice. When Francesca teaches three-year-old Addie to skate across the frozen lake, Cruz follows them, stepping out onto it, then comes to a halt. He stands as steady as he can, his legs rigid, his back hunched.

"Look, Mama, I'm skating!" Addie laughs as she shakes off her mother's protective grasp and moves in circles around the solid lake. She glides over the frozen surface, enjoying the freedom of soaring by her own power and heads toward Cruz, who stands like a dejected stray with his head lowered, his lips pressed together.

Just as Addie approaches him, however, she loses her balance by leaning too far forward, and her feet slip out from underneath her. She tries to hold on to her upright position by moving her skates rapidly back and forth, hoping to outrun the force and catch up with the increasing momentum. But she can't straighten up, and she falls first onto her knees, then onto her stomach, sliding the rest of the way, rather like a baseball player claiming home base. She comes to a halt beneath the motionless dog. He turns his head, looking grimly down at her. Before Francesca can get to her, Addie catches her breath, and rising to her knees as she has always done whenever she has fallen, she reaches up to Cruz, who braces himself as she grasps his back and pulls herself to her feet.

When Francesca joins them, she takes Cruz by the collar and escorts him from the ice. "You're always so patient, Cruz," she says as she ruffles the hair on his head. He looks up at her, barks twice and wags his tail. She steps back onto the frozen lake.

"Addie," she says, taking the child by the hand, "You need to lean forward to keep your balance, but not so far forward you fall. Come on, let's try again." Addie nods and holds her mother's hand, but only for a moment until the urge to fly pulls her away once more from Francesca's grasp. Effortlessly, she glides over the lake, laughing and twirling, extending her arms, embracing her freedom. "Mama, look! I can really fly!"

Cruz is happiest when he is with his family. He knows their routine whether it is their time for work or school. On those days, he calmly stays behind, the sole sentry, guarding their abode, sleeping in his comfortable bed and waiting. Waiting for them to return. Waiting for their life together, with him very much a part of it, to resume. But he also senses when they leave the house for an adventure which is not work or school related. And if they dare to exclude him, he abandons his role of guardian of the home and follows them, wherever it is they go.

On a late afternoon during Addie's fourth winter, they leave Cruz behind as they head out on the snowmobile for a lengthy ride.

"Why can't Cruz come?" Addie laments as her mother fastens the straps of her pink bibs and helps her into her pink jacket.

"Because the snowmobile goes too fast, and all he'll do is chase it until he's exhausted. Here, put on your gloves."

"He's too dumb to take care of himself," Ben says and snickers as they leave the house. Francesca looks back at Cruz who gazes after them from the kitchen where he paces back and forth. "He'd chase it until he dies."

"Cruz, stay," Francesca commands as she closes the door behind them. Cruz whimpers and barks in protest. "He's not dumb, just determined. He wants to be with us. Nothing wrong with that."

"But Daddy said he'd add something so Cruz could come." Addie points to the machine.

Francesca gives Ben a sidelong glance. "Yes, Daddy promised to make a cart we could pull so when Cruz gets tired, he could jump on and rest as we ride. Didn't you, honey?"

Ben nods. "Yeah, I'm working on it. But who has the time?"

"The season's almost over," Francesca needles, "and it'll be another year he can't come with us."

"He'll live. Come on. Get on."

Francesca climbs on to the snowmobile behind Ben; Addie snuggles into her father's lap. Ben revs the engine and guides it onto the trail. They glide across the meadow, into the woods, heading toward the lake. When they have put a great distance between them and the house, suddenly, he appears—like an apparition, a woodland specter—running toward the machine, barking. He comes to a halt in its path and, panting, wags his tail.

Ben stops the machine and turns off the engine. "Oh, for god's sake," he says, annoyed. "You forgot to lock the dog door again."

Francesca takes off her helmet, shaking her hair loose. "No, I didn't. I'm sure I locked it."

"You couldn't've, otherwise he wouldn't've been able to get out."

"I know I locked that door."

"Cruz can open it," Addie offers. "I saw him do it yesterday."

Her parents look at her, at the panting dog, then back at her again.

Francesca climbs from the snowmobile, cradling her helmet. "Why don't you two go on with the ride. I'll take Cruz back to the house."

"You sure?"

She nods. "Just don't stay out too long."

Ben scrolls through his phone and adjusts the GoPro camera he recently installed on the front of the machine. "I'll make a video and let you know if we see anything interesting."

Cruz moves around to the left side of the snowmobile and sits in front of Addie, his tail thumping in the snow. "Bad Cruz," Addie calls to him as she laughs and leans toward him, patting him on the head.

Francesca taps him on his neck. "C'mon, Cruz, let's go. Back to the house."

Suddenly, he stands and whips around, facing the opposite direction, his ears forward, his tail suspended in mid wag.

"What's up?" Francesca asks him. Through the silence she hears it: the church bells on the green in town chime, counting out the hours.

"They finally fixed the bell tower," Ben says. "It's been broken, like forever."

Cruz lifts his head to the sky, opens his mouth and howls.

"Ugh, I wonder if they'll chime all night." Francesca sighs and taps Cruz on the head. "Stop. They're only church bells."

Ben shakes his head. "No, I heard someone say when I was at the bank the other day, they'll only ring from six in the morning to six at night."

"Thank goodness!" She exhales, relieved. "Not sure I'd want him howling at all hours of the night!"

Francesca then turns to Addie who is nestled in Ben's lap on the snowmobile. "I counted four strikes. What time do you think that means?" She takes off her glove and holds up four fingers as the child squints at her mother's hand, concentrating hard. "There's one strike for every hour." Francesca hints and waits. Addie thrusts her arm high into the darkening sky and stretches out her fingers, made stiff by the thickness of her new pink gloves. Then she tucks her thumb as best she can into her palm, awkwardly holding four fingers aloft.

"Four!" she shouts. "Like me. I'm four in June!"

Francesca smiles. "That's right, you'll be four years old in June and it's four o'clock now." She pauses and looks up at the late winter sky. "It'll be getting dark soon. Don't stay out too late." She checks the zipper of Addie's jacket, making sure it is up as far as it can go, then pats her daughter's gray and pink helmet into place.

"We won't," Ben says, looking between the phone and the camera. "We'll be back in time for dinner and a fire." He starts up the engine and turns the machine toward the lake.

She struggled up to the surface and spat the water from her mouth. She sobbed. It was almost time for dinner and a fire. That's how she had planned to end this day, this Sunday. That's how they ended most Sundays in winter. A beautiful, comforting tradition to mark the beginning of a new week. But this Sunday was clearly different.

If only they had stayed home today, if only they had been more cautious about the conditions, if only they had taken the older, less powerful machine, if only they turned back when they noticed how rough the ride was, if only they had seen the glare ice in time. If only, if only, if only. . . .

As day faded into dusk, the church bells in the distance chimed four times.

The clock strikes four in her parent's restaurant as the dinner crowd gathers. Francesca, now fifteen, sets the tables in the rear dining room, folding napkins, placing forks, spoons, knives and crystal wine glasses carefully around the gleaming dinner plates.

"Francesca!" her mother calls to her. "Simone's here."

"In a minute," she answers, laying the bread dishes on the table, making sure they are the correct distance from the dinner plates. She wants each setting to be as perfect as possible.

Maria barrels in from the kitchen and takes the remaining plates from Francesca's hands. "No, no—you go. Now. I can have the boys do this. That's why I hired them."

"Mama, you hired me too." Indeed, Francesca's new part-time job is to help her parents in the restaurant waiting tables on weekends when they are at their busiest. This allows her to earn pocket money, as she gets to keep the gratuities the patrons leave.

"But today is Wednesday," Maria says. "And Wednesdays are for Simone. So go. Go. This is more important than setting tables."

Francesca senses how hard her parents work; she appreciates that they spend a lot of money paying an accomplished flutist to give her private lessons as she prepares for the state music competition. Her ambitions are no longer those of a child. She wants more than anything in the world to win a coveted place on the state orchestra by giving the best solo audition of her young life. She has dreamed about this for years. It is almost hers.

So once a week after school, at precisely four o'clock, Simone LeClaire enters the restaurant, her gold flute ensconced in the black carrying case.

Francesca nods, then heads toward the kitchen, where her teacher—and idol—chats with Dominic.

"Simone!" Francesca greets the gracious, slender thirty-something woman whose shoulder-length brown hair is still perfectly coiffed even though she has just entered the kitchen on this blustery November day.

"Hello, Francesca," Simone says as she moves toward her with a decided air of elegance, kissing her lightly on each cheek. She is everything the young girl hopes to be—sophisticated and cultured, successful and self-assured. Educated at the New England Conservatory and privately by the great Jean Pierre Rampal, she currently holds the position of principle flutist with the Orchestra of the New York City Opera.

"My apologies about last week," she says as she unbuttons her black winter overcoat. "I didn't expect having to leave so suddenly, nor did I expect being away for so long."

"That's okay. How was the trip? How was Paris?" Francesca's eyes take on a dreamy appearance.

"The trip went well. And Paris is beautiful, as usual, even for so late in the season!" Simone smiles, noting Francesca's expression. "You'll visit there someday. When you are playing with the great orchestras of Europe!"

"Well she won't be playing with any orchestra if she doesn't learn." Maria pretends to chastise them. "So shoo, the both of you. I'll send up dinner at around six."

"Oh, Maria," Simone protests. "You don't have to."

"We know we don't have to," Dominic says as he takes her coat and scarf from her. "We *want* to. So, go. Go and make beautiful music."

So Francesca leads Simone up the back staircase to a secluded room where they continue their ongoing work preparing Francesca for her solo audition. The room is bright but sparsely furnished. A

106   ICE OUT

walnut finished baby grand piano occupies the center of the room. It is flanked by a Queen Anne dining chair, which faces a Queen Anne style music stand. The piece Francesca is working on—Mozart's "Flute Concerto No. 2 in D Major"—rests open on the stand.

Francesca is single-minded and determined in her goal. She tries to stuff down and push away a sudden, rising self-doubt. She confesses this to no one, not even Simone.

"Let's begin with the Adagio," Simone says, settling herself at the piano after Francesca has warmed up by playing a variety of scales. "This is where you've lately been losing your focus." She points to the place in the music, and Francesca nods, bringing her flute to her lips. She plays the beautiful passage, but as she approaches the part that has given her trouble, she pauses and lowers her instrument. It is a hurdle she can't bring herself to jump over.

"Francesca?" Simone turns to her, concerned.

"I hear in my head how it should sound," she blurts out, exasperated. "But I, I just can't make it happen." A stray tear slips down her cheek. The biggest dream of her young life is slipping away.

"Francesca—I don't want to hear you say the word 'can't.' Ever."

Francesca wipes her cheek. "But what if I blow the audition? What if I *fail*? I want this more than I've ever wanted anything. What'll I do then?"

"The problem is you're *thinking* too much." Simone bends down and picks up the sheet music, which has randomly fallen to the floor. "You're thinking about the goal, of winning the competition and your life beyond it. You're forgetting about the music." She pauses and looks gravely at Francesca, who lowers her eyes. "Nothing should matter to you at this point except the music. The beautiful, sublime music. Everything else is inconsequential."

Francesca nods and sniffs. Simone continues. "You see, because you're concentrating on the goal rather than the means, you're *thinking,* not *feeling.* Music—art—is not something that can be thought about. In the beginning, yes. But ultimately it has to be *felt.*"

"How?"

Simone looks at her intensely for a moment, then looks away and says softly, "You must let it come from within you, and trust that it will in fact come. You must feel it with all your senses, and with every nerve in your body. You must meld with it. Become one with it. *Surrender* to it."

Francesca sighs, not quite understanding what Simone is telling her. Nevertheless, she brings the instrument to her lips again and, blinking away another tear, locates her place in the score. She attempts to force all thought from her mind, hoping to meet the music on its most fundamental level. She plays haltingly, struggling like a novice. Simone stares ahead.

For brief moments, when she relaxes, the music comes to her as it is meant to come. Here and there, scattered among the phrases, she glimpses the perfection she longs to achieve.

When she is done playing and the last note dissolves slowly into silence, she opens her eyes, lowers her flute and exhales, relieved.

"It was there. Briefly." Simone places a reassuring hand on her shoulder. "Did you feel it?"

Francesca nods. "It still eludes me most of the time, though. It's like a bird I can see, I can get close to, but flies away the minute I reach out to touch it."

"You need to concentrate on the one moment where you almost touched it. Eventually, it won't fly away. Eventually, when you open your hand, it will light upon it."

Francesca nods again. She worries that her self-doubt is stronger than the music itself. She wonders if anything can assuage her lack of confidence.

But she refuses to give up. Sometimes when she is bored, either in the restaurant or at school, she will drift inward where her music lives and note by note, theme by theme, she calls to it, and it sings to her. In this way, she practices even without an instrument in hand.

Her audition is set for the first Saturday in May and all year long, she struggles to keep up her confidence; her days are a continual fight to banish the demon of self-doubt. As the day approaches, Simone tells her she's ready, but she doesn't feel it.

When the morning of her audition dawns, it is thick with clouds and humidity. Dominic runs the car's air conditioner which fogs up the outside of the car windows. The oppressive spring air oppresses Francesca.

After a forty minute drive, spent mostly in silence, they arrive at the school where the competition is taking place—a large building which houses both a high school and a middle school. As he pulls into the parking lot, Dominic surveys the crowd.

"Looks like a full house today," he says as he steers the car into a spot some distance from the entrance.

"It's a big event," Maria says quietly, looking around in awe.

Francesca, seated in the back of their Plymouth Voyager, hugs the bag that contains her flute and originals of the sheet music as she looks nervously out the window at the crowd cramming into the front doorway.

"What if we can't find Simone in all these people?" she asks as they emerge from the car and walk toward the packed entrance.

"We'll find her." Maria puts an arm around her daughter. "Don't worry, honey, she'll be here."

After they enter the lobby, they are directed down the hall and up one level to the room where the audition will take place. Francesca trails her parents, cradling her bag as they search for room 202 amid the throng of other parents and students who are also navigating the unfamiliar corridor in search of their assigned rooms.

When they locate the room, Francesca hesitates. "We have to wait for Simone."

At that moment, hurrying toward them from the opposite end of the hall is her music teacher, who weaves in and out of the crowd, avoiding collisions with parents and students alike.

"Thank god you're here!" Maria exhales and opens her arms to embrace Simone, who slips into them with a smile. She greets Francesca with a gentle kiss on each cheek, then shakes Dominic's large hand. "I thought I left the City in plenty of time. There's always so much traffic on the LIE, even on a Saturday. But I never expected that much traffic." She looks at her watch. "We still have time, though. We're fine. Let's go in and get settled."

Simone enters the room; Francesca hesitates.

"It'll be okay." Dominic smiles and gently touches his daughter's pale cheek.

She nods and follows Simone into the room.

Maria and Dominic hover on the threshold. "Should we come in now?"

The Adjudicator, a portly, balding middle-aged man, stands behind the desk at the front of the room, cleaning his black-framed glasses with a large, white handkerchief as he greets Simone and Francesca then motions for Maria and Dominic to enter.

"You can take a seat in the back," he says to them, pointing to the chairs that are set up in place of the desks, which are stacked and pushed off to one side. "You can stay for the scales and solo portion of this, but you have to leave when we do the sight-reading."

Maria and Dominic nod as they take their designated seats.

"I'm Mr. Geller, by the way." He shakes Simone's hand and manages a faint smile as he glances at Francesca.

"How lucky for us to have a real piano and not just a keyboard," Simone says affably.

"Yes, I always try to get one for these auditions. I prefer it as well."
Mr. Geller looks at his watch. "We might as well get started. You can
warm up some if you'd like."

Francesca nods and gives a copy of the sheet music, one to Simone
and one to Mr. Geller, then takes a seat in front of the music stand.
Simone settles herself at the piano.

After Francesca has sufficiently warmed up, Mr. Geller instructs
her as to what scales she must play for this part of the audition. She
does so with precision and artistry. Then comes her solo. What she has
worked on for months. What she has feared for months. She pauses
and for the first time looks around the classroom. She notices post-
er-sized placards on the walls. Each has a quote printed in large black
calligraphic letters. These hang at even intervals and frame the room.

One reads: *"The mind is everything. What you think you
become." —Buddha*

Another one reads: *"Every strike brings me closer to the next home
run." —Babe Ruth*

And a third one: *"You can never cross the ocean until you have the
courage to lose sight of the shore." —Christopher Columbus*

Simone looks over at her and asks, "Ready?"

Francesca blinks, then nods and brings the flute to her lips. She
beckons to her music, and it comes to her. This time, it doesn't fail
her. With each note and phrase, she relaxes and yields to the seduc-
tion as if yielding to a lover; when she capitulates to the music and
truly *feels* it, as it drifts over her, around her, through her, *in* her,
there is no end or beginning to either her or the song. The boundar-
ies between them dissolve, and she surrenders to it completely. The
music comes as it is meant to come, as it wants to come, as she needs
it to come. Francesca exercises absolute control over it and over herself and doesn't have to wait to learn that she played perfectly or that

her score of one hundred assures her a coveted place with the state orchestra. She knows the moment the last note fades away. From this point on, she can control anything and has become the master of fate itself.

Francesca gazed up into the shrouded sky. She felt herself quickly weakening. She desperately needed saving. So did Addie. Yet every previous attempt she made to break free of the ice, failed. If she could just call to her music now, summon it from within her, make it rise, like a silvery god here on the icy lake, she believed—no, she *knew*—they would be saved. That's how she controlled everything. The insurmountable became attainable. Through her music, always through her music.

As the day dropped from her, slithering off into dusk, Francesca made one last attempt, bidding her beloved music to come as she had done on so many other occasions. But on this day, at this moment when she needed it the most, it abandoned her. She heard nothing but the lapping of the water and the cry of a crow as it glided free and fearless above her, taunting her. Realizing then that her power to control, to will, to accomplish the impossible no longer existed, she panicked and frantically flailed about, churning up the frigid waters around her, trying over and over to clear the ice which imprisoned her. Why did they venture out today, why didn't they turn back?

"Mama, Daddy!" Addie yells as she and Cruz tear into their bedroom on this Sunday morning in early December. She climbs onto the bed, rousing her sleeping parents. "It snowed last night! It finally snowed!" Cruz barks and wags his tail as he goes from one side of the bed to the other, nuzzling and licking Francesca and Ben in turn.

"Ugh," Francesca moans. "What time is it?"

"Too early," Ben mumbles from beneath the pillow he puts over his head.

Addie, unmindful that her parents are not sharing her excitement, wedges in between them, kneeling and tugging at their covers. "Come on, get up and look!"

Francesca opens one eye and raises her head a bit, glancing toward the window at the other end of the room. From her vantage point she sees the trees laden with snow. It looks heavy and wet. "We got a good amount even though it started out as rain."

Ben folds back the covers, lumbers out of bed and goes to the window. "Yep, a decent amount. Maybe we can take the new machine out for a spin." They had bought the large, two-up in the off season, for a very good price, and Ben has talked about nothing but riding it since then.

Francesca hesitates. She remembers hearing the rain pelt the roof as she was drifting off to sleep. It seems like the temperatures plummeted through the night.

Addie, her dark eyes full of wonder and excitement, tugs again at her mother. "Can we? Can we go? Please??"

Francesca yawns. "Maybe later. The conditions may not be good. We'll see."

"That machine's very powerful," Ben says as he gazes longingly out at the white landscape. "I'd love to see just what this new one can do. I've been waiting all summer to try it."

Francesca hesitates. "It won't be good if there's ice."

"It's still snowing," Ben counters.

"Is it sleeting?"

"Looks like snow, not sleet. Let's see how the day goes. Maybe this afternoon."

And even though Francesca has misgivings, she knows Ben and Addie will win out. They always do.

It is later in the afternoon when the snow stops. The day remains cold and gray. Ben convinces her it is safe for them to go for a ride. Addie dances around the house, ecstatic.

"Can Cruz come yet?" Addie asks her mother, as Francesca helps her to suit up.

"Not yet, honey."

"But Daddy said he'd make something so Cruz could come," Addie frets.

And indeed, Ben had promised.

It was now of Cruz, locked safely away in the house, that Francesca ruefully thought on this Sunday in early December as twilight closed in on her and the lake.

It happened so quickly. So suddenly. She could barely comprehend the sequence of twists and turns that had just changed their lives forever.

The trail emerging out of the forest on the eastern side of the lake was always tricky to navigate, especially with a larger snowmobile, even with a thick pack of snow on it. Once they cleared the trees, there was a short but steep drop which brought them to the water's edge. When Francesca first traveled this course alone on her own, less powerful machine, she hesitated at the top before finding the courage to slide down the incline. Ben knew it by heart, however, and always piloted the snowmobile with expertise and ease, instinctively understanding how fast to go, how to correct for any slipping or leaning. Having his young daughter ensconced in his lap and his wife seated behind him made him even more cautious.

But today, something went wrong. Perhaps it was glare ice that defeated them, perhaps the machine was more powerful than he could handle. When they first set off, he accidentally hit the throttle too hard, and they jerked forward with a force that threatened to eject them into the surrounding landscape. Francesca cautioned him to be careful. Whatever the cause, his instinct and his skill failed them. As they careened down the slope, the sled's skis caught something; it lurched and leaned; as hard as Ben tried to keep it upright and maneuver it away from the frozen lake, he was unable to do so. It bounced and went briefly airborne, then skidded over the frozen surface, catapulting and scattering the three riders onto and through the shallow ice. The machine sputtered and sparked and crashed through the surface, sinking out of sight.

Not realizing what happened at first, Francesca went limp as she plummeted beneath the freezing waters. Then instinct and her will to live arose; she tore off her helmet and fought her way to the surface. She tried to shout, but couldn't catch her breath. The world spun around her as she gasped and shivered.

"Addie!" she whispered, frantically looking around. She forced herself to stop gasping, to take long, steady breaths.

"Addie!" she shouted as her voice returned to her. Her desperate cry echoed over the lake. She scanned the expanse for her daughter. Francesca knew that Addie, at the age of four, was a skilled swimmer. But the waters were frigid; the heavy clothes she wore—the bibs, boots and helmet—would surely weigh down such a small child. She panicked. Addie was nowhere in sight.

Then she spotted Ben, not far from her, and called to him. He seemed dazed.

"Ben, I, I can't see Addie!" Francesca sought to move closer, but a segment of ice separated them. She tried to float on her stomach, hoping to clutch onto the ice with her arms, but her heavy clothes bogged her down. She attempted to leap out of the water, but she couldn't get the height. "Ben!" she screamed again. "Where's Addie? I can't see her!" One of them had to find her.

Francesca clutched wildly for his hand, hoping to grasp it, but he shook her off and shrunk from her without a word. Then he disappeared, descending beneath the surface. Within seconds he emerged, a mighty whale sputtering, twisting, leaping into the air from its watery haunt, only to crash onto the ice. She heard it crack as he lay flat, his limbs spread in all directions, reminding her of her beloved Cruz. But the ice held. Desperately, she grabbed onto his foot, hoping he would somehow drag her out.

But in a silent, delirious moment, he cringed and, shaking her off, recoiled from her as if she were death itself. He turned and stared at her long and hard, as if he no longer recognized her. Gone was the loving gaze that had always rained gently over her. His eyes were now hollow and foreign.

She let out a cry and again reached for him, but he scurried from her, moving beyond her grasp. There he unzipped his hip pocket and withdrew his keys, selecting the largest one, then plunging it into the ice like a spear. Slowly, deliberately, he crawled and dragged himself over the ice to shore.

"Ben," she screamed, tears streaming down her numb cheeks. "You have to find Addie! Save her! Please!"

But there at the water's edge, Ben lay still and face down in the snow. Francesca shivered and tried to leap onto the ice again, but again, she couldn't clear it. She sank farther into the depths. Despair overwhelmed her. Why was this happening? She mustered her strength and rose again from the water, looking around for Addie. She had to save her daughter, somehow. Some way. Anger bubbled up from within her. She raised tear-filled eyes to the heavens and screamed, a desperate cry reverberating through the mountains, echoing through the forest, a raging query that would not be silenced.

Why?

BEN

Why?

The frantic question echoed around him and through him as he lay face down in the snow. He moved his hands to his ears to block out the sound, but it crashed through the darkness, boring into his soul.

He shivered. Why had this happened to them? To him? It had just been a pleasant Sunday afternoon ride with his family. Now, as he heard his beloved wife's screams in the distance, he sensed all was lost. He wanted to move, to rise, to lift himself from the ice and away from this terrible reality, but some force beyond him tethered him to the earth. He loved Francesca. He loved Addie. They were his world. Yet he knew his world was gone. Vanished. As if it never was. As if it had already happened.

Just like Lucy.

They are born eighteen minutes apart. And except for those eighteen minutes when he is pulled from the womb first and lies alone out in the world, he has always had Lucy's comforting presence nearby. Hers is the first recognizable sound he processes—the distraught cry of the newly born, of one whose journey into life was as perilous as his own. Amid the unfamiliar background din, it reassures him. As he is roughly handled, poked and prodded, hers is the first touch he warms to, a familiar nudge, an assuaging pinch. He is no longer alone.

As they grow, people often remark on how similar they are: they sport the same thick wavy blonde hair, the same large, intense blue eyes, the same body type—tall, lean, and athletic. It is as if they are truly two halves of one whole.

But where Ben is shy and cautious, Lucy is gregarious and adventuresome, with a passion for life and a fearlessness that keeps her forging ahead, when he prefers to hang back. She is clearly the trailblazer. No one ever guesses she gives him the courage to do things he wouldn't ordinarily do on his own. He needs her strength, her passion in the same way he would later need Francesca's. Alone, he is useless and cowardly. But this is his secret. Admitted to no one. Not even to himself. And understood only by Lucy.

Though he is the older of the two, Lucy is the first to crawl, to walk, to talk. Like a restless, dauntless bird, she is more than eager to jump from the nest, fly out into the world where she seeks to devour life whole.

They are five when Lucy confronts Laura. Her arms akimbo, she stamps her foot for emphasis.

"I want to ride like a grown up."

Laura hesitates. "Those training wheels keep you balanced. Are you sure you're ready for a two-wheeler?"

"Yes!" Even if she isn't ready, her parents and brother know she will try anyway. She will force herself to be ready, will herself to stay upright. Laura worries constantly about her daring daughter.

Dan takes the training wheels from her red bicycle, turning it into the "grown up" bike she desires. He and Laura alternate running with her, holding on to the seat to help balance her, but she shoos their helping hands away, insisting, "Let me do it myself!" And so she does. She falls often and endures scraped knees, elbows, and contusions on her thighs and stomach. She even once lands on her face, sliding to a halt on the rough gravel. Shedding nary a tear, she brushes her blonde hair from her eyes, pats her bleeding cheek and laughs—always that infectious laughter—as she leaps up, kicks the bike before steadying it, then hops back on and rides away toward home, holding her head high. Her falls and bruises cause Ben to wince. But these never bother her. They only make her more determined. It doesn't take long for her to master the two-wheeler. Ben, standing in the shadows, looks upon her resolve in sheer amazement. He tries to emulate it, but a pervasive and elemental fear always stops him. Lucy, intuitively attuned to him, then takes his hand on these occasions, and guides him whether it is to his bicycle or to their first day at a new school, encouraging him, "Here, Ben, like this. . . ." Never critical or judgmental of his fear or his hesitancy, she instinctively aids and protects him. Her bond with him is unbreakable; they are truly two halves of one whole.

At the beginning of the school year when they are in second grade, Lucy once again begs her parents to allow them to ride the school bus, something she has desired ever since they were in kindergarten. Every day she looks with envy upon the students who come off the bus in the morning and who eagerly jaunt toward the large familiar yellow vehicles that await them every afternoon. It seems like a secret society from which she and Ben are purposefully excluded.

"Don't you like having your own private chauffeur?" Laura asks her daughter as she smiles and points to herself.

"What's 'chauffeur'?" Lucy frowns, stumbling over the word.

"A private driver. Me. I'm your *chauffeur*." She pronounces the word with a French accent, which makes both children giggle. "I take the two of you to school and drop you off and pick you up afterward. Don't you like that?"

"No." Lucy hops from one spot to another for emphasis.

"Why not?" Laura pouts, feigning rejection.

"Everyone says the bus is more fun."

"In what way is it fun?"

Lucy shrugs, pausing for a long moment. "Well, it passes this house on a corner where a hand goes up in a window and waves. The bus stops and honks its horn, and the hand waves back. I want to see it."

"It sounds too creepy to me," Ben says. He is content to have Laura drive them back and forth to school.

"Do you know why the bus stops at that house every morning?"

Lucy shakes her head.

"Probably to creep us out," Ben offers.

"All the buses, using the route, stop there. It's a ritual started a long time ago. A young boy, who was just a little older than you two are now, was in a terrible accident and became paralyzed."

Lucy's eyes grow wide. Ben looks away. He doesn't like where this story is going.

"You mean, he can't walk?" Lucy asks.

"He can't do anything," Ben says. "Can't move at all. Jason and Nick told me about him at lunch last week."

Her eyes grow wider, still. To her, movement is happiness. Movement is power. Over the world and herself. To bend, to stretch, to run is pure pleasure. It is liberation from the restraints that shackle her, the freedom to fly away from any situation. Like the birds she envies as they soar and glide above her, their wings beating to the rhythm of life, controlled and graceful, yet full of purpose, in command of themselves and of the heavens. It is the ability to make her dreams real, as she outruns a wicked stepmother when she plays at being a fairytale princess or brandishing an imaginary sword when she and Ben imitate a duel, the capacity to stride through the world propped up by her own will, as she etches a path over the earth, leaving a definite mark, to prove to herself as well as to others that she is real, that she is here. For Lucy, movement is life itself.

"Not only can't he walk," Laura continues, "but he can't talk, sit up, feed himself, or move his arms. Nothing. His parents didn't want to put him in a nursing home, so they chose to take care of him at home. Not sure how it started, but someone built him a mechanical hand. He can control it somehow, maybe with his mouth. When he was first hurt, the buses with all his friends and classmates would stop and honk to let him know they were still thinking about him, and he would wave back using this hand. Since then, it's become a tradition. So now, twenty-five years later, they still do it."

"Then I want to see the hand. I want to wave back."

Ben looks at his sister. "Well, I don't. It's too creepy for me."

Giving in to Lucy's insistence, Laura surrenders her role as her children's chauffeur and allows them to take the bus. When the driver opens the door on this first day of a new week, Lucy bounds up the steps with excitement, but Ben hesitates. He dreads this day; he has had nightmares about a giant hand that clutches at him, picks at him, pinches him in its large, forbidding fingers and crushes him, snuffing him out like an annoying insect. In those dreams he too is paralyzed, unable to move, unable to speak. Unable to save himself. Or others.

They take a seat next to the window on the side of the bus where they will have the best view of the house and the hand. Lucy's excitement builds as she chatters with her classmates nearby. Ben, however, is silent and breaks out in a sweat the closer they come to the disabled man and his mechanical hand.

The bus rounds the corner in a quiet suburban neighborhood after picking up its last group of children. Finally, they are there. The driver, Mr. Grissom, brings the vehicle to a halt in front of the house, a small, white ranch with well-trimmed shrubbery framing a large picture window. He honks the horn several times. The children crowd together, looking out with anticipation.

And suddenly, they see it. Like a fiend freeing itself from the deep, this enormous stark white hand, with its long straight fingers, rises from the bottom left corner of the window. It curves upward and sweeps across the glass, filling it as it goes, then glides downward until it disappears into the lower right corner, an alien sun dropping into the unseen sea. But like a persistent beast that refuses to be snuffed out, it rises again and again, following the same trajectory, back and forth, across the pane. Sweat drips from Ben's head to his neck and finds its way, drop by drop, down his shirt and onto his back, which makes him shiver.

"What's a matter, pretty boy?" A large, rotund sixth-grader mocks as he pushes Ben. "You afraid of the hand?"

Ben shrinks away from the bully as best he can without replying. Lucy, however, wheels around and moves toward the boy who is blocking the aisle, trapping them in their seats. "Leave my brother alone," she orders, her eyes narrowing.

The older boy laughs and so do his friends who have now joined him in the aisle.

"And if I don't, what are you going to do about it?" The portly boy laughs again, placing a heavy hand on her head.

Lucy answers him, though not in words. She takes everyone by surprise. Even Ben and especially the big sixth-grader and his friends when she crouches, escaping his hand and moves so deftly and so quickly he never sees the punch to his stomach coming even when it doubles him over, nor is there time for him to protect himself from the right blow to his head which catches him in the eye. When the final kick to the groin arrives, he is crying like a baby as he crashes backward, dragging his friends with him. The other children topple out of their seats and, drawn on by the ruckus, climb over one another, scrambling toward the combatants until Mr. Grissom, who bolts from the driver's seat and stomps down the aisle, thunders, "Knock it off, you miserable little . . ."

And that is the last time Lucy and Ben ever ride the bus.

Her protection is so complete even Dan and Laura never guess that such a demon lives within him, a determined beast he must always keep in check. Every moment of every day. He can never relax his vigil; he senses it will take very little for the ogre, like the hand in the window, to rise and overwhelm him.

But with Lucy by his side, he manages. Her lust for life overflows in torrents; it rains down and engulfs him so he, too, seems passionate and joyful. Their shared childhood is replete with many happy memories.

Where was that happiness now, he wondered as he lay immobile in the snow amid his wife's cries for help and the sudden carnage of his life. His childhood had been made joyous and peaceful by this place. The lake that had suddenly taken everything from him, was once their beloved playground where he and Lucy learned to swim and fish in, skate on; the surrounding woods where they romped in, ran through, loved. . . .

It is during the summer when he and Lucy are six that he first sees the lake and the property which would become their second home. His parents pack them and one-year-old Danielle into the car and head for a state he has never heard of for their month-long vacation: Vermont. As usual, Lucy is eager for a new adventure. In the previous weeks, Laura and Dan talk to their children about the family's upcoming vacation.

"Where's Vermont?" Lucy asks, her unfettered curiosity piqued.

"About four hours north of here," Laura tells her.

"Well, where's north?"

Laura brings both her and Ben outside to their front lawn, then turns them to the right. "That way."

Ben looks in the direction Laura points and sees only their neighbor's house. But Lucy looks up and above the neighboring house and sees beautiful Vermont. "There are mountains and lots of green trees!" She laughs and pointing, jumps up and down.

Laura, smiling, presses her cheek to her daughter's. "And beautiful clear blue lakes. And rushing rivers and streams. Nothing like we see on Long Island."

For weeks before their impending vacation, Lucy studies the map of the Northeast which Dan gives her, and soon she has learned by heart the route they will take, through Connecticut and Massachusetts into southern Vermont. She memorizes many of the cities and towns she locates on the map. Henceforth, dinnertime becomes a question-and-answer session:

"Where will we be staying? In Bennington? Or Brattleboro? Maybe Arlington? Manchester? Can we stop in Grafton? Ludlow? Windsor or Plainfield? I thought you said we could visit Island Pond and Grand Isle? And Lake Mem . . . Mem . . . Memgog . . ."

"Lake Memphremagog," Dan offers as he and Laura patiently answer their inquisitive daughter.

Her excitement builds every day until at last they arrive at the lake house they will rent for the month. She bursts from the car like a chick from the egg, and with arms outstretched she soars through the rooms trying to embrace everything—the beautiful curtains fluttering in the breeze of the open windows, the large country furniture, the very air itself.

For the last part of July and into August, they spend their days swimming in and boating on the nearby rivers, fishing in neighboring creeks and streams, and trekking through the surrounding woods. They visit country stores and working farms. They roam through covered bridges and old buildings that date back at least two hundred years. They hike up mountains, taking expansive aerial shots of the breathtaking views of New Hampshire seen from Vermont across the Connecticut River. In the evenings, they retreat to their rented waterfront house, weary but exhilarated wayfarers where they cook the fish they caught during the day over the camp fire they build on the bank.

In between their activities, Laura and Dan take the children along as they scope out properties in hopes of buying some land. It had been Dan's secret childhood dream to have a home in the country, and now that his family is complete and his business doing well, it is time to make this a reality.

They visit several properties in and around central Vermont, but when they come upon one which sports a large private lake, Dan knows this is where they will build their home.

Ben and Lucy hold hands as they stand in awe at water's edge.

"Wow! she says. "It looks like a sea."

"No, it's got to be the ocean!" Ben looks out upon the expanse with wonder. "There aren't any waves, though."

Laura places a hand on each of her children's shoulders, leans down so her face is level with theirs and she too looks out at the lake. "It's beautiful, isn't it."

"Mr. and Mrs. Bodin, glad you could make it."

Dan turns. "Mr. Austin? He stretches out his hand to greet the approaching man.

"Yep, that's me. But most people just call me Willy." He shakes first Dan's hand, then Laura's. "Perfect day for you to come to see this." He nods toward the lake and the forest beyond as he smooths his short, neatly cropped gray beard and mustache, then settles his thick gray hair which the breeze has ruffled.

"We were just remarking how beautiful it is," Laura says scanning the lake and surrounding woods. "So peaceful, so private. Like paradise!"

Willy smiles. "Yep, it is. Got lots a good memories from this place." He looks down at Ben. "When me and my brothers were boys, from the time we were this high, we spent lots of time here with my pop." He turns and points toward the trees on the opposite side of the lake. "We'd set up camp yonder. Slept under the stars, cooked the fish we caught over the fire we'd build. Pop always kept it stocked with rainbow trout. I do too. Never had a problem keepin' 'em fat and happy. They like it here, perfect environment for 'em, I guess. I've been able to get a lot of 'em to grow real good. Once, when I was your age, I caught one this big!" And he moves his hands far apart as Ben looks on with amazement. "Yep, they sure do like this place." He gazes across the lake, his eyes move back and forth, peering intently at images only he can see. "A few springs ago, a mallard pair nested over there by that cove." He points to the left, where the rocks make a discernable indentation. "All their ducklings made it. Now they come back every year. Of course, the herons come here too and sometimes steal the eggs. When I catch 'em dive bombin' for the fish, I try to scare 'em away." He smiles. "Don't always work, though. Sure is an active place, this lake. Even in winter. Every couple a years we have to drag a dead deer outa the water. They don't see how thin the ice is, they just walk out onto it and fall through. Sometimes we don't find 'em 'til after ice out in the spring."

Lucy's eyes grow wide. "Really?" she blurts out, concerned. "Can't you do something to make them not go out on the ice and fall in?"

Willy grins. "You mean like put up a sign or somethin'? We tried that, but the deer don't read English."

Ben giggles and nudges Lucy, who still seems upset.

"So, what made you decide to sell this property?" Dan asks, changing the subject.

"When my Pop died, me and my four brothers inherited this place. We'd bring our boys here when they were young. We talked for years about building a real camp. Never got around to it, no." He laughs. "Hard to get five grown men to agree on anything. Every year, it was just easier to pitch a tent, or in good weather, just throw sleepin' bags on the ground and sleep out under the stars. Like we did when we were boys." He pauses and looks down. "But things change. My two boys are in the military now. They're lifers. My nephews live all over the country, laid down their own roots, have their own lives. Me and my brothers, we don't spend too much time here anymore." He pauses, once again taking in the lake and the forest beyond. He puts his hand on his back and chuckles. "The old bones aren't what they used to be. Can't lay on the ground like I did when I was young." He pauses and whispers. "Guess it's time to let it go."

"Was this lake here when your father bought the property?" Laura asks.

Willy shakes his head. "Nah, the land's been in the family since 1863. Pop always wanted a pond. He loved huntin', but loved fishin' more. He had this built. It was supposed to be a small pond, but he got carried away," Willy chuckles. "Pretty much like everything he did in life. They kept diggin' and diggin' deeper and deeper and wider and wider 'til it got to be a lake. It's spring-fed. Fifteen full acres and drops to forty feet out there in the middle." He laughs again. "Pop always did things in a big way."

"He sure did," Dan smiles. "He sure did."

After the house is built, the Bodins spend every summer in Vermont, with Laura and the children staying on full time the moment school is out, while Dan remains on Long Island during the week, returning to the country for long weekends. It is a child's paradise. Ben and Lucy—and Danielle when she is old enough—spend their days exploring the woods. Every night they build a campfire at the edge of the lake, where Dan, when he is there, lounges with Laura, drinks in hand, and talks about everything and nothing. The children roast marshmallows and listen wide-eyed as Dan scares them with ghost stories as the shadows jump and lurch in the glow of the fire, and coyotes howl and barred owls hoot in the distance.

The surrounding woods hold a magic for them which nothing can dispel. There in the forest the children are transported to another time, another place. They bravely fight with swords made of fallen tree branches; the spirits and demons Dan makes them believe in are all around them. They inhabit the fairy tales Laura reads to them. They are at once Hansel and Gretel, King Arthur and Queen Guinevere, the Snow Queen, and Parsifal searching for the Holy Grail. They play Little Red Riding Hood being chased by wolves and come upon Snow White and the Seven Dwarfs. They hear Rapunzel cry from her woodland tower, they think they see Rumpelstiltskin stealing an infant. They are Bilbo and Frodo as they capture the ring; they meet the Frog Prince at the water's edge.

It is here, deep in the mysterious woods, where indeed the wild things grow, that Ben's love for photography burgeons. In the middle of play, he stops, pulls out his camera and takes photographs: of twigs laying amid brown leaves while the dappled sunlight falls over them, a rabbit scurrying back into its hole, a startled squirrel flying up a tree when the children claim the forest for themselves. He takes many pictures of Lucy. Lucy amid play. Lucy climbing a tree. Lucy jumping from a rock onto the forest floor. Lucy running with her arms outstretched, her blonde hair flying behind her like a kite caught in the wind. He wants these enchanting moments to last forever; he tries to capture them, pin them down, freeze them in time. But no matter how many photographs he takes, they always fall short. They never quite capture what he sees, what he feels.

Reluctantly, they emerge from the forest only when Dan or Laura insist they leave their woodland haunt and return to life on the outside, where reality forces them to relinquish their imaginary world.

It is Laura's father, however, who inspires them to believe in and embrace the magic and the mystery of the forest.

One of the happiest moments of their childhood is the time they spend with Laura's parents. Grandma Helen is plump and matronly, warm and maternal; she exudes the continuous scent of home cooking. In her youth, she aspired to be a professional chef and in pursuit of this dream, she attended the Culinary Institute of America. But after marrying and having children, she decided her family members were the only ones she wanted to cook for. And cook she does, her creative recipes often rival those of Julia Child. Any gathering, however brief, gives her the excuse to prepare elaborate culinary delights. She lays out an amazing spread of appetizers and baked goods even for a quick Saturday afternoon visit. Holiday dinners are major events; they are sumptuous meals which last hours through seven or eight courses.

Though Ben loves Grandma Helen and the way she fusses over her only grandson, always bidding him to eat more, because ". . . a growing boy like you needs good nutrition and as much energy as he can get. . . ." it is Laura's father whom Ben is closest to. A locally prominent neurosurgeon at a prestigious Long Island hospital, he appears much larger than his middling height and frame suggests. Perhaps it is his boundless passion and insatiable interest in the world around him which makes him seem larger than life. He exudes an unbridled energy which keeps him thin despite his healthy appetite and his wife's constant coaxing that he should eat more while she serves a never-ending savory banquet. And despite the gravity of his profession, he has managed through the years to retain a twinkle in his eye and a tall tale up his sleeve. Naturally, the children are drawn to him and his relentless interest in all things living. Ben is his namesake; the younger being named after Dr. Kinney as a tribute to him. In this way, Ben feels a distinct kinship with his grandfather, a special connection they both take pride in.

So Ben and Lucy delight in visiting their grandparents' home, a stately stone house set in the middle of a lush four acres on Long Island's North Shore, where gardens and greenhouses abound. They race up the stone steps, throw open the French doors, run down the hall to 'grandpa's study', where he gathers the children into his arms and lets out an effusive greeting. "My little loves are here!" he shouts and laughs, giving Lucy a long sloppy kiss on the cheek; his beard and mustache tickle her until she squirms with laughter. But he hugs his grandson to him and says, "You know you have a great name, don't you?" To which the younger Ben always answers, flustered, "Oh Grandpa. . . ."

Lucy eventually finds her way to the living room or kitchen where Laura, Danielle and Grandma Helen congregate amid the aroma of that day's cuisine. Ben stays behind with his grandfather and roams the spacious study, running his hands over the myriad hardcover books, sporting such names as: *The Complete Handbook of Neurosurgery, The Brain and Parkinson's Disease, A Short History of Stereotactic Neurosurgery.* An elegantly framed poster spans one wall. It is a sizable, colorful image of the human brain, dissected into several parts, each having its own color. Bold, black arrows point to the distinct areas; next to those arrows are the words: *Intelligence, Coordination, Vision, Judgment, Motivation.*

As if noticing Ben's interest anew each time he observes it, Dr. Kinney clasps his grandson's shoulder with his large, but delicate hand and, pointing to the image on the wall, utters the oft-repeated phrase, like a cherished, pious prayer: "There you see before you the most complex part of the human body. An intricate organ, the seat of our intelligence, the cradle of our consciousness. There in that small maze of tissue lies all the qualities which make us human. It is truly the crown jewel of the body." And Ben nods as if hearing this for the first time.

He loves it most, however, when his grandparents visit with them in Vermont. Every day is an adventure. His grandfather rises early and, with walking stick in hand and backpack slung over one shoulder, he coaxes the children out of their beds and into the dawn. Like a benevolent pied piper albeit without his pipe, he bids them to follow him, leading them deep into the woods, where he narrates nature's regeneration as it awakens from its nightly slumber.

"The one thing you must learn," Dr. Kinney tells them on the very day he brings them to meet the Little Elf, "is to listen."

"What if—" Lucy begins, but her grandfather leans down, placing his finger on her lips. "Shhh! If you listen and do so carefully," he whispers, "you'll learn everything you need to know." He points to the canopy and the brightening sky above. "Be silent and observe. Let the sounds of the forest wash over you, surround you, reverberate within you. Become one with the forest and its magic. *Surrender* to it."

They raise their eyes and look around. First, they hear the hoot of a distant owl, then the cry of the mourning doves, followed by the songs of blackbirds, robins, chickadees, and wrens.

"Hear that melodious song?"

The children strain to listen, then nod.

"Those are wrens, nothing special to look at. They're small and brown and plain but have big, beautiful voices."

A diminutive bird flits from one upper branch to another.

"Is that one?" Lucy mouths and points. It is very difficult for her at eight years old to remain silent and to listen.

He nods as he motions for them to follow him. He draws them deeper into the forest. It now teems with myriad sounds and movement.

"Where are we going?" Ben whispers.

"I'm going to introduce you to the Little Elf. It's time you met him."

Lucy looks at Ben who looks back at her and shrugs. Willingly, however, they follow their grandfather as he leads them through the woods, climbing through the thicket and over scrub.

They hike for a long time until they reach a clearing where Dr. Kinney stops, puts down his backpack and brings the binoculars to his eyes.

"Who's the Little Elf, Grandpa?" Ben asks, concerned. "Is he good or bad?"

"Always good." Dr. Kinney scans the top of the trees and points. "He lives in the heart of the forest. He rarely shows himself, but he makes himself known in other ways. Only to deserving children, though."

"Like us?" Lucy asks.

"Yes, like the two of you."

"Will we be able to see him?"

"Unfortunately, no. But you'll meet him, just not in the way you think. He does things in his own way and in his own time."

Ben frowns. He isn't quite sure the Little Elf is anyone he wants to meet.

"But I want to see him," Lucy laments.

"You don't have to see him to meet him. He'll make himself known to you. You just have to wait. Be patient. And believe."

"But if we can't see him," Ben reasons, "How can we ever believe in him?"

"Seeing isn't everything. You have to learn to listen and observe. And above all, to *feel*."

Dr. Kinney takes a large red handkerchief from his backpack. "This is why I told you to carry something red."

Ben looks down at the red bandana he tucked into his belt before they entered the forest. Lucy takes the red ribbon from her hair.

"If we wave something red, the Little Elf will know we are here for him. He will know we are friends, not foe. He'll respond. We just have to be patient."

Lucy waves the red ribbon in the air and laughs her infectious laugh. "Like this?"

Her grandfather smiles and nods.

"This is dumb." Ben scowls, reluctantly pulling the bright bandana from his belt and half-heartedly waves it in the air.

Dr. Kinney scours the canopy again with his binoculars. He gasps suddenly. "He's here!"

Looking upward, the children freeze.

"No!" their grandfather warns. "You mustn't look at him. Hurry and go stand by those trees. Close your eyes. Tight. That's the only way he'll come to you! We don't want to miss him as he flies over us!"

Ben and Lucy run to a nearby tree and, facing it, cover their eyes with their hands, their hearts beating with excitement and anticipation.

They jump as they hear a crash behind them. "Don't move!" Dr. Kinney orders. "Stay where you are. And don't look until I tell you!" They remain fixed in their positions by the tree, eyes shut tight.

"Wow," their grandfather says dramatically after a moment, "Would you look at this."

Tentatively, the children turn, and in the middle of the clearing, they spy two packages wrapped in colorful paper. One has Lucy's name on it written in large block letters, the other has Ben's, similarly marked.

"For us?" Lucy asks, afraid to move but longing to.

"Of course." Dr. Kinney motions for them to come. "This is his offering of friendship to you. He does this for only good children, children he loves."

They run to the middle of the clearing with the same excitement they exhibit on Christmas morning. Ben takes his present and unwraps it. He holds it out, looking at it incredulously.

"Wow! It's the camera I've been wanting. Like forever!"

"Well, the Little Elf knows everything." Dr. Kinney smiles. "Accepting this gift means you accept his offer of love and friendship."

"And this is the castle I wanted! My very own castle! Right out of the fairytales Mom reads to us!" Lucy holds up a replica of a medieval castle, then hugs it to her.

"Now the two of you, make sure you thank him," their grandfather instructs them.

"How?" Ben asks as he points his camera toward the heavens, hoping to find the Little Elf in his sight.

"First, you have to wave something red. That will tell him you are grateful."

Lucy jumps up and down, waving her red ribbon toward the heavens. "Thank you, Little Elf! Thank you!"

Ben, still pointing his camera upward, waves his bandana tentatively.

"The other way to thank him," Dr. Kinney says, "a better way, is by doing something nice, something good for the people you love. Your family. Your friends. You pass on the good deed to others around you, just like the Little Elf has done for you. That's all."

Every time they hike through the woods with Grandpa, the Little Elf visits and bestows upon them gifts from on high. On one occasion only, he made his appearance on Long Island, when they roamed their grandparents' property with their grandfather leading the way. But the Little Elf seems to prefer Vermont to Long Island, for that is where they typically find him, tucked away, deep in the forest where the magic and the mystery of life and nature—and the imagination— flourish without restraint.

But it is the natural progression of things that, as Ben and Lucy grow older, the magic fades, the dream ends, replaced by a steely truth and relentless reality which knows no mercy.

One night, when Ben and Lucy are almost ten, they lay awake in the upstairs attic room where they sleep whenever their Long Island house is full of guests as it is during this evening in mid-December. They are discussing their upcoming holiday stay at the Vermont house when Lucy mentions the Little Elf.

"You don't really believe in him anymore, do you?" Ben asks, surprised. He discovered the truth of things in all its rawness a while ago and assumes Lucy had, too.

"What do you mean?" She raises herself up on one elbow, facing her brother's bed.

"What do I mean? I mean he doesn't exist. He never has."

"That's not true," she blurts out, flustered.

"Yeah, it is true," he says pompously, as one who has just discovered a profound secret. "The Little Elf is Grandpa. Always has been."

Lucy, upset, repeats louder, "That's NOT true!" She stomps her foot into the mattress beneath the covers. The bed creaks.

"I thought you knew. I guessed it last year, but just played along to keep gramps happy."

"I don't believe you."

He laughs. "Then how come we never see him unless Grandpa's around?"

"Because Grandpa has a special connection to him, he's already told us that."

"He's told us we have a special connection to him, too. So how come he only shows up when Gramps is there and not when we're alone? And how come he always brings us the presents that Grandpa knows we want? Did you ever want something you didn't tell Gramps about?" He pauses. "Well, I did. I didn't tell him on purpose, the one thing I really, really wanted. The remote helicopter. I didn't tell anybody. Not Mom and Dad. Not even you. Just to see if the Little Elf would bring it to me. And guess what. He didn't. Why? Because Grandpa didn't know about it."

"That's not true," Lucy repeats, choking down tears. The truth of things was too much for her.

"I'm telling you, Grandpa's the Little Elf. It's just like Santa Claus, with Mom and Dad. They finally told us they buy all our Christmas presents themselves." He pauses. "Grownups like to make believe a lot, I guess."

"The Little Elf is different." Lucy frowns through the darkness, unwilling to let go of this one fantasy she has come to love. Her connection to the Little Elf is more than the gifts he showers upon her.

She feels his presence in her daily life, a benevolent and loving friend who keeps careful watch over her, who looks after her safety as she navigates an increasingly uncertain world.

"It's not different. It's all just make-believe. None of it's real."

Lucy drops back onto the bed and looks up at the ceiling through the darkness with savage determination.

"That's not true. The Little Elf *is* real," she says quietly. "My believing *makes* him real."

As the grayness of the late afternoon deepened, Ben glanced toward the woods, that enigmatic, otherworldly landscape of his childhood when he believed fully in the mystery and the power of the forest, of life itself. And he wondered ruefully where the magic was now. Now at this very moment as he lay immobile, melting into the ice, becoming one with it.

And then he saw it.

He raised his head with great difficulty to get a better look as a large buck stood motionless at the tree line staring down at him, it seemed, with patience and with pity.

And the church bells in the distance chimed four times.

Dan, who learned to hunt from his father, wants to pass his love for this sport on to his only son. When Ben is old enough, he enrolls him in a hunter's safety course. He instructs the child how to load and hold a rifle properly and safely, how to aim and shoot.

Ben loves the special attention Dan gives him; he basks in the time he spends alone with his father. Often when they are up at the Vermont house for the weekend, father and son retreat to the woods for an afternoon of target shooting. Ben loves the noise the rifle makes, the power of the bullet as it bursts from the barrel, slashing its way through the air, ripping through to its mark. Over and over he adjusts his site, loads, then pulls the trigger, perfecting his aim. Soon he is hitting the bull's-eye with a 98 percent accuracy. Dan, impressed by his son's natural ability, tells him he will be a fine hunter. He instills in him the importance of killing the prey with one shot. Their intent as hunters, he tells him, is not to inflict undue pain and torment on the animal.

"But doesn't it hurt them if we kill them?" Ben asks, pretending he is more curious than worried.

"Not if we do it carefully. One surprise shot is the key. They won't know what hit them. They won't suffer. I promise."

Ben says nothing, but Dan sees he remains unconvinced.

"Look, if no one hunts and the herd is left alone, they'll only overpopulate, and lots of them will suffer from illnesses or slowly die of starvation. Or they'll be pursued by coyotes and killed by the pack. What a cruel death it is if they're caught and torn apart by a group of hungry coys."

Ben shakes his head, his eyes cloudy with fear.

"A lot crueler than the one a skilled hunter can dispense," he continues. "That's why I say we have to kill responsibly. We can't just do it recklessly, we have to respect these animals and the land itself. And that's why there are rules about which animals we can take, which we can't, when we're allowed to take them. Most important, any animal we kill we have to use the meat. That way, we're not just killing for sport, but for purpose."

And indeed, Ben has seen enough of the spoils of Dan's hunting.

He and Lucy often aid in the gutting by holding flashlights as Dan carves away the innards of the unfortunate quarry, whether it be a bear, deer, or moose, draining the blood and packing the shell with ice. Laura has a difficult time with this at first; she recoils as she looks out upon the carcass of the dead animal hanging upside down from a nearby tree. She is repelled when Dan brings home the butchered meat wrapped in neat little packages and placed in the freezer. But soon she relents, pretending the meat is just another cut from the supermarket.

It is opening day of hunting season the year Ben is ten when he first sees his father take down a deer. He and Dan have come up to the Vermont house alone that weekend. A rampant stomach virus goes back and forth between Lucy and Danielle, keeping them and Laura at home on Long Island.

Both Ben and Dan are excited about this father and son weekend, and they prepare for the trip well in advance. On the morning of the hunt, the sound of the massive grandfather clock in the hall awakens them as it chimes four times. After a hearty breakfast of omelets, bacon, buttered toast, and coffee, they change into their camouflage clothing, accented with orange scarves. They stuff a backpack full with drinks and provisions, as they expect to be in the woods all day. With loaded guns, they set out for the spot deep in the forest on the western side of the lake where Dan has seen scrapes and rubs a few days before. He knows from the position of these scratchings that a large buck with a wide rack is in the area.

They settle into their places beneath the tall pines which border a small clearing. From this vantage point they quietly watch the new day dawn: black dissolves into gray, which fades to purple, then to pink and orange. The gloomy thicket brightens as shards of light flicker through the treetops, peppering the forest floor with specks of gold. Wordlessly, they listen as the woods come alive. Tree branches snap and leaves rustle around them as squirrels, chipmunks, mice, and hares shake off sleep and scamper eagerly from their beds. Crows screech nearby; over the treetops a hawk glides gracefully through the dawn. A woodpecker raps rhythmically above them as a mourning dove chants a plaintive hymn. All around them the forest teems with life as they wait in silence for the kill.

It is almost noon when they hear the cracking of a nearby branch. They turn, and at a distance of one hundred yards they see through the brush a large buck. He has come to a halt at a forty-five-degree angle to them; his horned crown, thick and labyrinthine, reaches majestically toward the heavens. He holds his head aloft, thrusting his nose into the air. His ears flutter as he takes in the sounds of the forest. There he stands, august and imposing, illuminated by the noontime sun which streams down on him from a break in the canopy.

Ben draws in a breath and stares at this magnificent creature who turns his head and looks in their direction. Mesmerized, he peers at the animal through the scrub and for a long, rare moment, their eyes meet and hold. Something flows between them: a thought, fleeting and imponderable; it gurgles up through the millennia and streams from one to the other. Here, deep in the forest, staring back at the buck who gazes steadily at him, Ben suddenly perceives the essence of existence. For a first time, he understands they are both one and the same and yet forever separate; ingenuous creatures, both, who have been arbitrarily thrust upon the earth and set adrift, alone, stranded on this tiny star, where, in the middle of a vast and unfathomable sea, they remain forever lost. He wants to linger in this moment where he is bound to this creature and all of life's sudden mysteries. He longs to fix in his memory the animal's beauty and nobility and innocence for all time. But the moment shatters, for out of the corner of his eye he sees the glint of the rifle as Dan raises the weapon, finding the buck in his sight. Horrified, Ben turns to his father. The word "No" forms in the very center of his being, coming together like a molten mass. It rushes up from his depths and pours out into the air, barreling toward its mark at the same time his father pulls the trigger, releasing the bullet from the chamber. But unlike the shot just fired, it falls short; it hurtles through the forest at the very moment the cartridge explodes; his long and desperate plea is swallowed up, drowned out by the mortal blast.

The buck remains still and, for an instant, Ben believes his father has missed. But suddenly the animal's eyes grow vacant as if a light has been extinguished, and he bows his head, prayer-like. His front legs buckle beneath him, his chest dropping to the ground. His hind legs kick and quiver, then also give out. The heaviness of the horns forces his lifeless head to the right and drags him down onto his side. There he lies, a felled king, sinking desolately into the earth.

Dan hurries to the dead animal. "Wow, he's huge," he says, amazed at the prize he has garnered for himself. "A twelve pointer. Ben, get your camera," he shouts as he goes behind the buck and, squatting, takes hold of the large rack and pulls the animal's head and chest upright. "Hurry and take a photo."

But Ben is unable to move. That one bullet kills more than a stag that day; it tears through him, too, burrowing its way into his soul. And there it stays, festering, tainting all life with the horror and randomness of death. It is the eyes that haunt him in future dreams and in all those thoughts which come to him intermittently through the years, those eyes that had spoken so much, that had brimmed with hope and possibility, those eyes that grew vacant when the bullet stilled the spirit within. And Ben understands then there is an unspeakable force more powerful than life. Darkness, it seems, is stronger than the light.

"Ben!"

He clawed the snow with his hands. His cheek, buried in the ice, was numb. Francesca's voice was desperate, though fainter and far away. He tried to move, but the force pinning him to the earth would not relent. He closed his eyes and moaned. They had awakened in the morning with such hope and happiness; this was to be just another one of their usual peaceful Sundays. It began with his homemade recipe for French toast and hash browns, which he proudly served them amid great appreciation and anticipation.

"Daddy!" Addie drags a kitchen chair over to the stove where Ben is preparing breakfast. "I want to dip the bread." She climbs up on to the chair and looks over the stove and the griddle with interest. Her face is almost level with her father's. He smiles and leaning toward her, kisses her on the cheek. "I'm getting it all ready for you, don't worry."

She giggles.

Cruz is standing nearby watching this Sunday routine, his nose in the air, taking in the scent of food.

Ben beats the eggs vigorously; the butter sizzles on the griddle.

Francesca enters the kitchen and yawns; she tightens the belt of her bathrobe and hugs Addie as she passes her.

"I made your tea," Ben says and nods toward the nearby mug.

"Oh, thank you." She takes hold of the handle and brings the white cup to her mouth. The steam rises in a perfect swirl, the tip kissing her lip. She blows it softly away before taking a sip, then puts the mug down on the counter. The black lettering which reads, "Trust in dreams, for in them is hidden the gate to eternity," is turned away from her, facing the window and the gray winter day beyond.

"Okay, you can dip now," Ben tells his daughter and places the large bowl near her. Carefully, she takes one piece of bread at a time and submerges it in the egg mixture, then with Ben's help, using tongs, she turns the bread over and over, saturating it.

"Careful, now," he says as they both place the bread onto the griddle.

Cruz moves closer, hoping to catch whatever might fall.

After breakfast, Addie plays with her toys and runs through the rooms enveloped in "make believe" as Cruz shadows her. Her squeals and laughter drift through the house, sweet music that fills their happy home as he and Francesca linger by the fire, drinking tea and coffee and reading the weekend paper.

It is a peaceful, ordinary Sunday. Just like so many Sundays before. Nothing indicates to them at all that this will be the day upon which they will die.

He wondered then as he lay immobile, if he had been wrong about everything. Wrong about life, wrong about love, wrong about death. Though he had hidden it well, Lucy's demise was a force so great it broke him. Outwardly, he carried on as did the rest of his family. After the initial shock, his parents refused to speak of her; they held their heads high and tried to go about their usual routine with a stoicism approaching denial. Their lives progressed in a seemingly normal fashion.

But for Ben, something was amiss. Her death posed an existential threat to his own life. It took something from him he could never regain. An innocence. A hope. There was an inexpressible emptiness within, as if the innermost part of his being had been carved out, excised, leaving only a barren shell. When he and Lucy's friends bore her casket up the steps and into the church, the weight of the heavy wooden box had no effect on him. He felt nothing, not the pressure on his shoulder nor the coldness of the brass rail he held to hoist and lower it. He could only stare blankly at the hundreds of people who packed the church to say goodbye to their beloved Lucy. The well his tears should have filled was cracked and parched.

He burrowed farther into the snow as if into his grave. All was truly lost.

The months after Lucy's death are bleak and desolate. Their once happy home has turned cold and bitter, as if a biting wind has blown in from a fissure in the foundation, extinguishing the fires of hope and life. Ben's sorrow is exacerbated by his parents' grief. They try to hide their misery because that is all they can think of doing, but it is palpable in every forced movement, in every unspoken word, in every vanished smile. Laura roams the house now, a lost and ghost-like figure, rubbing her hands repetitively over her forehead, an obsessive gesture that attempts to wipe away the obsessive thoughts and heartache which haunt her. She develops large circles beneath her eyes, her once straight and graceful form stoops from an inner weariness. She grows silent; her unspeakable sorrow eradicates any desire to connect with her family or the outside world. She goes about her duties out of habit; she cooks dinner each night and makes sure the pantry is well stocked, does the laundry, and runs clothes to the dry cleaners, ensuring the family has clean attire as they present themselves anew to the world each day. She waters the plants, pays the bills, keeps the house running efficiently, fulfilling any obligation that is required of her. But her movements are slow and labored; her gaze clouded and vacant. She is no longer there but has gone missing and is unable to be found. Ben despairs as he looks upon her, believing she is not long for this world; he suspects perhaps death has already claimed her.

Every evening, when the others retreat to different parts of the house, Laura ascends the stairs, opens the door to Lucy's bedroom, and enters, closing it tightly behind her. The room is now a shrine; in it she has amassed everything which belonged to Lucy in life: every photograph, every trophy, every scrap of paper that Lucy had drawn on, written over, scribbled across. Her daughter's laptop is plugged in and sits on the desk, along with an opened book and an unfinished assignment she was working on for her honors English class. Her folded clothes neatly occupy her dresser drawers, her shoes, organized with military precision, line the bottom of her closet in well-ordered rows. Stuffed animals and dolls, remnants of her childhood, crowd the nearby rocking chair, a chorus of inanimate companions who give the appearance of patiently awaiting her return. Discs of videos detailing every moment of Lucy's life are stacked in orderly piles by the television. Laura turns it on, loads the discs into the player and, lowering herself onto the bed, lights a candle. There, alone, in the flickering shadows, she consumes glass after glass of wine as she replays, on the screen and in her head, her daughter's life from beginning to end. She alternately laughs and cries as the memories and images wind around her like a noose, until finally, as dawn filters in through a chink in the drawn shades, she collapses into a fitful and dreamless sleep.

Dan, too, does what is required of him. He rises every morning and goes to work; he fulfills contracts, completes projects, talks to customers, writes proposals for future developments. But he does so routinely, also out of habit. He drags himself through each day, nothing more now than a shell of a man whose core has been expunged. He stays on at the office long after he needs to. It is his place of comfort where he is in control, a place of distraction and forgetting. He no longer wants to come home. To the silence. To the sorrow. To a wife who is fading away, dying a slow death from a grief he shares but cannot speak of. To a wife who stands on the brink, but who he is incapable of saving. Through the heavy fog of despair which envelopes him, he sees his family and everything he loves slipping away. He doesn't know what to do. So he works and sleeps and works again.

The spring following Lucy's death brings an end to a brutal winter, replacing it with a welcomed warmth, though there is still no relief from the sorrow that enervates the family. Dan, however, is nudged by the world's awakening. He doesn't notice it at first; it is an imperceptible prod as it rouses that part of him which has only slept and not died. Slowly, hesitantly, he welcomes the lingering light of day, the temperate breeze, the regenerating color.

So, on an evening in May, he arrives home late from work; Laura is in her usual nightly position, sitting amid the flickering shadows, locked away in Lucy's shrine. He ascends the stairs and hears a child's voice—his daughter's—as it emanates from the television in the sealed and darkened room. Instead of passing by the closed door and retreating down the hall as he has done on every previous occasion, this evening he drops his briefcase; it falls to the floor with a thud. He turns the knob, pushes the door open, and enters the room. Images of seven-year-old Lucy flit across the screen. It is a video of her first dance recital.

Without a word, he turns on the nearby lamp. Laura blinks and as if she has been in darkness too long, she shrinks from him and the light.

He picks up the remote and turns off the television. The sounds of Lucy's laughter intermingled with music are immediately silenced, and the image of her in mid-twirl freezes, then disappears. Laura looks in horror from the blank screen to him and back again.

"No!" she cries as she lunges toward her husband and the remote he still holds. Her nearby glass crashes to the floor, shattering, like their lives, into a thousand jagged pieces. The wine seeps out onto the white throw rug as if from a wound.

Dan takes her hands in his. "Laura, please. We can't go on like this. Lucy's gone."

She sobs, "No, Dan, no. . . ."

"She was my daughter, too." He pulls her close to him, blinking away tears. "We have two other children. They need us. Ben and Danielle. She was their sister, too. You're not the only one who grieves."

Laura pushes him away, but he holds her tight. She sobs again. "I, I can't. I can't go on. I don't know how . . . the pain, it's just too much. I can't. . . ."

"We have to. For them. Lucy wouldn't want it any other way. You know she wouldn't."

Laura shakes her head, "I can't. . . ."

"We have to."

"How? Tell me how? Please. . . ."

Dan lets her go; she collapses onto the nearby bed. She hangs her head as tears flow now unabated.

"I don't know how. But I know we can't live like this anymore. *I* can't live like this anymore."

Laura looks at him with dread as he roams the room, pacing back and forth, running his hand repeatedly through his hair. He stops and snuffs out the candle, then goes to the television and rips the disc of Lucy's recital from the player.

Laura bursts off the bed and goes to him, clutching at the sleeve of his jacket. "What are you doing? Please, Dan, stop."

Tenderly, he removes her hand from his arm, holds it for a moment in his, then bends down and kisses it. He straightens up, turns and hurries from the room, leaving Laura stunned and immobile. He returns shortly with a box of large black trash bags. He takes one and, prowling like a thief around the room, gathers up the things that are the sum of his daughter's life.

First, he takes the videos and tosses them into the bag. They clack as they descend, the blackness swallowing them up.

Laura, hysterical now, pleads, "Please, Dan, don't, don't. How can you do this?"

His face is solemn, his voice grave. "I don't see any other way. We can't live like this anymore. We have to go on."

He goes to the bookcase and pulls out the books one by one. They fall to the floor in a heap. As he reaches down to gather them into the sack, Laura charges toward him and the pile. She yanks one from his hands and, trembling, opens it. She pages through it, her tears staining the drawings and the words. "This was one of the first I read to her, she loved these fairytales." She looks up at him, hugging the book to her chest. "Please Dan, don't. Not this one."

He shakes his head, gently reaching for the book and, taking it, drops it into the bag with the others. "We have to."

He gathers the trophies Lucy earned from her many track meets and field hockey tournaments and places them one by one into the bag, then takes the rosettes from the wall, ribbons she earned at various country fairs in Vermont for the best chili recipe, the largest grown zucchini, the best tasting maple walnut cake. They flutter into the sack, falling, feather-like amid the books and the other keepsakes. He scoops up framed photographs which decorate the walls and tabletops; they clank and crash together as they descend into the bag's void.

Then he opens the closet doors. Laura rushes toward him, throwing herself in front of the clothes. "No! Not these," she shouts. Dan takes another large plastic trash bag from the box and shakes it forcefully. It opens, billowing amid the rustled air.

"We have to, Laura. There's no other way. It's time."

"No," she cries again. She buries her face in her hands as he steps around her, taking the clothes in clumps and dropping them into the open bag.

Hearing the commotion from downstairs, Ben makes his way to the upper hallway, where he pauses. Hidden in the shadows, he watches this drama unfold as his father rummages through Lucy's room, gathering the vestiges of her brief life into black bags, while his mother trails him, ringing her hands and begging her husband to stop.

Once Dan has seized everything that was Lucy's, burying it away forever in a multitude of sacks, he carries the overflowing bags in groups down the stairs and out of the house. Laura, distraught and heartbroken, sits slumped on the bed in her daughter's room and weeps.

Dan returns to the room with a variety of tools he has gathered from his basement workshop. He goes to Laura and, placing his arm around her shoulders, leads her down the hall toward their bedroom where he lays his sobbing wife on their bed, covering her with a blanket, then returns to Lucy's room. Gathering up the scattered bottles of wine, he empties what is left into the sink of the adjoining bath-room. The red stains the white porcelain purple. He makes his way back to the center of the room, where he pauses for a moment. Then he slowly turns, making a deliberate circle, absorbing every sight for a last time. When he halts, he closes his eyes; a solitary tear slips down his cheek. Wiping it away, he readjusts his glasses then slowly moves from the room, his shoulders stooping. He slams the door behind him and nails it shut.

From that moment on, all evidence of Lucy's life within their family vanishes. As if she never was. From that moment on, neither his mother nor his father speak of her.

Ben, however, unlike his parents, can't eradicate his sister from his mind and heart. Memories of her linger just beneath the surface. In those weeks and months following Lucy's death, he tries to ease the elemental fear which seeps in to fill the void within him. He tries to take comfort in the words everyone offers him and his family—time heals all wounds, everything happens for a reason—but none of this helps him make sense of her senseless passing; the image of her last pleading look, her outstretched arm that grasped for life and begged for saving before the light went out, is ever present in all his waking and dreaming moments. He cannot fathom how someone who tore through life with an unquenchable joy, whose laughter echoed through the world long after her last breath was stolen from her, could be stilled so suddenly and so completely. The pastor who spoke that morning at her funeral talked of God's will. But Ben recoiled from such an unkind god, who ignored him, who turned away in that one moment, when he silently begged for Lucy's life. It was evident then this hostile god was deaf to his pleas, for no amount of prayer could save her, no amount of longing could bring her back.

On this day, the summer following Lucy's death, Ben stands facing the chart in his grandfather's study. At eighteen, he towers over the older man who seems to have grown smaller and grayer through the years.

"I was so arrogant in my youth," the doctor tells Ben as he takes his place next to him, facing the poster without looking at it. "I truly believed with all the modern techniques at my disposal, armed with the most advanced knowledge, training, and skills that I would be able to control everything. And my object—as it is with any physician—is to save and restore people's lives." He pauses and glances at his grandson, who stands silently, his eyes boring into the wall. "And for a time, it seemed that's just what I did." He sighs. "But eventually I began to experience what I believed were failures on my part. Suddenly people who should have lived, who had no reason at all to die, just died. I was devastated. I spent all my free time obsessively reviewing their cases, trying to see where our team went wrong, what we might have done differently. But in the end, it was inexplicable. Then just as suddenly, I also began to see the opposite happening. People with the worst prognoses, people for whom there was no hope at all, lived and flourished. Despite all odds. Again, I spent hours poring over their cases, hoping to find a clue as to what we might have inadvertently done to help them live. But there was no explanation for this either. It seemed that sometimes people died for no reason I could determine when they should have lived, and others lived when, clearly, they should have died. I slowly realized perhaps there was another force at work, something far larger, certainly greater than all our combined knowledge, training and skills. Something I couldn't name. Something I couldn't control. It was truly a humbling experience."

Ben lowers his head and closes his eyes. "Why?"

The word catches in his throat like a bird trapped in the brush. It struggles up from his depths, freeing itself from the sinews and falls out into the silent room with a caw.

The old doctor turns to his grandson and touches his arm gently. "I can tell you *why* and *how* her body failed. I can explain the physiology of death and dying to you. But I know that's not what you're asking."

Ben, looking down at the floor, shakes his head.

"I don't know why it happened to her. Maybe there really is a thing called fate. It does seem that all the forces of the universe conspired to bring her to that one place at that one moment."

"But why Lucy and not me? It could have been me just a few minutes—no—a few *seconds*, before. What would fate or God or the universe care about her?" Ben raises his head, his eyes blazing with uncontained anger. "It's so unfair."

His grandfather turns back to the poster on the wall. "I don't have the answers to these questions, Ben. We are so limited in our knowledge of what exists." He waves his hand toward the diagram of the brain. "We know so much, but in the end, we know so little. Not enough, never enough."

Dr. Kinney pauses, then looks at his grieving grandson again. "My parents were very religious, and they brought the four of us up that way, too. I was the first to rebel. I could never accept the existence of a god who demanded we have blind faith in him. Why is it so important to such an omniscient power that we slavishly believe in him? I could never reconcile myself to such a being. But in recent years I've wondered if maybe we've gotten it all wrong. Maybe it hasn't got anything to do with mindless belief in the existence of a god. Maybe instead it's simply a code, a set of instructions for how to access a world that exists just beyond our senses. And I know that world exists. I've felt it, I've seen it. In the near-death and dying experiences of my patients. When we analyze these experiences in terms of the brain, we always come up against a wall. An insurmountable boundary we can't seem to cross."

He puts a comforting hand on Ben's arm again. "We're like the blind man and the elephant, touching only one small part of the large animal, we think we know the whole animal. But we don't. Our knowledge is so small compared to what is truly out there. And we're limited by our five senses. Only five. Imagine such a small number." He pauses. "But what if there are things beyond our senses we can't perceive because we just don't have the equipment?"

He pauses again.

"What I'm trying to say is maybe we don't really die. Yes, we die physically, and the absence hurts us beyond our ability to bear. But what if when we shed our physical selves, we then wake into our real lives?"

Wake into our real lives. Is all this nothing but a terrible dream? Ben scraped his hands through the snow.

It is homecoming weekend of their senior year—a year that promises to be at once exciting and demanding for both Ben and Lucy. They visited their chosen colleges during the summer; now they need only to apply and be accepted: Lucy is hoping to be admitted to Julliard for drama; she has fallen in love with Shakespeare, performing, and the excitement and the energy of New York City. She wants to pursue a career in theater. Ben has his sights set on the University of Pennsylvania for architecture.

The events of the long weekend begin Friday after school. As the shadows lengthen and the twilight creeps in earlier on this late September afternoon, students and faculty begin with a pep rally. They send special blessings to their football team—young warriors going off to battle, in a major encounter where they will meet their adversary the following day on their home field. The rivalry between these two teams is legendary, dating back half a century. It is such a profound and enduring conflict where students of one school refuse to date or befriend students of the other. On those rare occasions when such a friendship or romance arises, the offending parties are considered traitors by both schools and are ostracized ever after in the respective communities.

That evening the traditional bonfire is built, a massive pile of wood stacked in the middle of the field where it is set alight and burns like an eternal flame. Students and faculty hold hands and dance like pagans around the conflagration as they pay homage to the light, the life-giving, regenerative blaze as it banishes the night and drives away the fearsome darkness.

At noon on Saturday, the game commences, two sides battling for victory, undying rivals who struggle over a brass trophy that has gone back and forth between them each year. It is hard fought, hard won; young men earnestly warring to claim a small piece of turf. But victory is sweet; the winning becomes an end in itself. Their team wins this year, and the celebratory homecoming dance promises to be joyous and triumphant.

Lucy descends the stairs of their house; her long blonde hair is swept up elegantly, her powdery blue strapless sheath gown accentuates her expressive eyes.

Dan looks at his daughter and smiles. "Wow, you've grown up, Lucy. What a lovely young woman you've become." And he leans forward, kissing her on her head.

"Oh, Dad," she exhales, pleased by the compliment but embarrassed by it as well.

Ben comes downstairs next, dressed in a black tuxedo. Laura and Dan peer at their tall, handsome son with admiration and wonder.

"When did they grow up?" he whispers to his wife, who, smiling, shrugs her shoulders.

Dan insists on taking photographs of them together and separately before he hands Ben the keys to the car. "What time is the dance over with?"

"Eleven," Lucy offers as she glances in the hall mirror, pressing her lips together and turning her head from side to side.

"We'll probably have a bite to eat afterward," Ben says as Dan drops the keys into his open hand.

"Okay, but be back by one. No later. Are you going to the office tomorrow?"

"I'm planning on it. Thanks, Dad."

He has recently begun working in his father's office on weekends. This helps them both; it gives Dan the assistance he needs and provides Ben with an opportunity to learn the business he has committed to. It also provides him with a nice part-time income.

Laura kisses both her children goodbye, bidding Ben to drive carefully.

"Don't worry, Mom," he says as he pats her on the back, "I will."

On the way to the dance, they stop to pick up Karla, Ben's girlfriend of three months, then Matt, Lucy's love of the last year.

The four spend the evening mingling with friends, laughing, talking, moving to the beat of continuous music. The outer world ceases to exist for them. So does the future, which is very nearly upon them. They are caught up in the fantasy of this special night, snuggled safely away, wrapped in a familiar cocoon, unmindful that beyond this place and time awaits another world and their precarious voyage through it.

The evening ends with the ritual of selecting the homecoming king and queen. Ben's best friend, Jason, is chosen as king, and Gwen, one of Lucy's inner circle, is named as queen. Both Ben and Lucy are honored with a place on the court.

The thrill of a victorious battle still fresh in their minds, and with a sense of personal triumph, Lucy and Matt, Ben and Karla, along with a dozen of their other friends and classmates leave the dance at the end and head to a local diner. There they eat a late-night meal and drink enough coffee sure to keep them up for days. They laugh and reminisce about the weekend; they talk and plan for their futures. Whether they understand it or not, they are coming into the best time of their young lives where their future spreads out before each one of them, bright and full of hope. The stars shine down, large and luminous, on each of them, a beacon to guide them on their way. For some, the journey will twist and turn, leading them through dark and unsafe ports. But for now, for all of them, there is only the glint and promise of a golden future.

"I can't believe I got the part," Lucy gushes to everyone at the table as the waitress refills her cup.

"Why not?" Sarah, seated next to her, says. "You've been in a lot of plays in school and at the community theater."

"You're practically a pro." Megan laughs. "Well, certainly compared to us. We're the amateurs."

Lucy waves her hand in protest.

"But it's Shakespeare. You know how hard it is?"

"You just have to mumble a lot of thees and thous," her brother teases.

"Oh, stop." She shoots him a dirty look. "Not only do I have to play Kate convincingly," she tells the others, "but I have to make sure the audience understands what I'm saying. Not going to be easy."

"That's the one with the shrew, right?" Ben quips as he passes the beaker of milk to the other end of the table. "You won't have any trouble being convincing."

"Oh, shut up!" The others laugh as Lucy pretends to pout while hurling a crumbled napkin at him across the table.

"She's been practicing the shrew part all her life," Ben continues, catching the napkin and crushing it in his grip.

"Oh, shut up!" she says again. "I hope you go to college somewhere far away. Like California. Or maybe even Australia."

"Too bad. You're out of luck. I'm not even applying that far away. Pennsylvania is as far as I go." He grins across the table at her.

"Gee, too bad. The farther away the better." Lucy sneers at him.

"Wow, I wonder if you two are going to miss taunting each other next year," Matt says as Ben chuckles and nods. "Yeah, probably. She's such an easy target."

Karla, a pretty, auburn-haired senior with large green eyes that always seem to smile even when she doesn't, turns to him. "Ben, it's getting late. I've got to get up early for work. We should go." Since she is planning to study pre-med in college, she works part time at the local hospital as a nurses' aid. Reluctantly Ben nods to her. He gulps down the rest of his coffee, digs in his pocket and pulls out cash, which he throws down in the middle of the table. "See you guys on Monday," he says as he pushes back his chair and stands.

The others at the table bid them goodbye, settling back in their chairs, demanding yet more coffee from the harried waitress. They seem intent on continuing the evening well into the wee hours of the morning. Ben turns to Lucy. "Are you staying, or do you want a ride home now?"

Lucy snuggles into Matt, whose protective arm drapes affectionately around her. She pauses for a moment, then tells her brother,

"No, you go on ahead, I'll catch a ride with them." And she points to her friends seated opposite her.

Ben gives her an uncertain look.

"Don't worry, I'll be home by one." Lucy doesn't want the spell to break; she wants the evening of joy to last forever.

An unsettled sensation floods Ben then; danger is everywhere. The joy and happiness that has enveloped all of them abruptly dissipates as if the bubble they are drifting in has burst and they hurl down to earth with a crash. He is overcome with an anxiety he cannot tame; he wants to insist she come home with him. But when he sees Lucy sitting among her friends, radiant and joyous, laughing that infectious laughter as she entertains and dazzles her classmates, he pauses. She is the picture of grace and dignity, of happiness and innocence. Of hope and a thousand promises. Of life itself. He turns one last time and looks back at her, though he doesn't know why. She flashes him a good-natured smile that so defines her; an image which will haunt him throughout the years.

The following morning, Ben is up before anyone in the house except for Dan. After a quick shower and breakfast, he heads to the office, where he spends the day.

Even though the calendar indicates it is now autumn, summer remains beyond its time, like a cheerful guest who refuses to depart though the party is clearly over. The trees are still full and in bloom and the only hint of the season's shift is that the vivid green grass has taken on a tinge of late summer yellow.

It is almost four when Ben leaves the office, heading home. But the lingering summer glow intoxicates him, and he stops for ice cream.

He turns his car into the parking lot of the old-fashioned sweet shop which he passes every day on the busy highway. It seems out of place, nestled in the middle of a row of plain brick office buildings.

The quaint façade sports a large picture window with gold gothic lettering; an ornate red and white striped awning gives cover to the entrance and the Victorian tables and chairs, placed at neat intervals on the sidewalk out front. He goes into the shop and orders his usual root beer float. Once he has the overflowing mug in his hand, he takes a long spoon and straw from the counter and ventures outside to the sidewalk tables. It is too beautiful a day to sit inside.

"Hey, Ben!"

He looks to the right and sees Matt and Lucy already seated. They wave and motion for him to join them.

"What are you doing here?" he asks his sister as he pulls up the chair and sits next to her. "I thought you had rehearsals." He flashes her a smile then. "Or did they fire you? Like maybe you weren't shrew-like enough, though that's hard to believe."

She kicks him under the table and taunts him. "They would never fire me. I'm too great an actress. The world is just clamoring for my talent."

"Yeah, I'm sure it is." He dips his spoon into the large scoop of ice cream which precariously clings to the side of the glass and takes a sip of the soda through the tall straw.

"Logan fell down his basement stairs this morning and broke his leg," Matt says. "He's in the hospital."

"So, they suspended rehearsals until further notice," Lucy continues as she circles her spoon around the edge of her cup. "You can't really have rehearsals without a director."

Ben looks at Lucy's sundae. "Is there any ice cream in there or is it all just whipped cream?"

"There's ice cream in there, trust me." Lucy's sweet tooth is legendary in their family; she has a passion for hot fudge sundaes which she tops with so much whipped cream—a swirling white cloud towering high above the cup, masking all that lies beneath. For her, there is never enough whipped cream.

"How bad is he?" Ben asks them. "Are they canceling the play, or will they just postpone it?"

Lucy shrugs. "I think they said he broke the bones in his lower leg."

"No, his femur," Matt corrects her. "It's going to be a long recovery. It was for my mother when she broke hers in a skiing accident."

Lucy licks a large wedge of ice cream from the spoon. "No one's made a decision yet, since this just happened. I hope they don't cancel it, though. I don't think Logan would want that."

She reaches down and takes out an envelope from her bag. "Here, I bought a get-well card for him. We should all sign it. Might cheer him up. He must be so miserable right now." She pushes it toward Matt. "I hope the poor guy isn't in too much pain."

She dips the spoon again into the middle of the whipped cream and fudge and pulls out some more ice cream. "But I'm hoping they won't cancel the production. It's a great opportunity for me to learn Shakespeare."

The sun shines down brightly from the cloudless blue sky, warming them and their lives, blanketing them and all their hopes in a balmy glow. They take turns signing the card. Amid this summer-like afternoon, they talk and laugh about everything and nothing, all the while absently watching the cars pass on the busy highway before them.

"Oh, damn," Lucy says. She hasn't eaten the sundae quickly enough as she has been talking and laughing too much. The melting ice cream and fudge drip in tandem onto the table and down into her lap. She wipes it off her jeans, then holds her hand, now wet and tacky, away from her as she glances around the table.

Ben jumps up. "I'll go grab some napkins. I have to get rid of this anyway." He takes his empty mug and heads inside, looking for the napkins and a place to dispose of his cup.

It happens in an instant. A car driving much too fast doesn't see the car in front of him come to a sudden stop. The driver swerves hoping to avoid an accident but loses control of the vehicle; it lurches up onto the sidewalk coming to a halt only when it has crashed through the store's front window, dragging the tables—and Lucy and Matt with them. Partially pinned under the front wheels of the car, Lucy lies crushed and bleeding amid the shattered glass. Matt, unconscious, is rammed up against the counter inside the store where the force has thrown him. Ben, uninjured but stunned, clutching the napkins in hand, stands nearby, hovering above his sister. Her eyes follow him, boring into him, pleading. She reaches out to him, mouthing his name as her hand clutches the air. He remains immobile as the ever-widening pool of blood tinges her blonde hair brown. Her arm trembles, then collapses into the thick liquid encircling her, though her eyes never leave his. She gasps for air, but her gasping reverts to a gruesome rattle. Her full lips blanch white, her mouth distends and freezes into a silent scream, as if a cord that fastens it has been severed. It reminds him of a bird he once saw, who, having fallen out of its nest, gasped futilely for air, opening his bill wider and wider as he struggled to breathe until his little body relaxed as the fight ended and his beak, stretching beyond any normal capacity, expanded like a dark and secret entrance to another world. Lucy blinks twice, then her large, expressive eyes grow vacant and glaze over as they stare unseeing. Ben backs away in horror and, as if possessed by a force he cannot control, he runs. He bolts out of the store and speeds along the highway on legs he can no longer feel. He believes if he runs fast enough he can take flight, soaring above, soaring beyond and away from the sea of blood, the empty eyes, the silent scream, the sudden grief. He flies aimlessly down unfamiliar streets, through unknown towns, longing to put as much distance between him and the horror, yearning to rid himself of the powerful images he will never lose. He runs all afternoon, well into evening because he senses that if he stops, he too will die—of a sorrow he cannot bear.

He wanted to run now, away from the lake, Francesca's screams, and Addie's silence. But his every limb was frozen to the earth, an unrelenting melding of one spent mortal with the ice.

It wasn't that he didn't love Francesca. Indeed, he did. His affection for her grew and deepened during the years they had been together. So did his need for her. She, like Lucy, was his safe harbor, a friend he could count on no matter what her day was like. He loved to lie in bed with her, to watch the rhythmic rise and fall of her chest, the fluttering of her eyelids as she dreamed. At those moments, he wanted to clasp her to him and never let her go.

But he also sensed there was a part of her he could never quite touch, a veiled region that lay deep within her, a privileged room he could never enter. Though her every word and every deed was an invitation for him to meet her in that special place where her music and her passion for life took root and flourished unhindered, something prevented him. He would approach the threshold and even linger upon it. But he could never bring himself to cross over. He was afraid to descend so far. Addie, on the other hand, knew the place well and frequented it at will.

On a warm day in May, late in the afternoon, Ben comes home as usual from work. Francesca's car is in the driveway, her school bag is on the table next to the opened flute case, her work clothes strewn on the bed, evidence that she had in a hurry changed into something more comfortable. But the house is empty and quiet. Cruz is gone, as is Addie.

He lays his briefcase next to hers and goes from room to room in search of his family. Realizing they are not there, he looks out of the windows into the distance. After a long, seemingly endless winter, the world has burgeoned into spring. As if overnight, the mud has dried, the earth has grown firm, a vibrant green has overlaid the insistent brown hue. And in the meadow, the wildflowers have budded, suffusing the landscape with muted color. There, in the middle of this sudden beauty, he sees her. She sits on the bench they built out of stones they dug up from various parts of the property. She holds her flute to her lips. He doesn't hear the music; the house is too insulated and the meadow too far away for the soft sounds to reach him. But he senses it.

He should have looked there first. The meadow is her special place, the realm of comfort where she always runs to when her world has turned gray and troubled. It is the green fields of her longings and desires, a magic dwelling where hope blooms anew and sprouts heavenward, even though it is often buried deep beneath heavy layers of mud and ice.

Addie and Cruz run and play nearby.

He leaves the house and heads toward the meadow to join them.

"Daddy!" Addie rushes toward him with open arms and with laughter. He lifts his soon to be four-year-old daughter high into the air as she squeals. Lowering her to the ground, he kisses her tenderly. Cruz, too, bolts toward him, tail wagging and whimpering an excited greeting. Ben leans down, patting the dog on his head. Francesca lowers her flute but never leaves the bench. She musters a faint smile as he sits down next to her.

"What's up?" he asks, noting her frown.

She shrugs. "Just something at work." She fingers the flute's keys.

"Want to tell me?"

"One of my students, this little blond boy. Cutest kid you'd ever want to see. When he came in September, he wouldn't talk. Elective mutism, they call it. The counselors have been working with him. We were told his father had severely abused him. Which is why he's in foster care."

"Look, Daddy, look at this pretty flower!" Addie runs to him, and hands him one of the young blossoms.

"Addie," Ben says sternly, "you shouldn't interrupt. Your mother and I are talking right now."

"But I wanted to give it to you!" Hers is the look of dejection.

"You shouldn't interrupt. It's not polite."

She blinks and sniffs and whispers, "Sorry," then lets the flower fall to the ground.

Francesca places her hand on Ben's arm and shakes her head. She reaches down and takes the fallen flower. "Addie, this is beautiful. A pretty flower is always a lovely gift."

"Daddy doesn't think so," Addie pouts.

"Yes, I think he does. We just need to talk right now." She leans forward and kisses her daughter's head and smooths her hair. "We both love you, you know."

A wavering smile creeps into Addie's glum expression, and she bites her lip trying to suppress it.

"I see you smiling, silly girl," Francesca tickles Addie who giggles and squirms. "Why don't you throw the ball for Cruz? He'd like that."

She nods and calls to the dog, holding the ball aloft. "Come on, Cruz!" He wags his tail, never taking his eyes from the ball, waiting for her to throw it and, when she does, he happily runs and fetches it.

"He likes this game!" Addie calls over her shoulder to her parents; her spirits brighten.

"Yes, it's his favorite!" Francesca smiles at them.

"So, what happened with this student?"

"He's a victim of alcohol and drugs, among other things."

"Look at how fast Cruz runs!" Addie calls to them from the distance.

"Yes," Francesca laughs, "he can outrun all of us!" She pauses, turning her attention back to Ben. "But I worked with him diligently, and the music seemed to help. It brought him out of his shell. He responded to it. Since January, he's followed me around, talking my ear off."

"Well, it sounds like he's gotten over whatever problems he'd had."

She shakes her head. "No, unfortunately not. He's fragile, and now they're sending him back to his parents who are moving to North Carolina. Supposedly the father has gone through rehab. I just don't have a good feeling about any of this. And he's such a sweetheart." She sighs, looking down at the flute and fingering the keys again. "I wanted to teach music because I wanted to show children there's real beauty in the world. Even if they experience it only for a moment. I wanted them to know the power of music; how it can be a relief for everything that bothers them. It can *save* them." She sighs. "Maybe I didn't realize how terrible life can be sometimes, how disappointing people really are." She caresses the instrument. "Even music won't save this child."

Ben has no words for her. No reply. He puts his arm around his wife. Addie runs toward them as Cruz follows. "Did you see how far I threw the ball?" she asks her parents, trying to catch her breath. "Were you watching?"

Francesca looks at her and smiles. "Yes, we were, honey. You threw it a pretty long way."

"Soon you'll be ready for little league baseball," Ben teases, then turns to his wife. He wants this conversation to end; he wants to flee from her dismal story and her cheerless mood. "I have to make some phone calls. Coming back to the house now?"

Francesca shakes her head. "I have to think about dinner, but I need to stay here for a bit." She looks around. "I love it here. It's so beautiful, so peaceful."

"I'll take care of dinner," he says quietly. "Why don't we barbeque. Come on, Addie, want to go back and help me get the grill ready?"

"I want to stay here with Mama and Cruz." She dances around the bench. "Can we have hot dogs?"

"Well, I thought we'd grill the good stuff. Like steak. Wouldn't that be better?" He tilts his head, waiting for her to answer him.

"Okay," Addie says, drawing out the word. She snuggles close to her mother. Ben turns to go but stops to look back at them. Francesca and Addie have their arms around each other, and Cruz is settled at Francesca's feet, panting.

"I'll be back soon," Francesca tells him. "I'll fix the salad then."

Ben nods and turns from them, walking back to the house, alone.

He loves her more as he sees her blossom into motherhood for a first time, awash with devotion for this helpless little creature who is solely their creation. Caring for Addie comes as natural to her as breathing. When the infant cries and lets forth bloodcurdling screams which frighten him and make him back away, Francesca runs toward her, picks her up and rocks her, feeds her, sings to her, soothes her. It terrifies Ben to babysit during these early months. While he loves Addie, he feels inept in the face of her screams and howls.

"Ben, it's simple. Really." Francesca instructs him. "At this age, there are only a few reasons she's crying. If she's hungry, feed her. If she needs her diaper changed, change it. If she's tired, try to sooth and relax her. I'll know if she's sick or in pain, so don't worry." He tries to keep his wife's words in the forefront, but he is always glad to hand the crying child over to her. As if by magic, Addie's screams turn to whimpers and then melt into laughter whenever Francesca takes her in her arms.

The summer when Addie turns three, they visit Long Island for a week. On numerous occasions, Francesca has recounted to both Ben and Addie the many happy memories she has of the wonderful, long summer days she spent with family and friends at Jones Beach. So, on this visit, she plans to introduce her daughter to the place she has always loved. All four grandparents agree to join them, and together they plan to make a day of it.

They arrive early after having packed both cars with everything they will need for the day.

"Let's set up here," Francesca says as she marks out a large space in the sand away from the others who have already taken up their positions. She drops the chairs she is carrying, laying claim to that portion of the beach.

"This is perfect," Laura chirps as she dons a wide brimmed straw hat. She stares out at the beach and the ocean through her large sunglasses. "Not too close to the water, but not too far away either."

"See?" Francesca looks toward Ben. "I told you it pays to get here early. This is a great spot."

He shrugs. "Yeah, it is. I just hoped to sleep a little later, since this is *my* vacation, too."

"You can take a nap under the umbrellas once you get them set up." She winks and flashes him a smile. He smirks.

Dominic and Maria set down the large cooler full of food and drinks they are carrying, depositing it on the perimeter of the imaginary border of their turf.

"Mama! Look!" Addie points toward the ocean with excitement as she watches it retreat from shore, only to rush back a moment later, the swell crashing onto the sand, dissolving into a stream of white foam.

"Yes, those are the waves I told you about." She smooths the child's hair. "I'll show you how to ride them later. It's a lot of fun."

"That's the Atlantic Ocean," Maria tells her granddaughter. "It can be wild at times. But today it looks pretty calm, a perfect day to learn to ride the waves." She points straight ahead of her. "If we took a boat and kept going, we'd hit South America."

"Really?"

"Yes. Really." Maria turns and points to the left. "And over there is Europe."

"Can we swim there?"

"Well, no, it would take too long. But we could take a ship or fly over it in a plane."

Addie turns to the left and squints, hoping to see Europe on the horizon.

"It's too far away to see," Ben says as he takes an umbrella and drives the pole deep into the sand.

"Then how do we know it's really there, if we can't see it?"

Ben frowns.

"Because other people have flown planes over the ocean or sailed from here to there, and they've told us about it," Francesca says, opening the large beach bag nearby. "Nowadays we can see it in satellite view. I'd show you on my phone, but it's in the car. I'll show it to you on the computer when we get home. Here, Addie, here's your pail and shovel."

The child takes what her mother holds out to her and bending down, runs her hand through the sand, grasping a fistful. She watches, mesmerized, as it streams through her fingers into the pink and gray pail. Addie then uses the pink shovel to scoop more sand into the bucket. After she fills it to the brim, she turns it over and dumps the sand into a pile and laughs.

Dan and Dominic set up the remaining umbrellas while Laura and Maria spread out chairs and blankets beneath them.

Laura sinks into a chair and digs around in the cooler, pulling out a can of diet soda. "So Francesca," she says, "Are you glad school's over with for the summer?"

"Yes, of course! It always gets so stressful toward the end of the year, so it's great to finally have a month or two off to recoup." She vigorously applies sunscreen to her face, neck, arms, legs, and stomach, then hands the tube to Ben, who applies the lotion to her back.

"Look, Mama, look what I found!" Addie runs to her mother to show her.

Francesca takes the gift her daughter presents to her and examines it. "What a beautiful seashell, Addie. Come here, let me put this on you."

"I found it over there," she points while Francesca slathers her with the protective film.

"There are lots of them in the sand," Maria tells her. "If you keep digging, you can find some more pretty ones."

"I'm going to find lots and lots of them!" Addie laughs and grabbing her pail and shovel, runs to a spot just outside of their imaginary border. Singing to herself, she sets about unearthing the buried treasure.

"Don't go too far," Francesca cautions her.

"I won't, Mama," Addie calls as she exhumes the buried shells, taking them in her hands, examining them as seriously as an archeologist at a dig. Satisfied, she blows and brushes the sand from them, then drops the precious finds into the bucket.

Dominic, who has been talking baseball with Dan and Ben, slides into a chair near his wife.

"Psst, Francesca . . ." He leans toward her, trying to get her attention. "Angelo made a beautiful cake for this one—" he nods toward his granddaughter "—so we're all set for her party tomorrow night."

"Oh, how sweet of him," Francesca says, truly touched. She pulls out a bottle of water from the cooler and moves her chair next to her mother's. "Ben, isn't it nice of Angelo to make the cake? I'm so glad we decided to wait and have her birthday party down here."

Ben takes a seat on a blanket next to his wife's chair. "Isn't he the one who did our wedding cake? He's a real artist. He did a great job with that."

Francesca nods. "He's almost part of the family. He's made all our birthday cakes ever since we were children. And not just birthday cakes, but for any occasion we needed one."

"Communion, wedding anniversary, graduation," Dominic says.

"And now he's doing it for the next generation." Maria smiles fondly. "He's such a gem."

Francesca nods and glances toward the spot where Addie was digging moments before. "Addie?" she blurts out and leaps from her chair.

Ben rises and places a hand on his wife.

"I don't see her, Ben." Panic washes over her like rising floodwaters.

Dominic stands and looks around. "She was just here. Addie? Addie!" his voice booms out onto the beach from beneath the umbrellas.

Ben glances around in all directions, hoping to catch sight of the missing child. But Addie is gone, nowhere to be found.

The others jump from their chairs and take positions around the imaginary border of their turf like a pack of guard dogs. They strain through the late morning sun to see if they can spot her among the growing crowd.

Francesca bolts from their setup and heads toward the ocean, frantically calling her daughter's name. Ben follows her. People nearby take notice, stop what they are doing and look toward the water. One of the three lifeguards on duty sees the commotion and approaches them.

"I can't find my daughter. She's missing!" Ben shouts to him and gestures. "She's three years old. This high. Long dark hair, pink bathing suit, name's Addie."

The lifeguard nods and motions to the two others who, from their individual stations, scan the area with binoculars. He radios them, telling them it is a child who is missing and gives them a description.

"Let's go that way," Dominic says to Dan, pointing in the opposite direction. "That's where she was facing." Dan nods and together they rush out from under the umbrellas. They push their way through the crowd, calling her name over and over.

"We'll go this way," Maria says, pointing toward Europe. Her voice trembles, her body tenses. Laura nods and clutches onto her as they begin the hunt for their granddaughter.

The color in Francesca's cheeks fades as she grows pale with fear. Her eyes darken and muddy with tears and grief.

"Oh, Ben," she whispers anxiously.

He puts a firm arm around her. "We'll find her."

The lifeguard who has stayed with them, assures them, "Kids wander all the time on the beach. We usually find them hanging out by the food stands or by the bathrooms."

"She's only three," Francesca snaps. "I doubt she'd be 'hanging' by the food stands."

The young man looks away.

Suddenly, Francesca breaks free of Ben's grasp and heads toward the water; she can no longer bring herself to remain still and calm. She must do something. Anything. So, she roams up and down the shoreline calling Addie's name, hoping for an answer.

Ben remains behind with the lifeguard as he is fed information from the other two who are searching the beach for Addie. After ten long minutes, they are notified the child has been found.

"She's over there," the lifeguard informs Francesca when he and Ben have caught up with her. He points into the distance. "She was on the beach, not too close to the water. Samantha's bringing her back now."

It seems to take forever before Francesca sees the young female lifeguard approach. She and Addie are holding hands; they swing their arms and laugh as they walk and talk as if the two of them are old friends who have merely gone out for a pleasant morning stroll. Addie, hugging her pail to her, chats away.

"She was singing to herself and collecting shells from the sand," Samantha says as she hands the child over to her mother.

"Thank you, thank you!" Francesca says tearfully to the young woman, then she bends down and hugs Addie to her.

"Not a problem." Samantha turns to leave.

"Bye, Sam!" Addie giggles and waves to her new-found friend.

"Don't wander away again, cutie." She strokes the tip of the child's nose. "I don't think your parents can deal with all this excitement." She winks at Ben, who stares blankly at her.

Francesca clutches her prodigal child to her with a ferocity born of grief. Addie is unmindful of her mother's anguish, as she laughs and hands her a gift, "Mama, for you, these pretty shells!"

But all day long, Ben observes, Francesca's eyes remain dark and somber, her face ashen and grim, her lips press together and turn downward. It is as if Death has fleetingly grazed her and, like a petty pickpocket, has stolen a sliver of life from her.

And now, it seemed, the same thief had stolen from him everything and everyone he loved.

With all his might, he peeled his hands from the snow and ice and slowly, with great effort, pushed himself up. There he sat, his legs folded beneath him, his back toward the lake. He heard Francesca cry out again. He rocked himself back and forth and covered his ears with his hands. The vision which had haunted him for years now, the image he could never lose, arose before him and taunted him. Once again, he saw Lucy as she lay in the sea of her own blood, dying. He bent forward, holding his head in his hands. "Nooooo!" he cried out. With all the strength he could muster, he rose in stages upon unsteady legs. As Francesca's plea for help washed over him, thundering through him like a howling storm. He forced his feet to move, one in front of the other. Stumbling often, he fled from the lake, from the gruesome screams, the impending horror, the sudden, unrelenting grief. He knew, then, that all was lost.

For his fear of death was greater than his love for his wife and his daughter.

BENEATH THE
SURFACE

Francesca watched in horror as her husband ran from the lake, from her, and from Addie, disappearing into the advancing shadows. For a moment, she comforted herself with the belief that he was going for help, but the moment faded as quickly as it had come. Hope dissolved into panic and despair. In her heart, she understood the truth. He had answered her tearful pleas with nothing but a hurtful, intractable silence. A silence that flew over the lake toward her, landing like a purposeful blow, striking her to her core. A silence that inflicted a mortal wound from which she knew she would never recover. He hadn't once looked back at her or the lake. He just ran. Away from her and Addie, leaving them both to die.

She was overcome with sorrow and a crushing fear. She wanted to find Addie, to help her and to save her, but she felt her physical self weakening. The more exhausted she grew and the more fearful, the more she thrashed about in the water.

"No, no," Dominic cautions as he tries to stop her. "Don't struggle so much. You need to just relax. Relax."

"It's too deep," she frets as Dominic puts his arms around her and guides his six-year-old daughter to the middle of the pool. He has decided it is time Francesca learns to swim, so the first lesson takes place at the neighborhood recreation center. "Before you can really learn to swim," he tells her, "you need to relax. I'm going to teach you to be comfortable in the water."

He loosens his grip on her, and as she sinks, she flails.

"No, no, don't fight it." He props her up again. "See what I'm saying? You slipped down because you tensed up. Just relax."

"But how?" Francesca whines and pouts. Her every instinct is for life; her every impulse is to resist annihilation.

"I'll tell you how. You can't be afraid. If you are, you'll tense up. Your arms, your shoulders, your legs, all tighten up, and you fight it. But don't. Don't fight it. Don't struggle. Melt into it. Surrender to it." He loosens his grip on her again. "Once you relax, you'll begin to float. And once you float, you'll be safe."

He puts his hand on her back and nudges her shoulder into the water, encouraging her to lie on top. She giggles as her hair floats out around her. "That's it," Dominic assures her as she gives in to the sensation.

"Don't let go!"

"I won't." He smiles though neither hand touches her. She is floating under her own power. Then he holds up both hands. "You're doing it all by yourself. See? You're safe!"

Francesca wanted desperately to be safe now. She tried to heed her father's advice. Perhaps if she could relax, she could float far away from death and betrayal and find the strength she needed to save her daughter. With tears of fear and sadness, she gazed up at the gray late afternoon sky. She wondered then in an instant what it all really meant—this life. *Her* life. Her work, which seemed so insignificant now. Her beloved music which had vanished without a trace. Her love for Ben which seemed suddenly misplaced and unrequited. Her overwhelming love for her daughter, whom she was incapable of rescuing. She wished she could believe in something. Anything. So long as it was beyond herself and this terrible, heartbreaking, solitary moment. She longed to pray. But to whom? To what? She plunged down deep within herself, seeking to dredge up words of faith and hope. But she found only unformed fragments that washed up like jagged stones on the shore of her soul.

Once you float, you'll be safe. . . .

Her eyes fluttered like a bird's wings before flight and slowly closed. "Addie, oh Addie," she murmured as a long, quiet breath escaped from her, mingling with the cold, crepuscular air. Gradually, a calmness settled over her; her head drooped backwards, grazing the frigid water; her legs flowed slowly out from beneath her, rippling inertly before her. She lay there, still but buoyant, a sad and sleeping beauty, as if some insubstantial lover had reverently placed her upon this watery bed. But her heavy clothes—and heavy spirit—dragged her down, down to the murky depths.

And then it happened. It came to her softly, like a stray leaf floating upon the breeze. It was barely a whisper. "Mama!"

She sprang upright, though she was still far beneath the surface, her feet brushing the bottom. She looked desperately around. Addie! She heard a splash. She peered through the dimness toward the impact and saw a trail of white foam that stretched from the surface down toward the bottom and up again. To her utter surprise, she saw Cruz at the head of this white stream, rapidly paddling across the lake. In his mouth, like a large rag doll, was Addie, still dressed in her pink bibs and matching pink jacket, her gray Baffin boots, and her gray and pink helmet. He was heading away from her, toward the opposite shore. She needed to get to Addie; Cruz could drag her daughter from the water, but only she could imbue her with the breath of life. Francesca summoned all her strength and set off in the direction of the stream. Cruz was an angel, heaven sent, she was sure of that now. He had come to save Addie and lead them both out of this dismal prison.

She swam, keeping her eyes on the trail of foam and bubbles. Her journey through the lake seemed eternal; minutes passed like hours, like days and weeks and months. It took all her will to lift one arm, then the other, to kick her legs and propel herself forward. But when exhaustion nearly overcame her, and she believed she lacked the ability to go on, she saw a light shining down from the surface of the lake. It swirled toward the bottom, a ladder of hope. There, in this vortex, the white stream ended. Cruz and Addie disappeared from her view.

Francesca felt herself failing, but her desire to reach her daughter gave her the courage she needed. In one last surge, she stroked the water, forcing herself forward into the eddy. She looked up to see a break in the ice at the surface. With the last remaining ounce of energy, she pushed herself up, up toward the surface, up toward the blessed light. When she emerged from the depths, she coughed and gasped for air that had so long been denied her. She cried and laughed and cried again as she inhaled the cold early evening air. She took long draughts which made her dizzy with life. With renewed hope and stamina, she swam the last leg of her journey to shore, the fifteen feet that were miraculously free of ice. There she crawled from the water's womb, falling face down at the lake's edge.

"Mama!"

Francesca sat up, her numb legs folded beneath her, her hands pressed into the ice, supporting her. She scanned the deepening twilight but could find no evidence of where Cruz had gone. There were no paw prints in the snow, no trail that had been left behind to show he dragged Addie to safety.

"Mama!"

Francesca started; the child's mournful plea, full of longing and tears, clearly came from within the nearby forest. She forced herself to stand but didn't move until she felt her legs steady beneath her. Her black Baffin boots, outwardly wet, were now encased in ice. They had, however, performed as promised and kept her feet dry and warm. The outside of her jacket was soaked. She unzipped it, discarding it by the water's edge. The outer surface of her black bibs was also wet, but beneath them, the other two layers remained remarkably dry—the Thermaskin long underwear, her jeans and the white turtleneck she donned earlier in the day. The only thing that was wet was the collar. She ran her gloved hand around her neck to dry it as best she could and turned the collar down, keeping the moist portion away from her skin, then pulled off her black, heated, waterproof gloves. They too were wet only on the outside; her hands remained warm and dry. Reaching up, she unpinned her sodden hair, which tumbled down around her like a dark waterfall. The frigid December air immediately turned her long tresses white with frost.

Francesca gazed long into the gloomy woods before her. She knew she had come up on the other shore, but suddenly nothing looked familiar, not the forest before her nor the lake behind her. It was true, she hadn't spent much time on this side of the property and certainly never ventured into this part of the woods. But the sudden strangeness startled her.

Again, she heard the child's plaintive cry. Francesca realized then what she had to do. Though the afternoon had given way to twilight, and the eerie, lonesome shadows of night were now upon her, she approached the dark thicket on unsteady legs. Her heart was aflutter; a sense of dread and doom enveloped her. She paused. Then, amid fear and trembling, she made her way into the dark and unfamiliar forest. For her love of her daughter was greater than her fear of death.

In the distance, the church bells rang out five times.

THE FOREST

The newly risen moon slipped in and out of the clouds, a capricious child of the night, then turned its hazy eye downward upon this solitary woman. Its gentle light fell through the darkness like a luminous shower, setting the woods aglow, a lambent guide for the lost. Francesca, cold and fearful, stood amid the thicket and listened for any hint of her faithful dog or her beloved daughter. The forest, dusted white, was still—like death.

"Cruz, come!" she broke the eerie silence with the familiar command as she shouted into the void. "Addie! Where are you?" But the frantic words, shooting out through the trees like an arrow racing headlong toward its mark, turned cruelly back toward her without ever finding the target. They echoed around her and in her, gradually melting away like dewdrops after sunrise. And the woods grew quiet again.

Desperate to find a path which would lead her onward, Francesca warily stepped over the icy leaves, wet branches, and the decomposing logs of fallen trees that littered the forest floor. But if there was one, it was buried and obscure, hidden from her like a rare and secret gem that only the initiated were permitted to find. The way through the fearsome forest at this point was directly through the brush. The way back was useless. She had no choice but to go on. Somewhere in these dark woods, Cruz and Addie awaited her.

Minutes passed like hours. Like days, and months, and years. It seemed like an eternity that Francesca wandered, alone now, as completely and utterly as she had ever been. She had always been surrounded by people, an army of protection with her at its center, whether it was family or friends, students or colleagues, acquaintances or strangers. She was aware of herself only in relation to others; their presence lent her existence a reality which now seemed to be ebbing. They bore witness to her physical being, her words, her deeds, the things she loved and hated, desired and feared, her hopes and dreams. They were the gravitational force that held her to earth, keeping her bound fully to life.

But now her aloneness was absolute. There were no eyes to look upon her, no ears to hear her, no soothing words to comfort her, no hand to steady her as she stumbled through the woods in desperate search of all that was lost. Suddenly, her separateness from all things shocked her. As if imprisoned in a glass globe, Francesca was set apart from everything around her. She could hear, could see, but could not feel anything her hand fell upon, even though she grasped a branch of a nearby tree to steady herself while climbing over a slippery depression. She saw her hand around the limb, but it was numb to the thing it touched.

An invisible shield stood between Francesca and the world, keeping her separate and apart. She was overwhelmed by a strange and terrible lightness of being, as if her very physical substance was loosening and crumbling. Looking backward in the direction from which she had so recently come, even her footprints left in the snow were faint and ill-defined. It was as if she were fading from existence. Maybe this was nothing more than a dream—a nightmare—from which she needed to awaken. Yes, let it be a nightmare, she implored the heavens above and the earth below. Let Ben reach over and rouse her to remind her it was time to begin another day.

Ben.

No, no. This was real. *She* was real. She was sure of it now because the anger and bitterness that boiled within her toward her husband made everything real again. Francesca reviled him for his betrayal when he had promised to be loyal; she despised him for abandoning her and Addie when he promised to stay always.

A tear dropped down her cold cheek and froze there, a pearl of grief. Gazing up at the night sky which shimmered through the tops of the barren trees, she raised a belligerent fist to the heavens. "How dare you shine down on him like you shine down on me!" Francesca wept and shouted, a lone voice in the forest. Turning in a slow circle, her head still craned upward, her arms spread outward, she thundered, "How dare he breathe the same air as I breathe or look up at this same sky as I do!" Then lowering her head, still weeping, she brought her fists to her chest. Heartbroken and frightened, Francesca cursed him to the end of time and back again. For he had done this to them.

It seemed like months and even years that Francesca stood in darkness. Her head bowed, she cried and cursed and mourned and cried again. But as hard as it was, she had to go on. So stifling the sobs that rose relentlessly like waves within her, she wrestled with her grief and solitude. Holding back the flow of tears, knowing well the flood would drown her, she forged ahead, and though her fear was great, she stumbled through the torturous woodland drawn on only by her love for her child. All the while invoking the names of her lost dog and daughter, sending a call out into the world hoping for an answer in return. But always she was met with silence.

Francesca walked for miles, it seemed, losing all sense of where she had come from and where she was going. Everything looked the same; nothing looked familiar. She felt eerily lost, but pressed on until she could walk no more. Overcome with exhaustion that left her weak of body and empty of spirit, she sat down on a nearby stump, burying her face in her hands. He had left them both, her and Addie. She was trapped here, alone and cold, in this terrible forest, unable to find her daughter who needed her. Why? She should be home by now, cooking dinner with Cruz sitting attentively at her feet, while

Addie played by the fire, and Ben tinkered with the snowmobiles in the garage as they had done on so many a wintry Sunday afternoon. Afterward, they would prepare for another week—Ben at his office, her with her students, Addie at pre-school. Why hadn't their lives gone on as usual? Why couldn't they take back that one moment that had changed everything forever? Why had he, who once loved them so, done this to them?

She never would have done this to him.

The memory of their first moments together came back to her full force. Francesca saw him again, tall and handsome, as he tilted his head while shyly looking at her with the sidelong glance that lured her to him almost against her will. She spied the wisp of blond hair falling on his forehead like a stray vine, making him seem innocent and boyish. She caught sight of his intense blue eyes as they often smiled at her with love. She remembered his touch—his large hand on her back, her shoulder, the nape of her neck; the way his long arms enveloped her as he bent down to embrace her. She longed to hear his voice again, to reach up and smooth his hair as she had so often done in moments of tenderness, to see him, to touch him, to breathe in the scent of him again. She yearned to see the world through his lens once more. If he were here, the trees wouldn't seem so gnarled and ominous. They would rise instead, like stately sentinels above and around her, a platoon of protection. If he were here, the shadows which leapt around her, perilous and sinister, would be but a soft and comforting glow that banished this eternal winter and lighted her way to peace and happiness.

No, Francesca said to herself, shaking off the images of things that were gone from her forever. He had betrayed them; he had willfully put them here where death was their only companion. She knew then, there were some things that could never be forgiven.

Suddenly a long, plaintive howl broke the silence. It was faint and far away.

"Cruz!" she uttered aloud. Rising from the stump, Francesca turned toward the sound.

Again, she heard it. With renewed courage and energy, she sliced through the thicket, slipping over the sedge, hacking her way out of the frozen underbrush. The dog's cry echoed through the stillness like a siren, drawing her onward. But as she neared a clearing, it ceased. Francesca looked around. Once again, she was plunged into darkness and silence. There, at the opposite edge of this glade, she saw something through the gloom, a pack, a heap. Drawing near to it, she knelt. And then out of the shadows, she discerned her beloved Cruz lying on his side, his eyes opened but unseeing, his bloodless tongue dangling from his lips. His rigid body coiled protectively around a pink bundle.

"Addie!" she screamed as she pulled the child from between his legs and held her cold, stiff body in her arms. Francesca frantically tore the helmet from her daughter's head and, brushing the dark hair from her face, looked through the night into her open, empty eyes. "Addie!" she sobbed, shaking the lifeless form, trying to awaken her. Francesca kissed her daughter's colorless lips, forcing the breath of life into her. But the child remained still and unresponsive—like death.

"Oh Addie," she wailed and hugged her daughter tightly to her. "Why? How can this be? I never wanted this to happen to you!"

It seemed like hours that she knelt alone in the dark wood, clutching her dead daughter to her breast, her sobs and anguished laments permeating the forest like a raging storm. And when the last bit of her strength was spent, she crumpled to the ground, lying down next to her lost children, longing to die with them.

A wind stirred; dark clouds formed, blotting out the moonlight. Snow and ice tumbled from the tumultuous heavens. Francesca turned her face upward; the dense, frozen crystals fell heavily on her cheeks, still wet from tears and sorrow. They cut her like a thousand sharp blades, slicing through to her soul. "He did this to us," she whispered and sobbed through clenched teeth. "I'll never forgive him. Never." And so a terrible bitterness filled her aching heart. As a relentless fatigue washed over her, her eyes fluttered amid the squall; against her will, they slowly closed.

And winter, blanketing the heartbroken woman like a shroud, claimed her for its own.

"She's here," one from the group called out as she knelt to examine the still figure. "Over here!" She signaled to the others as she dug through the heavy snow to uncover a cold and lifeless arm. "Bring the light closer."

The others moved slowly, deliberately, toward the motionless form. The women, about thirty in number, encircled the entombed, unconscious creature, gazing down at her with pity. As they stood shoulder to shoulder, forming a tight ring around her, their long, gray hooded overcoats created a shield against the cold. The snow that had lain over the body melted.

"Does the Widow know she's here?" one from the crowd asked as she brushed away her unruly, long white hair which had crept out from beneath her hood.

The kneeling woman looked up at her companions. "I don't think so." She looked back toward the expanse of the forest behind her. "Someone needs to tell her."

The others nodded, their faces obscured by their large gray hoods.

"I'll go on ahead and tell her," another woman said from the crowd. She turned without waiting for anyone to consent and hurried away, the trail of her long cloak leaving a furrow in the snow.

The woman rose and turned to her companions. "We don't have a choice. We have to move her."

The others nodded again, then silently, some from the group bent down and in unison lifted the lifeless body onto their shoulders. The remaining women fell in before them and behind them as the gray forms advanced through the forest in a somber procession toward the familiar circle of light. Once there, the pallbearers released their burden, placing her on the ground not far from the White Widow, who was seated in one of the two white ladder-backed chairs which flanked the small white table. The Widow's arms rested on the square tabletop, her hands folded; she stared ahead as if she were looking at someone seated in the empty chair across from her. The messenger who had gone ahead stood at a distance in the shadows.

"Very unusual to find her so far away, isn't it?" the Widow asked half to herself as she turned and gazed upon the sleeping woman. Then she rose from her throne, tall and regal, and smoothed out the skirt of her long white gown that had crinkled from sitting too long. "I can't remember this happening before."

She shook her head, clearing the dusting of snow from the thin wreath of small white flowers which held her white, upswept hair in place. She let the gown's long train fall with a flutter; it swirled around her and behind her as she edged her way toward the unconscious woman in their midst.

The White Widow looked down at the lifeless form and frowned. "She's young. How sad."

"But we're all young," one from the crowd uttered as the others nodded in unison.

"Yes, even me," the Widow whispered, a touch of sadness coloring her words.

She knelt and gently brushed the motionless woman's hair from her ashen face. Then she laid a hand on her arm.

Francesca's eyes flickered; her arm quivered.

"That's good, that's it. Come on. Get up."

Francesca moaned, then awkwardly put her hand to her cheek. She woke as if from a dream; her spirit was heavy with sadness and a strange sense that something terrible had happened, but she couldn't remember what it was. She looked up and through the haze saw a crowd looking down at her. She shielded her eyes with her hand. In the center was a white light. It spoke to her kindly, "Come on now. Get up, get up."

Francesca sat up with a start, coming face to face with the woman dressed in white and from whom there emanated an unearthly glow.

"What—what's happened? Where am I?" She shook her head, trying to clear it, but the fog that enveloped her mind wouldn't lift.

The White Widow took Francesca gently by the arm, helping her to rise. "Come. Sit for a bit until you get your bearings." And she guided the unsteady young woman to the chair at the table.

Francesca slumped into it and stared at the ground. She rubbed her hands together, over and over. "I, I've slept long and without joy. Something terrible happened, something sad, I can't remember—"

"Maybe it's better you don't remember," the Widow told her. "All of us at one time or another have wanted to drown ourselves in the river of forgetfulness. It's easier that way."

The others nodded from beneath their hoods.

Francesca rubbed her forehead. "Something to do with my

daughter. And Cruz." She looked up suddenly, bringing her hands to her mouth in horror. "Oh, my god, my god! Addie's dead! They're both dead!" She looked frantically at the crowd, accusing them. "What have you done with them? Their bodies?"

The White Widow looked at her, perplexed. "I'm sorry, but you were alone in the clearing when we found you."

"No, it's not possible!" she shouted as she jumped up and faced the woman in white. "I saw them. I held them." She wiped away the tears that had begun to fall again. "Tell me what you've done with them!"

The White Widow took Francesca by the arm and coaxed her back into the chair. "Truly, you were alone when we found you." The others nodded and murmured "yes" in unison.

"I remember now," she whispered, heartbroken. "I remember. My husband left us to drown in the lake. Cruz pulled Addie from the water and brought her here to the forest. I followed them and finally found them, but it was too late. Too late." Her tears flowed from her, a deep and eternal spring that coursed unimpeded out into the world.

"Your daughter lives," the White Widow said. "We found only you."

"But, but, I saw them. I held Addie in my arms. She was—" Francesca hung her head and sobbed.

"Sometimes when we're lost in the darkness, the things we see are really only the shadows of our fears and expectations."

"I don't understand."

"There are so many things we don't understand."

Francesca bowed her head; her hair fell forward, almost covering her face. Trembling, she brought her hand upward, stroking her long tresses as if they belonged to someone else. Her hair suddenly seemed foreign to her; its texture and thickness seemed odd. She took hold of a section, clutching it between her fingers, and brought it closer to her eyes, examining it intensely. "It's, it's—white."

"Yes," the Widow affirmed. "Winter has you firmly in his grip." She looked across the table at the young woman whose eyes were turned downward, whose thoughts were turned inward.

"It was an accident," Francesca muttered, still clutching her hair. "He left us. To die. He never even tried to help us, he never once looked back. Not a word, not a thought, just silence."

She looked up and frowned across the table at the woman in white, as if noticing her and her companions for a first time. "Who are you? And who are they?"

"They call me the White Widow. And these are my sisters in spirit, the Vilas. We are those who have been betrayed. We gather here nightly to mourn for what has so grievously been taken from us. Our grief knows no end, nor does our bitterness. Like you, we all have unfortunate tales to tell."

She held Francesca's gaze and smirked. "Let me tell you my story. It was our wedding night. My husband threw me overboard."

Francesca frowned, looking at the Widow, perplexed.

"We were married only a few hours. He was a wonderful man. I couldn't have asked for anyone better. He was generous and loving and kind. It was the wedding of my dreams, aboard a cruise ship. All our family and friends were there. Then, as it neared midnight, we stepped out onto our private balcony to watch the moon over the water as we sailed to our next port. It was a beautiful sight. A romantic moment. I was the happiest I had ever been in my life. Our future stretched out before us, so full of promise—the home we would build together, the children we would have. I still don't know what happened."

She paused and collected herself. "He took his arm from my shoulder—he always had a lovely habit of putting his arms around me at every opportunity, as if he wanted to hold and keep me safe forever. But not on this night. He withdrew his arm from me, lifted me up suddenly. I thought he was going to carry me off to bed and make mad love to me. After all, it was our wedding night. Instead, he threw me over the railing."

"But they call you the Widow."

She snickered. "Yes. I held on. Tight. I took him overboard with me. Revenge is very sweet, my dear."

Francesca stared wide-eyed across the table at her.

A short, rotund woman with a large nose and ruddy cheeks stepped from the crowd. Her eyes, all but hidden beneath the hood of her cloak, darted back and forth between Francesca and the White Widow. She bowed, then spoke, faltering.

"My husband and I were married for fifteen wonderful years. We had two beautiful children, a son and daughter. Our lives were perfect. Really perfect. We had a beautiful home, successful careers. He was my best friend, my confidant. He was a very thoughtful person. His work schedule differed from mine; he was out of the house and on the road before I woke up, but he always took the time to fix my breakfast, leaving it and the coffee warming in the kitchen. Every day I'd find a note of endearment. It was such a wonderful way to begin each day. One chilly spring morning about ten years ago, he left a note next to the coffee just like he usually did. It told me to drink up and keep warm and be at peace, for he had brewed a special treat in honor of all our years together. So I drank it, smiling and contented. I was a very lucky woman to have such a kind and loving husband. It was more bitter than usual, with a strange almond taste. I assumed he had tried one of those new flavored coffees. Unfortunately, I learned too late what he had brewed for me. My beloved husband, my best friend, traded me in for someone else."

An attractive young woman stepped from the crowd. She smiled tentatively as she fixed her sad eyes to the ground and pulled up the gray hood over her long white hair. She tried to say something but emitted nothing except a rush of air where words should have been. She wiped away a tear.

"Jenn?" the White Widow called to her, and frowned.

The young woman stood tall and swayed, a tree breaking in the wind.

"Jenn," the White Widow said again.

"I remember when I first met Jamie," she began. "We were sixteen. He was my first love. My only love. We stayed together through high school, through college and married soon after graduation. We decided to take a year to travel, to see the country before settling down at permanent jobs, buying a house, having children. We spent several months taking the northern route, trying to visit every state between here and the West Coast. About half-way through our year, we found our way south to Yosemite. When we entered the park, it seemed like paradise—the meadows seen from the Tioga pass, the Mariposa Grove where the giant sequoias have lived forever. All of it was a breathtaking adventure. Since we were experienced hikers and climbers, we naturally wanted to conquer the summit of Half Dome. Not even part way up, when we had reached the Vernal Falls, I leaned over to look down at the beautiful sight of the rushing water—and felt a hand on my back." She lowered her head, stifling a sob.

"Then she found her way here, just as you have," the Widow finished for her.

Another one stepped from the crowd, bowed, then took a deep breath. "My husband put our two small children in the car one night and drove to my office. I often worked late, and when I did, I would come out alone. That night I was walking to my car when he sped toward me and hit me; the force threw me. As I lay on the ground, he backed up and ran over me. Again. And again. I thought I could hear him laugh as my torso flattened under the weight. The last thing I remembered were the screams of my children. Then I came here."

Francesca put up her hand. "I don't want to hear any more. What does all this have to do with me, anyway? I came here to find my daughter, and I'm not even sure now if she's alive or dead."

"Your daughter lives," the White Widow said harshly. "It's your bitterness and your sorrow that bring you here, not your search for your child."

Francesca bristled. "It's not true! All I want to do is find Addie and Cruz and bring them home!"

Home.

It had been a long time since she had uttered that cherished word. Unexpectedly, the images of her former life swelled and burst forth, like a butterfly from its chrysalis. The joyous memories flooded her, taunting her with a reality she could not deny. They flitted through her and around her until she yielded and followed them out of the dark forest. Suddenly she was standing in the middle of her living room, the fire crackling, sending light and warmth through the house, keeping the cold December night at bay. Addie, laughing a contagious laugh that always filled and overflowed her heart with a powerful love, held on to a tug toy as Cruz grasped the other end, emitting his silly play growls and head shakes as he tried to wrest it from her hands. Ben was there too, but distantly, at the far end of the room. He stood watching, not quite present, an indistinct and passive character in a drama which no longer belonged to him. The sight of him resurrected in her the old longings and a love which separation and hurt refused to diminish. Francesca sensed she had to sever the bond that held her to him, though it seemed even now after betrayal and abandonment, it was unbreakable. The aroma of a winter evening's dinner, beef bourguignon, wafted through the house. She saw both families gathered around her dining room table. Dominic, standing over her, bent down, and kissed her. His lips brushed her cheek; his thick arms surrounded her protectively, as they had often done when she was a child. She longed for them again, though she knew inwardly nothing could protect her now. She saw her mother's smile, which had always filled her with warmth and hope. "Mama," she called out, reaching toward the one person who could comfort her completely, but when she tried to touch her, the vision faded as quickly as it had come. She was overcome with a desolation that devastated her, for her home and her family and all that was meaningful and good in life disintegrated in front of her. Like an image drawn on wet glass, it dissolved, drop by drop, until she found herself again in the dark forest facing the White Widow and her companions. And the Widow's words echoed through her, slashing her like sharp spikes, "It's your bitterness and sorrow that have brought you here. Just like us. Just like us. . . ."

Francesca blinked.

"You're no different from us," the Widow spewed forth, her words heavy as stones. "We wear our bitterness like an outer coat. It wraps us up and keeps us safe and warm. But it also keeps us secure and separate from the world. A world that holds nothing for us but pain and anguish. And aching memories of good times gone. And of love and promises betrayed. That's why we're here." She stared at Francesca, whose misery was etched upon her countenance, rivulets of pain branching in every direction. The White Widow was unmoved. "Now you are one of us."

"No—"

"Now we have a wound which will not heal," a woman from the crowd called out.

"And a deep sense of betrayal which will never abate," another of the group shouted.

"There is an interminable ache which nothing quells, nothing eases," a young woman nearby whispered.

"No—"

Suddenly, the rustling of trees and underbrush echoed through the forest. Twigs and fallen branches snapped loudly underfoot. A torrent of sound barreled relentlessly toward them.

Everyone turned in the direction of the noise. They waited in silence as the footsteps came closer. A young man emerged from the dark wood. A woman from the crowd gasped. Sophie stepped forward; the hood of her cloak fell back, revealing her white hair tied up in a ponytail. "Martin!" she gasped. "My, my fiancé," she muttered to the crowd.

The Widow's eyes glowered. "Oh, *that* Martin."

Sophie narrowed her eyes and fumed, pointing to him. "Yes, *that* Martin. He hated my dog, Leo. Do you believe he was jealous of, of a harmless little dog?" She paused and put her hand on her chest. Her bitterness and hatred flew toward him like a bird of prey. "You took little Leo and threw him out of the car window when we were driving!"

Francesca brought her hands to her mouth.

Sophie turned and addressed her. "We were on a busy highway. I stopped the car and jumped out to try to save Leo. That's when a semi barreled toward us."

Martin stared at Sophie. "I hated that son of a bitch dog. I should have done it sooner."

Sophie looked down, stifling a sob. "Why are you here?"

The young man looked around. "They told me this is where I could find the White Widow."

The woman in white stepped forward and threw back her head. Her derisive laughter swirled around them, slicing through the silence like a well-sharpened dagger. "Why is it all of you eventually seek me out? Do you hope to wipe away your guilt with forgetfulness? Do you long to ease the discomfort your selfish acts have caused with a temporary ecstasy?" She circled the young man who looked down and looked away. "Come to me then, and I'll give you what you want." She held her arms open, and a silent but powerful force drew Martin to her. He twitched and jerked as he lurched unwillingly toward her, emitting a startled cry as his head fell heavily against her breast. She closed her arms around him as he stiffened, a fly caught in a flowery trap.

"Oh, yes, I'll give you then what you've come for—an unnatural happiness, a false peace. I'll call up the mist and throw a foggy veil over you like a shroud. You'll gaze at the world through it and see all things indistinct and illusory. Your guilt will vanish; you will laugh as you have never laughed before. You will laugh so hard and so long you won't be able to stop, even when your joy has turned to pain. You will dance with a madness you have never known and cannot escape. You will dance—and die, because in the end, nothing can erase the consequences of your deeds. For things once done can never be undone." She squeezed the frightened man until he cried out, begging to be released. Laughing again, she shoved him; he fell to the ground with a thud. He raised himself on his elbows and looked up, terror-stricken at the crowd which now encircled him.

Francesca rose unsteadily from her seat as the Widow walked toward the fallen man. "What are you going to do to him?" she asked frantically.

The White Widow swung around and pointed a menacing finger at her. "Quiet! You have no power where he is concerned!" Francesca jumped back, startled.

Alarmed and frightened, she fell back into the chair as the Widow turned her attention now toward the ill-fated man. The vengeful crowd parted as the woman in white neared them.

"Get up!"

The man shook his head.

"I said, get up!" And she extended her arm toward him. A force beyond his power dragged him upright. He cried out in fear and pain. The White Widow rolled her arm thrice and suddenly the forest reverberated with sounds. Francesca looked up and glanced around; from all parts of the dark wood came music—*her* music, the melodies of *her* flute and *her* chamber group. Her beloved music that had always stood at the center of her life and brought beauty and comfort to her when she needed it the most. The music that had abandoned her at the lake, when she was unable to summon it to save herself. But here amid the gloom, the White Widow beckoned, and it came forth, like Lazarus from the tomb. Gone was its beauty, though, its grace and its artistry. Rather, it was discordant and disjointed—an eerie dirge that sang silent through the trees. Francesca covered her ears with her hands.

The White Widow raised her arms above her head and rolled her hands over one another twice as she laughed, then pointed toward the doomed man. "Dance," she commanded, "and be happy. Dance and laugh. Until you die!"

Suddenly the young man's head fell back; his mouth dropped open. Tears of fear and hurt washed down his cheeks as his unwilling laughter roared through the forest, melding with the cacophony, forming a grotesque tapestry of torment and death. His feet tapped frenetically to the dissonant music; his legs twitched, his arms flailed as he twisted and jerked like a misbegotten puppet on a string. He spun and leapt in paroxysms of pain to the clapping and the cheering of the crowd that surrounded him. Francesca watched, horrified, as the frenzy swirled before her, unstoppable. Even from the beginning, she knew how it would end. She turned her eyes away.

This dance of death seemed to go on forever amid the fevered cries and manic applause of the crowd. Francesca wondered if somehow, someway, she had accidentally found her way into hell. There was no inferno here, though, no fiery depths or red-hot blazes to consume her. Instead, she was trapped in an icy darkness, forced to bear witness to an anguished death amid unnatural laughter and harrowing ecstasy. And she was powerless to stop it. As powerless as she was to find her daughter, as powerless as she was to find her way home again.

Home.

Suddenly, the music stopped, and Martin's body fell to the ground with a thud. His eyes were open but empty and unseeing; they had long ago grown lifeless and vacant. The White Widow's countenance burned with pure pleasure as her laughter crashed through the forest, an avalanche of contempt. "Get this trash out of here," she ordered with a wave of her hand as some from the group scurried toward the body. They hoisted it above them and, in a haphazard procession, carried it off into the darkness.

Francesca rose to face the woman in white as she approached the table again. A pervasive anger smoldered beneath her controlled exterior. "I can't stay here," she announced with steely determination and a look of disdain that bore through the woman to her soul.

The White Widow laughed again and threw her head back. "You're free to leave here any time you want. Nothing holds you here but yourself." Then she drew close to Francesca, her eyes narrowing as she returned and held the young woman's defiant gaze. "This young man got what he deserved. He brought it upon himself when he robbed Sophie of everything she loved and cherished. And for no other reason than his own cruelty and selfishness."

"You didn't give him a chance to apologize."

"Apologize?" the White Widow uttered and blinked incredulously. "He stood there before us, remorseless and hard of heart. I heard no words of regret. And even if he had, it would have been of no consequence. Do you really think you can wipe away a hurt with a kiss or beg forgiveness with a tear? We didn't inflict this harm on him. He chose it the moment he robbed Sophie of her very being. He caused an intractable pain, a devastating wound that will never heal. And he did so willingly. We were merely the instruments through which he embraced his own demise."

She circled Francesca, whispering in her ear.

"Just as you have chosen to come here and wear your bitterness as we do, like a warm and comforting cloak wrapped round and round us. . . ."

Francesca swung around to face the White Widow. "That's not true. I told you, I've come into this god-forsaken forest for one reason only—to find my daughter and to take her home."

"But your husband has destroyed the only home you have ever really known. And you hate him for it, as well you should."

"Yes, but —" her voice trailed off.

"And he killed so much in you, you will never recover; he has left you too with a wound that will never heal."

Francesca grimaced and turned away. The Widow's words caught her off guard. The burning truth of them sparked an inferno which rose and engulfed her, scorching her through to her core. Desperately, she pulled away, trying to smother the blaze before it consumed her.

Suddenly, a cry, soft and plaintive, reverberated through the dark wood, filling up Francesca's empty heart. It called out: "Mama!"

She looked around. "Addie!" She drew her hands to her chest; she felt as if she would faint. "Is it really true?" she beseeched the White Widow. "Is it Addie? Is she really still alive?"

"I told you already she lives."

"Then he hasn't killed everything I've loved, if she still lives. I have to go and find her and bring her home. And yes, despite what you say, I still have a home, just beyond this forest."

Francesca turned quickly away from the Widow. The gray-hooded sisters now stood shoulder to shoulder in a straight line; as she hurried passed them, they bowed their heads one by one. And when she had disappeared into the thicket and was swallowed up by the blackness of the forest, the White Widow sat down again by herself at the table, looking across it to the empty chair opposite her and said, "She'll be back. I know she'll be back."

Francesca found herself alone once more, surrounded by darkness and silence. The soft cries of her daughter melted away into the surrounding stillness as if she had never heard them, as if they existed only in her dreams. Closing her eyes, she leaned against a nearby tree, and wondered then if anything was real. She was weary beyond her years; she felt as if she had lived forever and yet not really lived, but only slept. Was there nothing that was real to her now except eternal darkness and endless repose?

She tore herself away from the tree and, stumbling, forced herself onward. The fires of betrayal had nearly consumed her. They burned her to her core and turned everything she held dear to dust. Yet somewhere inside her, in a place so deep where even she had never ventured to go, there remained a lone ember of hope among the mountain of ashes. Here, lost in the dark wood, Francesca plunged down within herself and gripped the last cinder, wrapping her hand around all that had been and, with a fading breath, vowed to restore her life as it was. She would never let go of that hope and all she had once loved. Never.

She forced herself to go on, calling her daughter's name, longing to hear a reply. But as always, she was met with only silence. There was a time, not long ago, when her world was full and happy and safe. It was filled with the sounds of music and laughter and all that was good and joyous in life. Her very being, so intertwined with both Ben and Addie, was bathed in color and light. Blessed, life-giving light. But in an instant, everything vanished. As if it never was. Now she wandered long where stillness reigned, through a world so steeped in shadows she felt buried alive, entombed in this dark, cold world of endless night.

Losing count of the minutes and the hours which seemed again like weeks and months and even years, Francesca stumbled on. When exhaustion threatened to overtake her once more, she paused. At some distance ahead of her, the forest opened out into another clearing, and she spied a familiar light. *Could it be?* she thought, stunned. Could this be the soft glow from the stained-glass lamp which stood like a guiding star in the middle of their dining room window? It had always been her evening ritual, the moment twilight descended, to turn on the lamp and watch peacefully as the soft colors flowed together into a red-orange flame that would dance and gleam and point her family's way toward home.

Suddenly, Francesca heard a rustling nearby. A child's exuberant laughter bounded through the woods toward her, a torrent of mirth and joy. "Addie!" she shouted into the silence, straining through the mist to see what was real. There she glimpsed a child—her daughter's age and stature. The little girl danced in and out of the brush amid the shadows, a woodland elf whose merry laughter bellowed through the night, her arms outstretched like the wings of a soaring bird, her long dark hair flowed behind her like a black veil caught in the breeze.

"Addie!" she called again. This time, the child stopped and turned to look at her. Francesca was certain now this was in fact her daughter, for what mother wouldn't recognize her own child, even through the thickness of gloom and shadows?

"Addie! Are you all right?" But when Francesca moved toward her, the child only laughed again and danced onward toward the lamp, which glowed fiercely in the night. Francesca followed, fighting her way through the icy brush.

She watched as Addie ran toward the house, opened the door, and entered, disappearing from her view. Francesca halted. She had not left the forest; none of the surroundings seemed familiar, yet here before her was the home they had struggled so long and worked so arduously to build. Could it be? Had she really found her way back to her old life? Was it simply that things looked so different in the dark than they did by the light of day? She drew near to the building, laying her hand on the clapboard. Truly, this was her own house. She knew it by sight. She knew it by touch. They had built it from scratch; they had both been an integral part of the process and knew every nail and timber, every shingle and every stone. She had worked tirelessly to find the right color and texture of the wood and shingles. At their request, the workmen searched all over the property, digging up the large, heavy boulders from which they fashioned the front walkway. She looked down now at those very stones. Could it be? Had she truly found her way home? Yes. At last. Her terrible journey was over. The instant Francesca understood that her odyssey through the dark wood had ended, she sprinted with a long-forgotten energy along the path toward the door, flying like an unencumbered spirit up the porch steps, finally gripping the latch in her unsteady hand.

"I'm safe," she thought as she turned the knob. Tears of happiness flowed down her cheeks. "And Addie's safe, too. Now we can put this terrible day behind us."

No sooner had she whispered those words to herself than her overwhelming joy tumbled away and scattered like debris blown afar on the wind. The door wouldn't budge; she pressed her shoulder into it and jiggled the handle, but it remained closed and unyielding. She knocked, at first softly, then louder and more firmly. "Addie. Addie, please open the door. I know you're in there!"

Again, only silence.

Francesca moved to the large picture window on the porch and peered in through the lace curtains, past the stained-glass lamp and into the vacant dining room and beyond that, the vacant living room. She rapped on the window, gently at first, then harder as her desperation grew. "Addie!" she shouted. "Addie, open the door! Please!"

But no one answered her forlorn pleas. She circled the house, stopping at each window to stare into empty rooms. She tapped on the glass but again was met with only silence. In the kitchen, she hoped to find Cruz sleeping on his cot, his food dish nearby, but all she could see was the deserted bed, his kibble untouched, his water bowl still filled to the brim as if he too had been long absent.

The house that had once been her home, where her daily life bustled, busy and happy, was desolate now and closed to her, shutting her out while keeping every part of her former existence in. Francesca stood outside, a trespasser, an unsavory intruder who brazenly begged for entrance into a place where she no longer belonged. She went around to the garage and keyed in the familiar code to open the doors. Her plan was to grab the hidden key and let herself in. In, to her own home. But when she pushed the familiar numbers, the garage doors didn't move. Could she have forgotten the code? Accidentally entered the wrong numbers? She tried again and again, but nothing happened. Francesca went around the back, and once more banged on the French doors, but her desperate knocks were met with only silence. Sinking down onto the deck in despair, she slowly felt her old life departing from her. How many houses were locked to her now? Houses where she had once been welcomed. Her childhood home, her in-laws', not far from here. Houses she had so freely entered by simply announcing her arrival, and where she had always been warmly greeted. Were all the doors closed to her now? Now that she had been gone for so long? Perhaps she had been absent from the world longer than she realized, so the world had lost all remembrance of her. Perhaps she wandered in solitude and in darkness so completely that her very being was fading. For there was no one to bear witness to her existence and, having no eye to see her and no ear to hear her, her elemental self crumbled and dispersed. All that was left to her now was to stand longingly outside, a dimming spirit, looking in at rooms where once she had had her play.

She could accept anything as long as she understood it, but this was beyond any understanding.

Burying her face in her hands, she cried for everything that was lost.

"Shhhh," came a comforting voice and a steady hand on her shoulder. "Please don't cry."

Francesca looked up with a start. She was no longer on the deck, leaning against the doors to her locked house, but was rather propped up by a tree in the dark forest where she had wandered for so long.

"Who are you?" Francesca blurted out through her tears.

Scurrying to her feet, she came face to face with the heavy set, disheveled woman who had spoken.

"Please don't be afraid," the woman begged her, smoothing the ends of her gray matted sweater which bulged over her protruding stomach. The hem of her long gray skirt was stained and wet as it dragged through the snow and mud.

Francesca stared at the unkempt hag. "I asked you who you are."

The fat woman grinned. Most of her teeth were missing; those that remained were yellow and crooked. Francesca drew away from her. "My name is Lisee. When I lived in the world I was a seer; many a fortune I told, for good or ill."

"If you have special powers then, can you tell me where my daughter is? Do you know? There was an accident at the lake. My dog dragged her from the water and brought her here. I've been searching for them ever since, but I can't find them. I feel like I'm going in circles."

"You are."

"I am, what?"

"Going in circles."

Francesca frowned but continued. "She's a little girl, this high. Only four. She might be hurt, and she must be cold. Cruz was with her. He may still be, I'm not sure—he's a golden retriever. Have you seen them? Please. . . ."

Lisee shook her head. "My powers have grown faint and dim with the years. I haven't come across anyone but you."

"You must have some powers left. I'm desperate, please—"

"I'm sorry. I've lived in darkness and solitude too long. I have little to offer."

Francesca looked around longingly. "This forest, this cold night that never seems to end. Once it was a place of comfort and great joy.

We used to walk in these beautiful woods. Picnic at the tree line. This land meant so much to us as a family. To me. I was so privileged to live here. But now, now . . ."

"Ah," Lisee said as she lifted her skirt and sat down on a nearby boulder. "What was once your paradise is now your hell."

"I'd give anything to be out of here with my daughter, to be home again, to have things back the way they were."

"But you understand that can never happen. We can never go backwards in time."

The old woman's words landed like an icy slap on her soul. Francesca blinked and looked at her as if seeing her for a first time. "Why are you here?"

"I've been condemned to darkness and solitude."

Francesca glared at her. "What are you talking about? Who condemned you?"

Lisee sighed. "It was my own doing, I'm sure. When I lived in the world, I saw everything. Do you know what it's like to see truth in all its rawness? The good and the bad? Everything? I saw things I never wanted to see. Terrible things I could do nothing about, only acknowledge and accept but never change. Like you, I was unwilling to accept things as they were. That unwillingness forced me here, where I dwell alone in darkness."

Francesca bristled. "I'm not like you at all."

Lisee threw back her head and laughed, loud and harsh. When she looked again at the young woman, a glimmer of pity flashed in her eyes.

"It was my inability to pry my hands and my heart from yesterday that condemned me to live all my tomorrows in solitude and darkness."

Francesca spoke, hurried and hostile. "I have no idea what you're talking about. These sound like the ravings of a madwoman. This day hasn't even ended for me. I have a good life, a happy life, and I have every right to reclaim it. I'm here only to search for my daughter. I'm going to find her and bring her home."

"Ah."

"I used to know this forest well. We walked in it, we played in it. But I never ventured into it this far, never at this time of night when it's so dark. Once I get my bearings, I'll find my way out. I'll find Addie and take her home." Francesca turned away. "I have to go now."

Lisee sprung from her perch and advanced quickly on the young woman, taking hold of her hand. "Not so fast!" In one deft movement, she swung her around, yanking her close. Startled, Francesca let out a cry and tried to pull away from the hag and from her foul breath. But she remained locked in Lisee's unyielding grip. The old seer turned Francesca's hand over and ran her crooked finger around her palm. She met and held the young woman's gaze, her eyes boring into Francesca's, burrowing into her soul.

"You will never find your way out of this forest," she spat, "unless you let go of all that was and accept all that is."

Francesca twisted and squirmed and wriggled, a butterfly whose wings were pinned to a wall. "Never."

"Then you are doomed as I have been doomed."

"No," she cried out, full of hate and bitterness. "All I've ever known in my life were good things, and I've gotten them because I refused to accept things as they are. If I didn't like something, I'd change it. For the better. If I wanted something, I'd work hard and get it. I can't accept this. I *won't*. You're telling me I should yield to this terrible night? How can I embrace the darkness when I have been bathed so long in the light? Never."

"Then you will never find your way out of this forest."

"I will," Francesca spewed, freeing herself from the gypsy's grasp.

She wiped her hand roughly on the leg of her bibs, trying to obliterate Lisee's touch as well as her warning. Without a word, Francesca turned, and stumbling over a large log, steadied herself on a nearby tree. "Never!" she called to the old woman, but when she looked back, Lisee was gone as were all traces of her existence. There were no footprints in the snow where the heavy woman had stepped, no trail where the hem of her dirty skirt had dragged. The large rock where the old hag had sat was still covered with undisturbed snow. Francesca shivered and shook her head, trying to rid herself of the images. "A dream," she mumbled into the darkness. "Just a dream. I'm cold, I'm tired, I'm scared. That's all it is. Just a dream."

As much as she tried to believe she would soon find her way out, find her way home, deep within her the well of hope that had sustained her thus far was drying up. In its place sprang abysmal waters of despair and bitterness.

"Addie! Cruz!" she shot into the darkness through tears which seemed now not to end. Gone was the certainty, though; no longer did these names hurl through the forest as a command. Instead, they fell quietly from her as an uncertain plea, a fitful prayer for the lost.

Francesca stumbled on, carefully cutting her way through the thicket. But soon her plodding became a trot, and her trot became a gallop, until blindly, without direction, she broke into a run. She flew through the woods, heedlessly, chased by the furies of darkness and solitude, no longer drawn on by a desire to find her daughter or her dog, or even to find her way back to her old life, for she sensed they were gone for good. But now her sole motivation was to escape this terrible night.

Francesca saw a light in the distance and headed for it, a moth toward the flame. The faster she ran, though, and the more ground she covered, the more the light retreated. The same span remained as when she first spied it. Francesca ran and ran, frantically flying through the dark wood, a last streak of life amid death.

How long she ran through this darkest night, she couldn't tell, but like a bird shot down in mid-flight, her running ceased abruptly when something unseen in her path felled her. A rock or perhaps a log. There, sprawled face down on the forest floor amid rotting, ice covered leaves and strewn brittle branches, she raised her head and watched, dazed, as blood flowed from her bruised lip, spilling onto the snow.

"Are you all right, Mama?" came a familiar voice from behind her. Francesca sat up and looked around. "Addie?" She was afraid to hope.

Out of the shadows of a nearby tree stepped her daughter who stood resplendent in pink and smiled radiantly down at her.

"Oh, Addie!"

The child flew to her, effortlessly, as if on wings. Francesca rose to her knees and embraced her. She wrapped her arms around her daughter, hugging her tightly, never wanting to let her go. She kissed her forehead and lips and cheeks. She caressed the top of her head, her eyes, her chin as if trying to assure herself this was not a dream. Lovingly, through tears and laughter, she brushed the child's long hair from her face and murmured, "Oh, Addie. Addie. You're real. You're alive!"

Addie nodded and hugged her mother and laughed. Then pushing herself away, she bent down and plucked the flowers which sprang up where Francesca's blood had fallen, amid the rotting leaves and deadwood.

"For you!" And she held out the small bouquet of anemones.

Francesca took them, lifting them to her nose. "They're, they're beautiful!" She smiled through her tears and, drawing in long, deep breaths, inhaled the scent of the multicolored flowers.

"Oh, Addie," she exhaled, hugging the child to her again. "You've come back to me!" She stood and wiped her eyes, then took her daughter's hand in hers. A sense of urgency enveloped her. "Come on. Let's go home. Cruz might be there waiting for us. If we find the path that brought us here, we can find our way back." She turned and moved forward, but the child didn't budge.

"Addie?"

"There *is* no path back. Only a way forward."

Francesca looked quizzically through the darkness at her daughter, not sure she heard correctly.

"Addie, we have to go home. Now," she said firmly.

But the child remained still as if rooted to the earth. Francesca softened and looked lovingly toward her. "It's all right, sweetie. You don't have to be afraid anymore. I'll get us out of here. I'll find the path I took to get in here. It'll bring us out by the lake, even though we'll be on the other side. The one we're not familiar with. But once we're there, I'll be able to find the way home."

"No."

"No, what?"

"That's why you can't find your way out."

"What?"

"You're looking in the wrong direction. You're looking backward, not forward."

"Backward, forward, it doesn't matter." Exasperated, Francesca raised her voice. "Don't you want to go home?"

"Home is back."

"Of course it is." She closed her eyes and let out a long sigh. Why was a normally agreeable Addie giving her such a hard time now? Now, when she needed her to behave.

"You'll find your way out of this dark wood," the child spoke with a sudden gravity, "but only if you accept things as they are."

Francesca dropped Addie's hand and reflexively stepped away from her. She looked down at the bouquet as one by one the blossoms withered and crumbled. She let out a startled cry and tossed the flowers from her. "Addie, please—you, you're scaring me. Let's go." She reached for the child's hand again.

"No amount of longing can change what is."

Francesca, her hand still extended, said sternly, "Let's go. Now. I'll never accept this. We have a family, and I have students who need me, a home I love —"

"And if I tell you all of those things are passed?"

"I can't accept it. I won't."

"You have to. Because things once done can never be undone."

Francesca's hand flew to her chest and froze there. The words the child spoke cut into her like a thousand pointed knives. She let out a muffled cry.

"Somewhere out there beyond this forest, deep in the wider world lives a Power who rules us all."

Francesca backed away from the little girl in pink and shook her head.

"Perhaps His is some whimsical or preordained plan of which we know nothing and of which we can change not a particle."

Francesca sank to her knees and put her hands over her mouth. She looked at the child who now seemed so foreign to her. She was swallowed up by a torrent of grief. "How, how—do you let go—of—everything you love?"

"I don't know," the child replied. "I only know that things happen as they are meant to happen."

Francesca's heart raced; she buried her face in her hands and wanted to cry out in a panic. But the moment passed, and she regained her composure. Her hands dropped from her face. When she opened her eyes, Addie was nowhere in sight. Once again, she was alone. Francesca sank to the ground and lay face down in the snow, her arms covering her head, breathing in the scent of the dying flowers that were strewn amid the woodland debris not far from her. At first, she was still like death, but soon, haltingly, she stretched out her arms and curled her hands into fists, weakly pushing them into the ice. Soon her labored efforts became stronger and more steady; she struck the earth softly, then forcefully, until the pounding resounded through the forest, the rhythmic roar of a thousand hammers striking a thousand anvils. Francesca sat up, no longer beating her fists into the ice, but the clamor continued, flooding the dark wood with a persistent roar. She brought her hands to her ears, trying to block out the sounds she had begun but could not end. The pulsing thunder reverberated around her and through her; the earth beneath her quaked and quivered. Her head dropped back as she looked up into the night. Amid the din and tears that seemed now not to end, she forced herself up on trembling legs and ran unsteadily toward the distant light.

"There is still something of the darkness about you," the White Widow remarked as Francesca stood before her at the center of the circle of women, her shoulders bowed, her eyes lowered. "Patches of night cling to you yet."

The Widow cupped Francesca's chin in her hand, raising the sad woman's face toward hers. "I knew you would be back. We are your sisters in grief." She turned to the others and stretched out her arm. One from the crowd stepped forward, placing a cloak over it. The Widow wrapped the long gray mantle around Francesca. She pulled up the hood, tucking the young woman's hair into it and, drawing it forward, covered her face from sight. "Now you are one of us."

And the church bells on the distant green rang out six times.

Minutes passed like hours. Like days. And months. And years. Deep within the forest, concealed from the outer world, the Vilas languished and Francesca with them. The small ember of hope she had clung to during her journey fluttered away unnoticed. She stood, withered and hunched and hidden from the world that had broken her. A hollow, brittle tree awaiting the final storm that would upend her, lay bare her roots and grind her bit by bit into the cold earth. From her lethal wound, she bled all the promise and joy life had given her. Now it streamed non-stop and pooled like black water through this darkest night.

Their bleak existence was punctuated by unexpected intrusions of those whom the women had known in the past, those who had so betrayed them.

One by one they came, willingly and always, for the same reason. All of them sought vindication; none sought forgiveness. And so, none was given. As they flew toward the light they were snared; the powers of revenge and bitterness wove a complex web from which they could not break free. They were forced to dance, all of them. Until they died.

Francesca felt nothing now at the intermittent carnage. Certainly not the horror nor the disgust she had previously known. She had become one with her sisters, bowed and broken and gray. She was indistinguishable from them. From the night. From the forest itself.

So, as she stood apart on the outskirts of the clearing, solitary and still, she no longer flinched at the rustling of dead leaves, the snapping of branches on the forest floor, or the sounds of approaching footsteps. She remained unmoving as a tall, blond man bolted from the tree line, chased, it seemed, by the forces of grief, of guilt, of remorse. He came to a halt behind her. As exhaustion set in, he covered his face with his hands and sank to his knees.

Through the gloom, she heard it. It rose like the soft mist of early morning and floated toward her.

Francesca!

A fragment of a life, long stilled, stirred within her. She raised her head slowly as the sound once again strayed near, falling over her like a gentle rain.

Francesca!

She turned and though the night was thick with shadows, she saw him.

Startled, she murmured his name. It seemed foreign and meaningless as it seeped from her, a forgotten vestige of a vanished life.

He raised his head; he thought he heard his name, but it was faint and far away. Slowly, he forced himself up until he teetered on unsteady legs. He looked around, turning in the direction of the sound, but saw nothing. He stretched out his flailing hand, a blind man groping in the dark.

Francesca stepped back. The hand she had so longed for, to grasp, to save her in her hour of need, the hand that had instead pushed her away, robbing her of all hope, now reached out toward her. For what? For salvation? Mercy?

"Why are you here?" she asked, slowly circling him.

He turned again, following her voice. But he did not see her.

"Francesca?" he asked, faltering. "Is, is it really you?"

She kept her distance, remaining beyond his reach. "Yes. It's me. I'm here. What do you want?"

He swung around, following the muffled sound. He stared into the empty shadows.

"Please—"

He hurled the plea into the night, hoping to light up the woods with his appeal, to ease the pang of regret with his fitful prayer. But it was not to be.

She closed her eyes. So much enmity, so much bitterness toward the one who had harmed not only her but her daughter, and yet . . . and yet . . .

And there upon her bereft soul, a deadly battle was waged between anger and hatred on one hand and the tender remembrances of love past on the other.

He stretched out his arm toward her again. She hesitated.

"I know you're there," Ben said. "Please."

She hesitated again then moved closer until his hand came to rest upon her shoulder. The veil of darkness that separated them was drawn back; he saw her for a first time. His yearning made her palpable; his touch made her real.

"I've missed you."

She pulled back the hood that had so long hidden her; her white hair tumbled down around her like an icy squall. Her eyes bored into his, a barbed drill into blighted wood.

"You left us. To die. . . ."

"I was afraid."

"So was I. So was Addie." She held her breath, drawing her hand over her heart. "Is Addie—?"

"She's okay. Cruz—"

Her breath flowed from her, a stream of relief and sadness and longing. It had visible substance amid the cold night air; it puckered and swirled above them, hovering briefly, then gradually drifted away, like the spirit of all that was.

"That's your reason then," she said, disheartened.

He turned away, ashamed.

"You can't stay here. It's not safe."

"It's not safe for me anywhere since you've been gone." His eyes mined the darkness in search of hers.

"Addie needs you. The powers here are too great. They're beyond even my control. I won't be able to help you if you're caught. For her sake, I'm asking you to leave."

"No, not when I've just found you again. I don't want to leave. There are too many memories, all of them good." His eyes blazed through the night and rolled over her lovingly. "I remember what it's like to hold you, to touch you, to kiss you. To reach over in bed and feel the warmth of you. All those Saturday nights before Addie was born when we'd lay on the couch wrapped around each other while we watched old movies."

Francesca closed her eyes and shook her head, trying to rid herself of the unwanted remembrance.

"And all those weekends in Maine," he continued quietly. "We'd walk arm and arm on the beach, the two of us and then the three of us. The four of us when we brought Cruz. Addie would collect stones. It was her favorite thing to do. Cruz would run ahead of us, jumping in and out of the water, then run back to us." He paused, his eyes blazing through the night. "And you'd always ask him why he waited till he was next to us before he'd shake the water off his coat. Did you really expect him to answer?" Ben laughed. "But you always asked him."

"He answered in his own way," Francesca said sadly. "Yes. I remember."

"And the time I got stopped for speeding by a cop patrolling the area on a bicycle. On an actual bicycle. We couldn't believe it."

She looked down. "Yes, I remember. I remember it all." Francesca turned away. "But I don't want to remember any more."

He drew close to her and, leaning down, wrapped his arms around her. "Why?"

She slipped from his embrace like water through cracked glass and, standing at a distance, she turned her back to him, hurling her words toward the woods. "Because it's too soon for them to be memories."

Ben hung his head and said nothing.

Francesca swung around, facing him. "You have to leave. This place isn't safe for you. I won't be able to help you, should you need it."

Ben's smile faded; he looked at her perplexed. But before he could answer, the edge of the forest where they stood brightened. The White Widow hurried toward them, lighting up the woods as she stepped. Following closely behind her were her sisters.

"Ah, we have a guest," she snickered.

"He was just leaving." Francesca moved to block her.

"It doesn't look that way," the Widow said, her eyes narrowing. The sisters advanced slowly, deliberately, forcing Francesca and Ben apart as they surrounded him. Overcome by a sudden exhaustion, Ben dropped to his knees and bowed his head.

"Him, too?" Francesca asked, a sliver of the old tenderness, long absent, crept up from her barren soul.

"He's come here of his own volition. No one compelled him to do so. Once they come, there's no escape."

The crowd parted as the White Widow moved toward him. Ben stared steadily at the ground, supporting himself with his arms which trembled from weakness and fear.

"Just as no one forced him to run from you and your daughter at the lake." The Widow's eyes glowed with joyful revenge.

Francesca sighed, her head lowered, her heart empty.

The White Widow, towering above him, stretched out her arm. "Get up!" she commanded.

Ben, growing weaker, scraped the forest floor with his hands as he tried to rise. Instead, his arms twitched from the weight, then collapsed beneath him. With a grunt, he fell face down into the cold earth. Faintly, he called out to his wife, a muffled plea that filled up the darkness with regret. "Francesca!"

She closed her eyes. Why had he come now? After such a long time? Now when she was powerless to help him. Now when it no longer mattered. For the fires of despair and bitterness had drained the well that once overflowed with her hope, her longing. And her love.

The White Widow's laughter echoed through the woods as she mocked him. "So you beg now for the very help you were once too selfish to give. There is only one just fate for someone like you." And she paused, looking down upon him with disgust. "Get up!"

He shook his head, but a power beyond his will, a force outside himself, dragged him upright. He cried out in fear and pain.

Francesca winced. For a moment, she saw the two of them again, younger and hopeful, standing amid the wildflowers in the meadow she loved. His lips brushed hers, his large hand touching her back. She turned away, wanting to rid herself of the unwelcomed memories. He called out to her again and, when she looked over at him, the gentle eyes that had always searched out hers with longing were now etched indelibly with sadness and grief.

"I'll tell you your fate," the White Widow spoke through gritted teeth.

Francesca moved forward, coming to a halt again between him and the Widow. There, facing the woman in white, she drew herself up and pleaded, "Let him go."

"Why?" the White Widow asked, surprised, her eyes flaring with contempt. "Are you so weak and craven that you're afraid to punish his poisonous deed?"

"No, not weak," Francesca countered. "It's just—once, once—" she hesitated. So much had been snuffed out in her "—I still remember—once I loved deeply."

The Widow threw back her head and laughed. Her derision flew through the woods like a winged beast annihilating everything in its path. "You think you're the only one who has ever loved deeply? We all have. And, like you, we were all betrayed. Their selfish deeds killed what was best in all of us. But now we hate just as deeply. Now we do unto them as they have done unto us! You're such a foolish woman, if you truly think there's another way!"

"I don't know if there's another way, or if this is really the only way," Francesca spat. "I only know I've been here too long. I just want this to end!"

"It will end as it has to end," the White Widow sneered. "With his death. The only way you will ever be free is if the harm he has done to you is avenged."

"Just like all of you have been set free?" Francesca jabbed. "Odd, but I don't see any freedom here. And certainly no peace."

The White Widow, caught off guard, flinched. "Revenge and bitterness are all we have. It's all that's left to us." She blinked away an unwanted tear. "What else is there?" She cleared her throat, regaining her composure, then stretched her arm out toward Francesca. "You have no power here." Against her will, Francesca was pulled from Ben whom she shielded and forced to the opposite side of the clearing.

The White Widow turned to Ben and pointed. "I'll give you then what you've come for. An unnatural happiness, a false peace. I'll call up the mist and throw a foggy veil over you like a shroud. You'll gaze at the world through it and see all things indistinct and illusory. Your guilt will vanish; you will laugh as you have never laughed before. You will laugh so hard and so long that you won't be able to stop, even when your joy has turned to pain. You will dance with a madness you have never known and cannot escape. You will dance and die, because in the end, nothing can erase the consequences of your deeds. For things once done can never be undone." The White Widow rolled her arm thrice, and the woods came alive with music. Francesca's music. She realized what this meant; she covered her ears with her hands, not wanting to hear. She closed her eyes and bowed her head, not wanting to see. But suddenly, as if a curse had finally been lifted, something deep within her that had long been stilled, awakened. From the ashes, her broken will arose, whole and undaunted. It hurled her through the night, an unrestrained projectile tumbling back through time until she once again stood in the classroom of her Long Island school, surrounded by her young pupils. Francesca brought her flute to her lips and began Massenet's "Méditation" from Thaïs. Ben and his father and Josh looked on enchanted, as the soulful notes reverberated in her and through her. The lilting melody filled the air, echoing through eternity.

"Let the music come from within you," Simone's voice resounded. "You must feel it. Meld with it. *Surrender* to it."

And so she did. She saw nothing, heard nothing, felt nothing. Except the music. The beautiful, impassioned music which she had become one with. It seemed to go on forever, the ethereal notes quivering through the night. But when the last one hovered delicately in the air, she opened her eyes and, standing in the forest which she had never left, amid the darkness which had not ceased, she saw the White Widow and the Vilas were now transfixed and inert—like death.

In one frantic movement, Francesca rushed to Ben where he

had fallen again and, as he lay trembling on the ground, she called, "Hurry, you have to leave this place now."

He shook his head weakly. "I, I can't."

"You have to." And as she stood above him, extending her hands toward him but not touching him, she forced him to rise on unsteady legs.

"Hurry," she bade again, and stretched out her arms toward the dark woods. "Go and live."

In an instant, he vanished from the clearing. His voice rang out with the sound of her name; it reverberated through the forest as he shouted it over and over. But with each repetition, it became more faint until it faded into silence. "Go. And live," she whispered ruefully when the night had grown quiet again.

She didn't know how long it was she stood alone amid the darkness and hung her head in sadness, but eventually an icy hand fell upon her shoulder, at once comforting and constraining her. "You wish him life," the White Widow hissed, "when all he did was leave you to die. There are some things that can never be forgiven."

Francesca looked steadily down. "How much hate is the heart supposed to contain? How much bitterness will it take to wipe away a deed?" She turned to the White Widow, earnestly seeking an answer. "Please. I need to understand."

"Oh, I will tell you how much hate the heart can contain." The Widow drew her hand to her chest. "It's immeasurable," she spewed through clenched teeth. "It's like an infinite and regenerating well that knows no end. The more you mete out, the more there is." Her eyes glistened. "And there is no amount of hate large enough to ever wipe away a deed such as his." She snapped her fingers, and the Vilas turned in unison toward the dark wood. "Bring him back," she ordered, "and let him meet his fate."

Francesca watched in silence as the avenging army moved in formation toward the trees, where they were swallowed up by the darkness.

It seemed like an eternity that she stood solemnly facing the edge of the clearing, The White Widow's hand resting heavily on her shoulder. Out of the shadows, it eventually came, this death march through the night which could not be stopped. The Vilas advanced two by two, in long columns, snaking through the gloom, carrying their quarry gravely on their shoulders. In the middle of the clearing they paused and laid their unconscious prey down upon the cold earth, forming a loose circle around him.

Francesca, her eyes boring into the Widow's, asked quietly, "Tell me, how long can I keep this bitterness alive before it poisons me? Tell me, because I just want this terrible night to end."

The Widow looked at her, bewildered. "You are already poisoned. That's why you're here with us."

The White Widow's words flew toward her, striking her like a sharp, heavy blow. Francesca gasped and put her hand to her cheek, as if stung, then stepped back and, blinking, looked around for a first time. She glared at the trees, the Vilas and the Widow. She shook her head, and said quietly, "No."

Looking around again, she shouted, "No!"

Then without hesitation, she went to Ben, knelt close to him, and leaning over, kissed him.

And in the distance, the church bells on the green chimed six times.

MORNING

The White Widow cringed and shielded her face with her arm. "It comes!" she shouted as she glanced up at the canopy.

"First light!" The Vilas called in unison as they moved skittishly around the clearing.

Francesca, kneeling beside Ben, raised her eyes heavenward and, through the intertwining branches, saw the black sky yielding to a soft blush. She put her hands to her mouth to stifle a gasp and slowly rose. Could it be this terrible night had truly ended? She turned, looking for affirmation. Instead, she saw the Vilas were now fixed and rooted, anchored to the ground, a grove of gray and broken trees. The White Widow's light had gone out as she stood motionless and iced over, her arm suspended in mid-air, nothing more than the hollow limb of dead wood in winter.

Ben's eyes fluttered. He sat up, dazed. Francesca held out her hand to him. He hesitated, then took it. She helped him to rise.

"Come with me, Francesca," he whispered haltingly, holding her close. "Come back to me. Please, come back."

She looked up into the eyes that had always gazed upon her with affection. She shook her head and pulled away from him.

"I can't," she said sadly. "I understand now. We can't change anything. What is done is done. Forever."

He looked down and begged, "Please. . . ."

"I'm sorry. I have to go."

"No!"

He reached out toward her, but she stepped back, eluding his grasp.

She brought her hands to her chest. A stray tear slipped down her cheek. "Tell Addie I love her. She is and always will be my heart." She swallowed hard. "Tell her I'll always watch over her; I'll always be near to her. If she looks for me, she'll find me—my kiss will be the soft breeze wafting over her on a summer's day; my embrace will be the noon-tide light warming her on a winter's afternoon. My tears will be the gentle rain falling over her on gray days, soothing her troubled heart and driving away her hurt. My voice will be all the songs of the earth reverberating over the mountains and echoing through the valleys. If she listens closely enough, she will hear me tell her everything she wants to know. And when she needs me the most, I'll flow toward her, the ocean flooding the shore at high tide, washing away her pain, making her heart strong and whole again. We'll be apart only for a little while, but one day we'll be together again. Tell her all of this. For I love her so."

Ben, looking down and grimacing, nodded.

Francesca went to him and touched his cheek gently. "I have to go now."

"Please!" he begged again and held out his arms to her, but she had already turned from him and, spying first light through distant trees, she unbuttoned the long gray mantle, letting it slip from her onto the icy earth. Its heaviness had imprisoned her for so long; without it she was suddenly free and buoyant.

She didn't look back. Instead, she turned her eyes and heart forward as she moved cautiously through the night toward morning. She stepped carefully over snow-laden logs and frozen brush. Her heart pounded; she worried that the light might elude her, that she would be unable to outrun the darkness and free herself from night and from winter. But her fears were unfounded; with every step she took, the shadows that had lain over her for so long ebbed. The more distance she covered, the warmer the woods grew. As the snow melted, the ice that had turned her hair white and brittle dissipated, and her long tresses grew dark and supple again. All around her, the still forest burst into life. Small woodland creatures darted back and forth underfoot, scattering around her as they emerged from their long sleep. Robins, blue jays and chickadees soared from one branch to another as they sang out their ode to a new day. The coral rose of dawn filtered down through the treetops that were now thick with leaves. In the distance, she saw the edge of the forest and hurried toward it. There, the golden rays of morning flooded through the greenery; shafts of yellow and orange streamed down and warmed the moss-covered forest floor. And on the outskirts of the woods, two figures loomed. They stood motionless, backlit and veiled by the newly risen sun. As Francesca approached them, they grew more distinct, and she recognized them. The tall, young woman, in a gray skirted suit, her jacket sporting a Peter Pan collar, her blonde hair woven in an intricate braid that fell behind her to her waist, stood beside a dog. The woman held out her arms, and Francesca, slipping into them, embraced her. "Lucy!" she uttered as a stray tear fell from her eyes.

"Francesca!" The young woman looked upon her with love. "We've been waiting for you. You're safe now. Nothing will ever hurt you again."

Francesca nodded gratefully then turned her attention to the dog who slowly, methodically, wagged his tail. She bent down, gently petting his nose, his head, his ears.

"He went back for you." Lucy smiled and stroked Cruz's back.

Francesca buried her face in his neck. Then she laughed and laughed as she ran her hands through his coat, pausing now and then to hug him. He licked her wildly, and his tail moved so rapidly his hips swayed from side to side.

"Come on. It's morning now," Lucy said and, placing her arm

around Francesca, helped her to rise. "You can put this terrible night behind you forever."

Francesca paused for a moment, then nodded. With Cruz brushing against her leg and Lucy holding her, the three of them walked into the morning and into the light. They came to a halt in the middle of the meadow, that beloved tract where she had often danced in and run through, taken strength and comfort from. Now it was abloom with wildflowers that spread out before them, dense and lush, a thick carpet of color as if a rainbow had just fallen to earth.

Francesca turned her face to the heavens. It had been a long time since she felt such warmth and beheld such beauty. She smiled, then. She laughed. She brought her hands to her cheeks as she basked joyously in the newly found light. She had finally come home.

Home.

And there in the glow of that solemn dawn, once dead, she lived again.

Acknowledgments

First, I would like to thank the faculty of Lindenwood University's creative writing department, where this book took root and grew. I am especially grateful to Eve Jones who, kindly and gently, helped me to find my inner poet. My prose has been made richer for it. I am also grateful to Dr. Wm Anthony Connolly, whose guidance helped me transform this story into its present form.

I would like to thank Eugene Scott and Romeo Enriquez for their encouragement during this process, and also Diana Power and Debi Barton Haverly for their insights and suggestions during the early stages of this manuscript. The perspectives they brought to this story as readers were invaluable.

I am forever indebted to Brooke Warner and the entire She Writes Press (SWP) team for providing me with the opportunity to get Francesca's story out into the world. I am honored to be part of this community of exceptional women authors, and I especially value the support and friendship of my sister SWP authors, Isidra Mencos, Lindsey Salatka, Elisa Stancil Levine, and Catherine Drake.

About the Author

© Gail Hynes

@susansperanzaauthor

@susan_speranza_castleriggpekes

@SusanSperanza

Susan Speranza was born in New York City, grew up on Long Island, and went to college and for a time worked in Manhattan. For years she enjoyed the hectic pace and cultural amenities of the City, but after a great upheaval, she escaped the urban/suburban jungle and claimed her piece of the country in Vermont, where she has now lived happily for more than twenty years. In between the demands of life, she's authored two other books: *The City of Light*, a dystopian story about the end of Western civilization, and *The Tale of Lucia Grandi, The Early Years*, a novel about a dysfunctional suburban family. She's also published numerous articles, poems, and short stories. Along the way, she managed to collect a couple of master's degrees. When she is not writing, she keeps herself busy exhibiting and breeding her champion Pekingese.

SELECTED TITLES FROM SHE WRITES PRESS

She Writes Press is an independent publishing company founded to serve women writers everywhere. Visit us at www.shewritespress.com.

Magic Flute by Patricia Minger $16.95, 978-1-63152-093-8
When a car accident puts an end to ambitious flutist Liz Morgan's dreams, she returns to her childhood hometown in Wales in an effort to reinvent her path.

The Lucidity Project by Abbey Campbell Cook $16.95, 978-1-63152-032-7
After suffering from depression all her life, twenty-five-year-old Max Dorigan joins a mysterious research project on a Caribbean island, where she's introduced to the magical and healing world of lucid dreaming.

Water On the Moon by Jean P. Moore $16.95, 978-1-938314-61-2
When her home is destroyed in a freak accident, Lidia Raven, a divorced mother of two, is plunged into a mystery that involves her entire family.

Shelter Us by Laura Diamond $16.95, 978-1-63152-970-2
Lawyer-turned-stay-at-home-mom Sarah Shaw is still struggling to find a steady happiness after the death of her infant daughter when she meets a young homeless mother and toddler she can't get out of her mind—and becomes determined to rescue them.

In the Heart of Texas by Ginger McKnight-Chavers
$16.95, 978-1-63152-159-1
After spicy, forty-something soap star Jo Randolph manages in twenty-four hours to burn all her bridges in Hollywood, along with her director/boyfriend's beach house, she spends a crazy summer back in her West Texas hometown—and it makes her question whether her life in the limelight is worth reclaiming.

Center Ring by Nicole Waggoner $17.95, 978-1-63152-034-1
When a startling confession rattles a group of tightly knit women to its core, the friends are left analyzing their own roads not taken and the vastly different choices they've made in life and love.